A COLD CASE

A Maurice Mundy mystery

Peter Turnbull

severn
House

This first world edition published 2016
in Great Britain and 2017 the USA by
SEVERN HOUSE PUBLISHERS LTD of
19 Cedar Road, Sutton, Surrey, England, SM2 5DA

Trade paperback edition first published 2018
In Great Britain and the USA by
SEVERN HOUSE PUBLISHERS LTD
Eardley House, 4 Uxbridge Street, London W8 7SY

British Library Cataloguing in Publication Data
A CIP catalogue record for this title is available from the British Library.

ISBN-13: 978-0-7278-8683-5 (cased)
ISBN-13: 978-1-84751-787-6 (trade paper)
ISBN-13: 978-1-78010-856-8 (e-book)

ONE

Two men walked casually side by side although with a greatly noticeable gap between them. An observer would note that the two men were of the same age group, being in their middle years, and the observer would further note that the two men were both dressed in casual, durable but also comfortable-looking clothing. The observer would also note that both men were tall, being just under six feet, and that both were of large, stocky build. The observer would note a striking difference between the two men in that one walked with his eyes downcast, looking only at the road surface just ahead of him, while the other man walked with his head up, glancing keenly in all directions, looking ahead of himself both in the near and middle distance and also searching for detail from side to side. Both men kept their hands in their pockets. The man who kept his eyes downcast was wearing a green wax jacket, while the keenly searching man wore a trilby and a camel-coloured duffel coat against the chill easterly wind which blew across the flat landscape that was the vast open space in the centre of the village of Matching Green in the county of Essex. As the two men walked they encountered a large puddle in the road which was the consequence of recent rainfall, and the man in the duffel coat deferred to the other man and fell in behind him as he walked over a narrow stretch of tarmac between the puddle and the raised boundary of the village green. The observer would then doubtless deduce that the man who walked with his head down knew the area and was possessed of knowledge and/or seniority which the second man, the wearer of the camel-coloured duffel coat, did not possess.

When they were beyond the puddle the two men recommenced walking side by side in a casual but confident manner, with the outer of the pair – the man in the duffel coat – continually turning his head as he surveyed his surroundings.

The man saw the large – exceedingly large – village green and, bringing to mind a parcel of land with which he was very familiar, and knowing that said parcel of land was approximately one third of an acre in respect of its expanse, he was thus able to estimate the village green to be approximately two acres in size. It was the largest village green he had seen, though he would not dispute that there would probably be larger, he being a city dweller all his life and unversed in the sights of rural England. Surrounding the green were houses, the man noted, each well-set, proud and well-maintained, detached from its neighbour and clearly the possession of a moneyed owner. Beyond the houses lay the flat expanse of farmland that stretched away to the skyline. At that time of the year it was deeply and neatly furrowed, awaiting the sowing of winter wheat, and all at that moment under low, grey, swiftly scudding clouds. Once again the two men fell into single file as a black mud-bespattered Range Rover approached and drove past them, being driven by a muscular-looking, well-built man in his middle years who was dressed in a dark green, military-style woollen pullover and a well-worn grey, torn flat cap. The driver of the Range Rover did not look at the two walking men as he drove by at a safe and a sensible speed. Upon the passing of the Range Rover the two men once again began to walk side by side and, continuing to keep a comfortable and a relaxed silence, they carried on until they drew level with a pond set in the village green, close to the southernmost boundary beside which the men were strolling. When they were level with the pond the man in the green jacket stopped walking, turned to his right and faced the pond. The second man stood beside him and gazed at the dark, still, chill-looking water. He thought that the pond was perhaps thirty feet long by about fifteen feet wide. A stand of reeds protruded from the surface of the pond at its furthest, northern end. The man noticed a stark sign, of black letters on a white background, affixed to a post beside the pond at eye level which read Private Fishing. The two men read the sign and glanced at each other.

'Essex,' growled the wax jacket-wearing man. 'This part of Essex anyway. Here be money and ownership rules, it's just the way of it round this place. Mind you, I suppose it's fair enough – the sign, I mean. If they didn't limit the number of licences this little pond would soon be fished out, or there would be too many people crowding the edge of the pond. That would spoil the peace of a day's fishing, so I can readily understand it.'

'What's in it?' the man in the duffel coat asked. 'Do you know?'

'Dunno . . . I don't fish. Are you an angler?' the man wearing the wax jacket replied.

'I'm not passionate about it like some guys are but I have cast a hook now and again,' the second man explained. 'So, yes, I dare say that I am a bit of an angler. I reckon this pond will contain the likes of perch or roach, but there could equally be trench or carp in that sort of water.'

'I see . . . I'll take your word for it.' The man wearing the wax jacket looked at the still water, which was occasionally rippled by the wind but in the main was still. 'Well, this is where he was found . . . floating in the water, head down, on a wet, dark night, raining heavily . . . you can imagine it. His body was apparently part hidden in the reeds . . . over there.' The man pointed to the vegetation at the far northern end of the pond. 'The boy was wearing a dark blue school uniform raincoat with nothing else of him being visible. The poor visibility and the colour of his raincoat served very efficiently to camouflage him. The police had a search party out looking for him by then, of course, a missing twelve-year-old . . .'

'Oh, indeed.' The man wearing the duffel coat also gazed out across the forbidding-looking water of the pond. 'Indeed,' he repeated.

'But, as they subsequently found out, they were looking in the wrong place. They were apparently searching the fields and woodlands between here and Matching Tye, which is a smaller village . . .' the man in the wax jacket pointed to the west, '. . . in that direction. It's about a mile away,' he explained, 'perhaps a little more, but an easy walk for a twelve-year-old.'

'Yes, quite easy.' The man in the duffel coat looked curiously to the west. The village and the surrounding area would, he felt, be very fetching in high summer, but on that day it all looked cold, desolate and deserted, save for him, his guide and the driver of the black Range Rover who had just passed. 'The boy had apparently gone to visit a school friend and left his friend's house to do the walk home at about eight thirty p.m.'

'Not too late?' the man in the duffel coat commented, glancing at his companion.

'Not too late at all,' the first man replied. 'The walk should have taken him only about twenty minutes . . . perhaps half an hour, and when he had not returned by nine fifteen his father phoned his friend's parents, who confirmed that he had left their house at eight thirty p.m.' The man in the wax jacket continued, 'So his father went looking for him, as indeed any parent would have done.'

'Of course . . .' The man in the duffel coat nodded. 'It must have been awful for him.'

'He took the family dog and together they walked to Matching Tye and back,' the first man explained. 'And, not finding him anywhere on the road, the boy's father raised the alarm upon his return home. The police from Hounslow duly arrived and went to the pub—'

'The Chequers?' the man in the duffel coat enquired.

'Yes.' The man in the wax jacket smiled. 'You noticed it?'

'Of course . . . red brick building over there.' The second man pointed to the public house. 'Thirties roadhouse style, I'd say . . . it is significantly younger than the buildings around it, most of which seem to date from the Victorian period.'

'Are you an architectural historian?' The first man raised his eyebrows.

'Heavens, I wouldn't go that far . . . but,' the second man gave a slight shrug of the shoulders, 'I have, over the years, developed more than a passing interest in buildings, especially smaller, domestic buildings. For some reason I can't explain, I'd be happier looking round a perfectly preserved house from the twenties than I'd be looking round a castle, for example.'

'I see.' The man wearing the wax jacket inclined his head. 'Anyway, they – the police – asked for volunteers and, despite the time of night and the foul weather, not a man nor a woman refused to help. The fields from Matching Green to Matching

Tye were searched as much as they could be . . . they had a few lamps and fewer dogs, but the search continued until well after midnight.'

'Nothing?' the second man asked.

'Nothing at all,' the man in the wax jacket growled, 'and that is because by then he was most likely already in here.' He nodded to the dark, cold-looking water of the pond. 'Anyway, the search was resumed at first light with more police officers and more dogs, the officers equipped with poles to help search shrubs and woodland.'

'Yes,' the man in the duffel coat replied softly, 'I've done that a few times.'

'We all have . . . we all have,' the man in the wax jacket replied dryly. Then continued, 'The farmers in the vicinity were asked to search their outbuildings and the householders in the village were similarly asked to search their sheds and garages as a small number of constables did door-to-door inquiries.'

'I get the picture,' the man in the duffel coat replied.

'So it seems that the search was well under way by about eleven a.m. that morning when the postman came riding up to the mobile incident room on his bike, panting for breath because, sharp-eyed man that he apparently was, and knowing of the search for the missing boy, he'd been glancing in all corners as he did his walk delivering letters, really keeping his eyes peeled . . . and he'd seen the body floating among the reeds.'

'So the search was being undertaken on the wrong side of the village?' the second man replied.

'Well, yes, as I said, but only in hindsight. At the time it was sensible of the police to search the area between Matching Green and Matching Tye,' the man wearing the wax jacket responded with a defensive tone of voice.

'Of course . . . of course,' the man wearing the duffel coat stammered.

'The search would eventually have been widened and, at some point later that day, the body would have been found,' the man in the wax jacket explained, 'but in the event it was found by the sharp-eyed postman before the search was widened.'

'Good for him,' the man in the duffel coat offered.

'Oh, indeed . . . indeed . . .' The man in the wax jacket once again growled his reply. 'So . . . for some reason the boy had left his friend's house, walked home, seems to have walked beyond his parents' cottage and been found in this pond. At first, people thought that it had been a tragic accident. They thought he'd lost his way in the dark and stumbled into the pond, but at the post-mortem the pathologist found head injuries . . .'

'Yes.' The man in the duffel coat glanced around the village green again and was struck once more by its size. It was surrounded by houses yet it seemed to him to be a very lonely place to die. Especially for a twelve-year-old. 'I read the report . . . skull fractured in two places. So then it became a murder inquiry.'

'Yes, and a murder inquiry with no suspects.'

'None at all?' The man in the duffel coat glanced at the first man.

'None, although the feeling was that it had to be a local culprit . . . and that is still the feeling.' The man in the wax jacket also looked at the village green. 'I mean, just look at the place . . . just look at this village, will you? It's in the middle of nowhere.'

'So I saw on the map.' The second man took another glance over the expanse of rough pasture that was the village green.

'There are seven roads leading into it, or out of it, depending on which way you look at it,' the man wearing the wax jacket breathed deeply, 'so it's like a hub with seven spokes but the seven spokes don't go anywhere – not anywhere significant, anyway. They just lead to neighbouring villages or hamlets . . . or lead from neighbouring villages or hamlets. Matching Green, this village, is not on a route from one significant place to another. There is hardly any through traffic. If there was significant through traffic the police might have considered an opportunist attack by a stranger.'

'And the place where the body was found . . . this pond.' The man in the duffel coat considered the cold, still, dark water. 'It seems to imply local knowledge, I would have thought.'

'So the police also thought, and I would agree. The pond can't be seen from the road – only the Private Fishing sign indicates its presence and that looks quite new . . . though it might have replaced an older sign which was in place at the time.'

'So, no leads at all?' the man in the duffel coat asked.

'None.' The man in the wax jacket shook his head. 'All the men in the village were able to give a good account of themselves. The forensic pathologist who was consulted said that the attack was almost certainly done by a male. The head – the skull, I should say – had been fractured in two places with a flat object. She said it was consistent with being smashed over the head with great force by the blade of a spade.'

'A very masculine sort of attack indeed.' The man in the duffel coat nodded in agreement. 'Did the family have any enemies?'

'None,' the man in the wax jacket grunted. 'None known, anyway. They were local people – they grew up locally, settled locally and then lived quietly. Eventually, as you have read, the police drew a blank,' he explained. 'The case was put to one side and sadly, but dare I say inevitably, it began to lose its core temperature. Would you like to see the family home?'

'Yes, I would,' the man in the duffel coat smiled briefly. 'It will help me to get a clearer picture, which is why we are here. And since we are here anyway . . .'

'Very well, this way . . . we'll have to walk past the pub.' The man in the wax jacket pointed to the top left of the green from their vantage point. 'If it was drier we could walk across the green. As you can see, there are a few well-worn paths . . .'

'No . . . no,' the man in the duffel coat replied. 'I'd rather walk on the road. It will be less messy. It'll take longer but we both have the time these days.'

The two men glanced at each other and grinned warmly and broadly, then turned to their left and continued walking. At the end of the southern boundary of the green they turned to their right and followed the road past the pub, keeping the village green to their right. Once at the top of the village green they turned left and put themselves on the narrow road which led to Matching Tye. All around them was drab, end-of-year landscape, leafless trees with a murder of crows cawing loudly and relentlessly in the black branches. Shortly after leaving the village green the man in the wax jacket stopped and turned to his right. 'This,' he pointed to a small house, 'is where the little lad lived with his parents. It was the family home. Still is, in fact.'

The man wearing the duffel coat considered the building. He saw a single-storey cottage, sunk beneath the level of the road so that his eyes were level with the eaves of the house. Steps led down from the road to a gravel-covered pathway which led directly to the front door. The doorway was encased in a trellis which held climbing plants – clematis, the man thought. The cottage walls were painted white with a shiny black door and the window frames were similarly painted in gloss black. The roof was tiled, dulled with age, and moss grew upon it liberally in scattered patches. The modest-sized garden which surrounded the cottage was, the man felt, untidy, but he could detect more than the suggestion of a once-neatly-kept and hard-worked-upon garden.

'It is quite small by comparison to the other houses around here, as you'll note,' the man in the wax jacket commented, 'but it will still cost you a tidy sum if you wished to buy it.'

'I'm quite happy where I am,' the man in the duffel coat smiled, 'which is just as well, I dare say, because I do not possess the tidy sum in question.'

'I'm happy for you . . . being settled, I mean, but Matching Tye is down there . . .' the man wearing the wax jacket nodded to his left, '. . . so he was walking from that direction to his home, to the cottage here in front of us, but his body was found in the pond, to our right and behind us.'

'So I see . . .' The second man looked up and down the narrow road.

'And, as I said,' the first man continued, 'it was a filthy night; he'd just want to get home, to the warmth and the dryness. Heavens, I know I would . . . and to his bed, it being a school day the following morning . . . oh . . .' He paused in mid-sentence.

'Something?' The man in the camel-coloured duffel coat asked.

'Yes, the window to the left of the door . . . the silver-haired lady.' He held up his hand in greeting. 'That is his mother, Mrs Walwyn.'

The man wearing the duffel coat smiled and nodded at the elderly-looking lady who stood looking out of the window of her cottage and up at the two men who stood outside on the road surface.

'I was going to wait before introducing you to the personalities in the case,' the first man explained, 'but since we have been seen we ought to pay our respects and take the opportunity to allow me to introduce you.'

The man in the wax jacket went down the steps followed by the second man, and the door was opened just as he arrived at the trellis. 'Good afternoon, Mrs Walwyn.'

'Hello, Mr Ingram.' The woman was short, wore a yellow shawl, a black skirt and heavy black shoes. 'Do come in, please . . . or Tom, I should say. I keep forgetting you prefer things to be informal.' The woman stepped nimbly aside and the two men entered her home. The man in the duffel coat swept his hat off as he entered the cottage and glanced curiously round the living room. He saw that it was cluttered, noted it to be cleanly kept but smelling musty as if it suffered from rising damp, the possibility of which did not surprise him.

'May I introduce you.' Tom Ingram indicated the man in the duffel coat. 'This is Maurice Mundy. He has just joined our little team. I am bringing him up to speed on the case. Maurice, this is Mrs Walwyn, Oliver's mother.'

'Pleased to meet you, Mr Mundy.' Mrs Walwyn held out her hand. Mundy found her grip to be firm but not overly so. 'It is so very reassuring that the police have not forgotten us . . . or Oliver.'

'We never forget anyway,' Tom Ingram smiled, 'and we don't close cases until we have secured a conviction.'

'Thank you.' Mrs Walwyn returned the smile. 'Well, it's cold out there – that east wind's a real biter. I imagine you two gentlemen could use a warming cup of tea?'

Over tea, served in plain blue cups and matching saucers, and when all three persons were seated in deep armchairs round a small log fire which burned slowly on the grate within a tiled surround, Mrs Walwyn asked, 'So I assume that you're a retired police officer also, Mr Mundy?'

'Yes.' Maurice Mundy smiled as he replied, 'Very recently retired . . .'

'And brought your expertise to the Cold Case Review Team?' Mrs Walwyn pressed.

'Well, I hope I can make a contribution.' Mundy continued to smile.

'I hope you can as well.' Mrs Walwyn sighed deeply. 'After ten years things can get very cold, very cold indeed.'

Maurice Mundy glanced at Mrs Walwyn: frail looking, silver-haired, a yellow shawl about her slight shoulders, and yet, he thought, ten years ago she was the mother of a twelve-year-old boy. She was, he realized, younger than she looked, or had aged prematurely. Probably both, he thought. She appeared to be in her sixties, or even older, but was likely to be still in her forties. Life can, he felt, sometimes deal a very cruel hand.

'That's Oliver,' Mrs Walwyn continued in her rich East Anglian accent as she pointed to a framed photograph of a smiling boy in round-lensed spectacles which stood centrally upon her mantelpiece. 'That photograph was taken just before . . .' she paused, '. . . just before he was taken from us. He was just a child – it was all still ahead of him. I was quite old when I had him, as you may notice. I mean, old for a parent, we both were . . . we were both elderly parents. It made the gift he was to us all the more precious . . . and his loss all the harder.'

'Yes,' Maurice Mundy replied softly. 'Yes, I can imagine.'

'I knew when he'd been found,' Mrs Walwyn announced.

'Really?'

'Yes, I told Mr Ingram . . . I told Tom but I'll tell you if you like . . . Maurice, isn't it?'

'Yes.' Maurice Mundy smiled. 'It's Maurice. I also like things to be as informal as possible.'

'Well, Maurice, it was when I saw the postman cycling past

the house. He was the postman round here for years. He knew where Oliver lived and he was cycling as fast as he could . . . not his usual, slow, I've-got-all-the-time-in-the-world speed but standing up in the pedals, leaning forward in a hurry . . . a real, tearing hurry – and him a middle-aged man. I was standing at the window and as he went past he looked at this house. Our eyes met and I saw his face was drained of colour and that there was real fear in his eyes. I knew then that Oliver's body had been found and I knew that the postman had found him. You see, the police and local volunteers were searching out towards Matching Tye but the postman rode from the opposite direction. He rode from our village to where the search was going on . . .' Mrs Walwyn paused. 'He'd come from Matching Tye earlier . . . he has deliveries there . . . he would have seen the search party as he rode from there to here with the post in the pannier of his bike. He always leaves the bike outside the pub and walks his walk round Matching Green, does his delivery here, collects his bike and cycles back to Matching Tye. That's his walk . . . the three Matchings: Matching Tye, Matching Green and Matching. He gets a lift in a van from the sorting office in Harlow, him and his bike, and he gets dropped off at Matching Tye and starts delivering each morning except Sundays. He cycles past our house . . . then that day he cycled in the opposite direction, back towards Matching Tye, with a face as white as can be, cycling back to where the police were searching, and he glanced at this house as he rode past. I said to myself, "He's found Oliver and he's not where they are looking for him. They're looking for him in the wrong place".' Mrs Walwyn paused as if reining in a difficult memory. 'So then, a few minutes later, a police car went by at speed with its blue light flashing. Evidently it was checking on the postman's report, and a few moments after that . . . no . . . not moments . . . a few minutes after that a whole convoy of police vehicles drove past this house going towards the village green. My husband was part of the search party but they didn't let him go with them to the pond. He had gone to help the search and I had stayed here to answer the phone in case anyone rang with news . . . but after the convoy of police vehicles had gone past, a police car stopped

outside the house and my husband and a policewoman got out
and both came in here and we waited in silence, just the three
of us. We just sat in complete silence. Later, a police officer
came and told us that a body had been found which matched
Oliver's description.' Again Mrs Walwyn paused and clearly
fought to control her emotions.

'Yes,' Tom Ingram spoke softly, 'we are both very sorry.'

'Indeed.' Maurice Mundy once again glanced round the
small cottage. 'Very sorry indeed.'

'He'd be twenty-two years old now . . . I might even have
been a grandmother. Imagine that. Me and my husband both
agreed that we would encourage Oliver not to wait as long as
we did before starting a family . . . and we were so proud of
him. He was already shining at school; his teachers said that
they recognized university potential in him. This is not just a
grieving mother talking, you understand. He really was going
to go somewhere very special in life.'

'Your husband isn't home, Mrs Walwyn?' Maurice Mundy
asked quietly, and by doing so he noticed that he had caused
Tom Ingram to glare at him.

'No . . . no . . . he isn't.' Mrs Walwyn slumped forward.
'No, his heart gave out . . . that was really quite a shock
because he was such a strong man. In fact, his doctor had told
him just a few weeks earlier that if his body was a motor
vehicle it would be a Land Rover or a farm tractor . . . you
know, rugged and just keeps going. But, well, they put cardiac
arrest on his death certificate. I dare say it was as close as
they could get to saying he died of a broken heart but you can
take it from me that that's what he died of – a broken heart.
He and Oliver were very close, you see. They loved each other
. . . they were more than father and son. They were very good
friends to each other and you know, sir, as I told Mr Ingram
. . . Sorry, as I told Tom, I didn't want him to go out that
night. It was more than the dark night and the rain battering
on the roof and the window panes . . . I had a strong presenti-
ment that something dreadful was going to happen. I have
never felt such a thing before . . . it was very strong, very
strong indeed, but Oliver was insistent and my husband said,
"Let the lad go, he knows the road to Matching Tye and a

little rain won't harm him." He felt bad about that, my husband, very bad . . . blamed himself, he did . . . but it's so, so very reassuring that Oliver has not been forgotten. Thank you, gentlemen.'

'It is as I said,' Tom Ingram replied in a soft voice, 'we don't ever close cases until they are solved.' He stood up slowly.

'Yes, thank you.' Mrs Walwyn forced a smile. 'I am so pleased.'

'It was nice to have met you.' Maurice Mundy smiled as he also stood up. 'I'm sorry the circumstances were not more pleasant.'

'We'll see ourselves out,' Tom Ingram added. 'We will, of course, keep you informed of any and all developments as soon as they occur.'

'Thank you.' Mrs Walwyn nodded gently while remaining seated. 'I appreciate your calling on me.'

Outside the cottage, Ingram turned to Mundy. 'I dare say I should have told you about her husband but I wasn't expecting to go in. Would you like to see the house he visited?'

'Yes.' Mundy glanced up at the low, grey sky. 'Yes, I would, and more importantly, I'd like to see the road to the other village. I think he was very likely murdered somewhere along that road.'

'I'd be inclined to agree,' Ingram replied. 'Walk or drive?'

'Oh, drive.' Mundy grinned. 'Though at some point I'd like to walk the route. I'd like to walk the little lad's last walk . . . but for now I am content to drive.'

'Likewise,' Tom Ingram replied. 'On both counts.'

The two men walked unhurriedly side by side to where they had parked their car beside the village green and Tom Ingram drove at a sensible speed along the road to Matching Tye. As the road unfolded before them Maurice Mundy observed that it was narrow and winding with no buildings on either side once they had left Matching Green. A watercourse ran along the southern side of the road and the low, flat fields of Essex expanded outwards at either side, beyond the shrubs and the trees.

'It's a very lonely road,' Mundy commented, scanning the view from side to side. 'It has a loneliness about it.'

'It is,' Ingram replied. 'These bends – you can see no more than one hundred yards ahead of you before you turn, and with hardly any buildings to be seen. You know, he was a brave lad . . . young Oliver Walwyn . . . even as a grown man and a copper I wouldn't like to walk this road on a dark, rainy night, even if I knew every inch of it. But for a twelve-year-old . . . local or no local, it must have been frightening.'

'He would have had to be very determined.' Mundy glanced to his right as they drove past a solitary house. 'A very plucky little lad, or desperate to get home . . . or both.'

'Seems likely that it was both . . . and it's not a short walk,' Ingram commented. 'It takes half an hour at least. In those weather conditions . . . those bends, no lighting . . . that's not actually an easy walk . . . not for a twelve-year-old.'

'As you say.' Mundy once again glanced to his right, this time at a concreted-over entrance to a farm driveway and then to his left at a thick stand of trees, black against the grey sky. His eye was caught by a heron flying with clear effort against the wind. 'It's not a short walk for a twelve-year-old.'

Ingram slowed the car as he approached Matching Tye. He kept it to the left as the road divided and Mundy noted a line of local authority homes to the right and a children's playground accessed by a wooden bridge over the stream to his left. He observed that Matching Tye did not seem to be possessed of the level of wealth enjoyed by Matching Green. Ingram halted the car when level with the playground with its brightly coloured equipment and indicated a modest house in a terrace of similar houses which stood on the opposite side of the road. 'That house there, with the yellow door, is the home Oliver Walwyn visited on his last night.'

'What's the family like?' Mundy asked as he looked at the house. It seemed to him to be neatly kept, as indeed all the houses in the terrace were.

'Don't know yet.' Ingram took a deep breath. 'It's still early days. We did call last week on the off chance of finding someone at home but we were out of luck. Shall we try now?'

'Why not?' Mundy released his seat belt.

The two men left the car and walked slowly across the road and up the driveway of the house with the yellow painted front door. Ingram knocked reverently, yet with some degree of authority, on the door, which was opened a moment later by a short man in his mid- to late-forties, or so Mundy guessed. 'Yes?' The man showed no fear of the two strangers who had called on him. 'Can I help you gentlemen?'

'Police.' Ingram showed his identity card. Mundy did likewise.

'Oh?' The man became concerned. 'What is it? What's it about?'

'It is nothing to be alarmed about,' Ingram replied soothingly as he put away his ID. 'We are making enquiries about the murder of Oliver Walwyn.'

'Oh, yes, Oliver Walwyn. Poor lad. His body was found floating in the fishpond at Matching Green . . . they . . . we still talk about it round here. He was here that night. Please, come in.' The man stepped aside, allowing Ingram and Mundy to enter his house. 'You take me as you find me, I'm afraid,' he added in a strong Essex accent. 'It's the maid's day off, you see.'

Maurice Mundy read the man's sitting room as he and Tom Ingram accepted an invitation to take a seat. He saw many chrome-coloured items of amusement on shelves and the mantelpiece; he saw a large chrome television set; he saw modern, lightweight, inexpensive furnishings; he saw no reading matter at all, no magazines, no newspapers and no books. He found there to be no depth to the house and he was instantly ill at ease.

'So, have there been developments?' The man sank, rather than sat, back into a scarlet armchair.

'No . . . none.' Tom Ingram glanced around the room. 'It's been handed to us to have a second look, to check and see if anything was overlooked during the first investigation, if witnesses have now remembered things they didn't then think significant and/or which they didn't tell the police at the time . . .'

'Or subsequently saw something months or even years later which they think might have a significance to the crime and have not thus far reported it,' Maurice Mundy added. 'That's our brief, our remit.'

'I see . . . well, he,' the man spoke with a helpful tone of voice, 'Oliver . . . we knew him as "Ollie", visited us that night. He and my son were good friends.'

'Your son is . . .?' Mundy asked.

'Luke . . . Luke Kells,' the man replied. 'I am Sidney Kells. Unemployed – damned unemployable at my age – but the wife works, good woman that she is, so we scrape by.' Mundy thought Kells was an early middle-aged man, medium build, dressed in a red pullover and white summer trousers and blue slippers. He wore a shiny imitation gold watch. 'Luke's in the army now and loving it . . . best thing with clothes on, he says.' Kells grinned. 'He was always physical and Ollie, well, he was brainy so they made strange mates. I always thought it was a case of "birds of a feather flock together", so the sporty ones stick together, the brainy ones stick together . . . but with Luke and Ollie it was different. They hadn't a lot in common but they just clicked . . . like opposites attract. My lad was a team player while Ollie was quiet and bookish, but he had backbone, walking home on a night like that . . . Ollie had backbone all right. You'll never take that from him.'

'We said much the same thing driving here,' Ingram replied. 'It took a lot of courage to do that walk, especially on a night like that night.'

'Yes. If I'd had a car I would have run him home, of course I would, but I hadn't and he was up for the walk. He walked here in the rain and the dark and was quite willing to walk back in the rain and the dark. He had good shoes and a duffel coat . . . a blue one . . . not like yours, sir,' Kells indicated to Maurice Mundy's coat, 'not a light coloured one but dark blue, dark trousers and black shoes, as I recall.'

'So not easily seen at night?' Mundy commented.

'No . . . no . . .' Kells glanced upwards. 'Come to think of it, he wouldn't have reflected a car's headlights. Wonder if that was what happened . . . a motorist knocked him down and in a panic picked him up and threw his body in the pond at Matching Green. Maybe that's what happened?'

'That didn't happen.' Mundy continued to find both the man and his house irritating. 'The injuries would be different and if a motorist had run him over he would have driven off in a panic, not picked Oliver's body up and dropped it somewhere else. But Oliver would have been hidden from view on the road by his clothing . . . I find that quite interesting. It might be significant.' Mundy paused. 'So he left here at eight thirty p.m. that night?'

'Yes, that was approximately the time he left . . . I am positive,' Kells replied. 'I told the police that was the time that he left our house. His parents wanted him home by nine p.m. and you have to allow a good thirty minutes to walk from here to his house. So, yes, he left here at around eight thirty p.m. It had quite an impact on the folk round here, I can tell you. Really quite an impact.'

'I can imagine,' Ingram replied. 'I can well imagine.'

'Yes, like I said, people still talk about it.' Kells swept his hand over the top of his head. 'Nothing ever happens round here . . . nothing . . . no crime at all, nothing, and then we get two murders in the same night.'

'Two murders?' Mundy repeated. Beside him he sensed Ingram sit up in interest. 'Two murders, did you say? Two?'

'Yes.' Kells looked at Mundy. 'There was the murder you gentlemen are interested in and the murder of the street girl from Chelmsford. Her body was dumped near here that same night. I can't remember her name but I recall that they found her body more or less at the same time they found Ollie's body. The woman was found out towards Chelmsford . . . nearer Chelmsford than here. I believe it was the case that the police linked her murder to other murders of women and so that was taking all of the police's time . . . looking for their murderer. Not heard much about that business for a long while,' Kells added after a moment's thoughtful pause. 'Not for a long while.'

'Did you know about the other murders?' Mundy turned to Ingram.

'We did not.' Ingram sat back as if deflated. 'That's news to me . . . that really is news to me. I wonder why we were not told of it?'

'It's because the murders of the women are not a cold case. It's as simple as that,' DCI David Cole of Essex Police replied with an air of calm indignation. 'In fact, it is still a very warm case, very, very warm. We were and are satisfied that the murder of Oliver Walwyn and the woman who was murdered on the same night have no connection; they have no forensic link at all. So we handed the murder of Oliver Walwyn to you blokes . . . Scotland Yard's Cold Case Review Team, but we are keeping the murders of the street girls open as a hot case . . .'

'Murders?' Ingram leaned forwards in the seat in which he sat in front of DCI Cole's desk in Chelmsford Police Station. 'How many murders are you talking about, if you don't mind me asking?'

'Six,' Cole replied calmly.

'A serial killer? There has been little publicity about it,' Mundy commented.

'Or killers, but we can't definitely link them. So we don't know . . . we just don't know. You see, street working is a very dangerous game. As you gentlemen will know . . . one sex worker a week is murdered in the UK and those, of course, are the ones we know about. Others just vanish – again, as you gentlemen will know. I mean, a working girl gets into a stranger's car . . . well, then, she puts her life at risk. Most get out again, job done, money earned. Others don't get out. Their bodies are thrown out; most times they are found but sometimes, *sometimes*, they are never found.' Cole was a large man; he wore a light blue shirt and a dark blue tie which showed the police logo of a candle burning at both ends. His office window looked out on to New Street towards the railway bridge.

'But six,' Ingram protested. 'That's a serial killer.'

'Is it?' Cole smiled knowingly and stood up. He walked casually to his filing cabinet and took out a slender file. 'The actual file is a lot bigger than this,' he explained. 'This is just an overview file I made for my own use.' He resumed his seat and opened the folder. 'You see, in the midst of the attacks on street girls, which happen on a regular basis, we have isolated six who might . . . and I emphasize might, be linked. All are from the East Anglia region, not localized round Essex, so we are liaising with other, neighbouring police forces.'

'Understood.' Mundy nodded.

'So . . . it goes back twenty years,' Cole advised.

'Twenty!' Ingram gasped.

'Yes . . . and that is part of the puzzle. Reading from this, I can tell you that the first girl was Pamela Deary. She was twenty years old, from King's Lynn.'

'Wide area, as you say,' Mundy commented. 'King's Lynn, indeed, that's quite a long way north.'

'Yes. Then seventeen years ago, Sonya Machin, twenty-four, from here in Chelmsford, was murdered . . . the third was Denise May, eighteen, from Norwich. She was murdered fourteen years ago. Then Janet Laws, twenty-one, another Chelmsford girl, in fact. She was murdered ten years ago . . .'

'On the same night that Oliver Walwyn was murdered?' Ingram asked. 'That was the girl?'

Cole nodded. 'Yes. Then Davinia Dredge, nineteen, another Norwich girl. She was murdered six years ago, and the last girl . . . well, hardly a girl, was Gillian Packer, forty-one years old, and she was also from Chelmsford. I knew her, in fact . . .' Cole added after a pause, 'I knew her quite well.'

'You did?' Ingram asked.

'Professionally speaking, I mean.' Cole smiled. 'And that is my profession, not hers . . .'

'Of course.' Mundy grinned. 'We realized that.'

'And we put a question mark against her name . . . twice the age of the five previous victims, which means that she does not fully fit the victim profile. The others were aged between nineteen and twenty-four. She was forty-one . . . So . . .' Cole laid the file down, '. . . are they linked or are we seeing something that is not really there? These murders are well spaced out in both time and geography . . . one murder every three or four years and, unusually, not increasing in frequency. As you gentlemen know, we would expect a serial killer to strike with increasing frequency and take his victims months, not years, apart.'

'Yes.' Mundy nodded. 'I see what you mean. So what is it that does link them? What are the similarities?'

'All were sex workers,' Cole explained. 'All were abducted, all were left naked outside the town in which they worked and

all were strangled. So it's the same MO which links them . . .
possibly. But only possibly.'

'Did any clothing or other personal items ever turn up?'
Mundy asked.

'No.' Cole shook his head. 'We never found anything. Not
a trace of any of their clothing or possessions.'

'Was there anything similar about the way they were left
. . . I mean, were they in a pose or anything like that?' Ingram
enquired.

'No,' Cole leaned forward, 'not that we have been able to
determine anyway. All were left by the side of a minor road
and they were left as if dumped . . . so not in a pose or anything
of that manner, and a side road is not unusual. I mean, no
murder victim is ever dumped on the side of a main road . . .
all those cars going past.'

'Any CCTV footage?' Mundy asked.

'Good point.' Cole pointed his index finger at Mundy.
'CCTV only arrived in Chelmsford in time to record the
goings-on when Gillian Packer was murdered but we have not
identified any vehicle or pedestrian of interest. So either they
are the victims of the same person or persons, or it is the case
that on an average of once every three or four years one person
or persons acting alone will abduct a sex worker off the street,
strangle her and dump her body in a remote location a few
miles out of town, be it Chelmsford, King's Lynn or Norwich
or wherever . . . All that amid the plethora of crimes of violence
which take place annually in our little corner of England which
is known as East Anglia.'

'I see your difficulty,' Mundy murmured. 'You've either got
a serial killer or you haven't.'

'That about sums it up.' Cole smiled and nodded. 'We have
or we have not. As you say, no hallmark, nothing to let us
know that all the victims were murdered by the same person
. . . no taunting of the police . . . and, like I said, there is no
increase in the frequency of the murders. The murders are not
localized but East Anglia is flat and if the murderer had a car
they would travel, so that may not be a significant argument
in favour of different perpetrators, but the victims were all
strangled whereas Oliver Walwyn was battered over the head.

The women were dumped where they would be easily seen while Oliver's body seems to have been deliberately hidden from view . . . so, we are quite certain that the murders of Oliver Walwyn and Janet Laws are unconnected. It is just coincidence that they both occurred on the same night and in the same approximate location.' Cole paused. 'Oliver Walwyn is a cold case, so over to you gentlemen with that one. Janet Laws is hot. It stays with us. It's part of Operation Moonlight. We are seeing if we can find a definite link between the murders of the six women.'

'Would you mind if we looked at the file?' Mundy asked.

'Of Operation Moonlight?' Cole sounded surprised. 'I'd have to get clearance, of course, but I can't see why not. You are still police officers, technically speaking, but I don't need to remind you gentlemen that you're investigating the murder of Oliver Walwyn. Please don't go plunging your little hooves into Operation Moonlight.'

Walking away from the concrete slab-sided new build that was Chelmsford Police Station, Ingram asked Mundy why he had asked to look at the file on Operation Moonlight.

'It's not the whole file that I want to read,' Mundy explained. 'I really want to look at the file on the murder of Janet Laws. Same night, you see, and in very close proximity to Oliver Walwyn's murder. It occurred to me that there might be some link, not seen at the time. Anyway, it's been an unexpectedly long day. Let's get back to London, shall we? We only came up here for you to show me a pond in a village green, remember?'

'Suits me.' Ingram took the car keys from his coat pocket. 'That more than suits me.'

TWO

'**W**ell, as you know, it's still very early days, boss.' Ingram cleared his throat. 'By that I mean, of course, that it's very early days for us.'

'Yes, of course.' Fred Pickering smiled his response. 'So where next, do you think?'

'I really don't know.' Ingram paused. 'Speaking for myself, I have the distinct impression that it's going to remain a cold case until a local person comes forward with a confession, possibly even a deathbed confession . . . but I think Maurice has a notion?' Ingram turned to Mundy.

'Yes, sir.' Mundy sat forward and clasped his meaty hands together. 'I would like to investigate any possible connection with a murder which took place on the same night. Essex Police are assuming it to be coincidental – different victim profile, different method of murder, you see . . . but I'd like to turn the stone over. Essex Police have obtained clearance for us to look at the file.'

'It's an ongoing case?' Pickering frowned. 'I confess I don't like the sound of that.'

'Yes, sir,' Mundy replied. 'It's ongoing . . . possibly linked to other similar murders.'

Pickering glanced out of his office window at the buildings on the south bank of the Thames, at that moment dulled in focus by a relentless drizzle.

Pickering was a short man for a police officer, and a man whom Mundy had found to be serious-minded. After a brief pause, Pickering turned to Ingram.

'Tom, could you give me and Maurice a moment, please . . . if you don't mind?'

'Of course.' Ingram stood up. 'I'll wait outside.'

'Maurice,' Fred Pickering folded his arms when Ingram had closed the door behind him, 'I read your file. I had to when you joined the CCRT. But you know that.'

'Yes, sir.' Maurice Mundy nodded briefly.

'Do be careful about getting involved in ongoing investigations,' Pickering cautioned.

'Yes, sir.' Mundy glanced downwards at the worn carpet in Pickering's office.

'Don't eat out of anyone else's nosebag . . . don't drink out of anyone else's trough . . . keep inside your traces.' Pickering spoke solemnly.

'Yes, sir. Understood. Thank you for the advice.' Mundy looked up at Pickering. 'I hear what you say.'

'You know the rules,' Pickering continued. 'If you do uncover any new evidence, you must hand it over to the boys and girls who are still working towards their pensions. Remember, we're the old fogies who have been given some old cases to play with before we get dementia. We have no right to conduct formal interviews and no power of arrest.'

'Understood, sir.' Mundy held eye contact with Pickering. 'Fully.'

'Understand, remember . . . and,' Pickering added sternly, '. . . observe the rules.'

Mundy stood up. 'Yes, sir. Will that be all?'

Outside in the corridor, Mundy approached Ingram. 'I'd like to nip down to Criminal Records if you don't mind,' he said in a calm, pleasant voice.

'Of course.' Ingram smiled.

'I can meet you in the canteen?' Mundy suggested.

'If you like. How long will you be?'

'Fifteen minutes, half an hour,' Mundy replied. 'It won't take long . . . not long at all.'

'That'll give a little more time for the traffic to clear. Yes, all right.' Ingram smiled again. 'I'll see you down in the canteen.'

Mundy took the lift down to the basement of New Scotland Yard and walked along the narrow, quiet corridor to Criminal Records. At the enquiry desk of Criminal Records Stanley Kinross limped up to him wearing a wide and a ready grin.

'I see you made it.' Kinross shook Mundy warmly by the hand. 'Well done, you.'

'Yes.' Mundy smiled, shaking Kinross by the hand equally

as warmly. 'The pension's mine, all mine to have and to hold
. . . can't be taken from me. Mine until I croak but it's not an
awful lot – it's hardly a king's ransom, which is one of the
reasons why I applied for the CCRT. It provides a little stipend
on top, makes for a living income, keeps my old hand in
and it helps to fill the days. I am certain that I'd rot away
otherwise. I feel that there's still life in the old dog yet.'

'Yes, I must say you're looking fit,' Kinross observed. 'Me,
I won't have that option – another eighteen months and they'll
kick me out to grass. No extended service for little old me.
I'll be out of the door asap on a police constable's pension
. . . full service but still a police constable's pension. Can't
say I am looking forward to it – money will be tight and no
option to continue service in the CCRT for little me. I have
no criminal investigation experience. I was never out of
uniform.'

'Yes, that was bad luck, Stan . . . a lot of bad luck.' Mundy's
jaw was set firm.

'Was it?' Kinross raised his eyebrows. 'I survived . . . patient
killed, mental health officer left with permanent brain damage,
but I survived. I have to look at it that way – unfortunate
maybe but also with a big slice of luck thrown in. I look at
it that way . . . I try to keep a positive outlook.'

'But still, it was a bad show all round,' Mundy insisted. 'A
very bad show.'

Kinross pursed his lips. 'Yes . . . yes . . . I was angry at
the time, I don't deny it – I don't deny it at all. But now . . .
well, I have stopped being angry. It does you no good. I have
had a full life . . . two perfect children, both at university and
a very good marriage which still has a lot of passion in it.
I've a lot to be thankful for. It really could have been an awful
lot worse.'

'Well, yes, you beat me on that score.' Mundy inclined his
head. 'I can't compete there.'

'You should have got married, Maurice,' Kinross said
matter-of-factly. 'I can wholly recommend it.'

'No one would have me, Stan . . . and I always think that
it's better to be happy and contentedly single than unhappy
and malcontent in marriage.' Mundy paused. 'Well, we must

have a beer one day, as we keep promising we will, but right now I wonder if you can help me?'

'If I can.'

'I'd like to look at the file of Joshua Derbyshire, convicted of murder twenty-eight years ago,' Mundy explained.

'Twenty-eight years ago. That's going back a long way.'

'Yes, but he's still inside,' Mundy added. 'He's still doing bird.'

'Still!' Kinross whistled. 'Is he a multiple murder . . . a serial arsonist?'

'Nope, just one murder. He hacked an old lady to death. It was very, very messy . . . and then he went in front of a hanging judge who gave him life and set the minimum tariff at thirty years.'

'A throw-the-key-away number.' Kinross turned and reached for the requisition form. 'You'll have to complete this form, Maurice. Is it a CCRT case?'

'No, it's just something I want to check . . . something personal.' Mundy took out a ballpoint pen and began to fill in the requisition form. 'I won't keep the file long.'

'It can't be removed from CR without authorisation,' Kinross advised as Mundy completed the short form.

'Yes, I know.' Mundy handed the completed requisition form back to Stanley Kinross. 'I just have to check a detail or two. Won't be a jiffy.'

Tom Ingram drove at a steady speed out of London on the Great Cambridge Road. The journey passed largely with a comfortable and relaxed silence existing between himself and Maurice Mundy. Only when the built-up area of north-west London was behind them and they drove out between ploughed fields near Cheshunt did Tom Ingram ask, 'So what was down in CR that you wanted to look at? Was it something to do with this case?'

'Who really, not a what,' Mundy replied, 'and no, it has nothing to do with our little job. I hope you didn't mind waiting?'

'No, not at all.' Ingram fixed his eyes on the road ahead. 'As you said yesterday, we have more time now and I rather

enjoyed my cup of tea and bacon sandwich. I didn't have
much of a breakfast, you see, so it suited me. You have a
friend down there . . . down in the void?'

'Yes . . . a "there but for the Grace of God go I" sort of
friend,' Mundy explained.

'Oh?' Ingram asked. 'A close shave?'

'Yes, it was, and he's a geezer called Kinross, Stanley
Kinross – a very nice bloke. Very nice bloke indeed.' Mundy
looked out across a ploughed field to a small wood on the
skyline. 'In fact, you might have seen him from time to time
over the years. He's a bald-headed geezer with a pronounced
limp.'

'A copper with a limp.' Ingram turned to Mundy. 'No, I
would have remembered seeing him.'

'Well, the limp is the story.' Mundy returned his gaze to
his front. 'We were on duty, me and Stan, both uniformed
constables. I'd just joined the Met. Stanley was a year or so
younger than me but he already had a few years in. Anyway,
we were about to go off duty . . . it was approaching ten
o'clock . . . when we got a call from control. One constable
was required for a Mental Health Act escort; it was either me
or Stanley. I was keen on a young policewoman at the time
and had promised to take her out if we could both get off duty
on time. Stanley had just got married and was anxious to get
home so we tossed a coin. Stanley lost and he said, "Oh, well,
I dare say that the overtime will come in useful". He had just
taken on a mortgage, you see, so there was some compensation for him in working late.'

'Indeed.' Ingram kept his eyes fixed on the road.

'Anyway, it turned out that the patient had just been sectioned
under the Mental Health Act as being a danger to others but
he was apparently quite placid and cooperative. Stanley told
me later that he, the patient, suffered from a delusion that he
had "special powers" and that he had been arrested when he
was reported for stopping women in the street and telling them
that they had to give him their handbags. But he wasn't
snatching their bags and running off with them, you understand,
just very calmly telling them that they had to surrender their
bags to him because of his special powers.'

'I've got you.' Ingram continued to drive at a steady pace, in keeping with the traffic flow.

'So the police arrived, sized up the situation and bounced him into custody. He kept telling them about his special powers so they called the police surgeon, who said that it was definitely a mental health issue. He said to get a mental health officer and request him – the patient, that is – to be sectioned. "It's a clear Section 24 . . . forty-eight-hours' detention for observation . . ."'

'Yes,' Ingram replied, 'sounds like it was.'

'Anyway, the mental health officer was called and had a chat with this geezer who kept asking to be allowed to go because he had special powers so the MHO consented to a Section 24. The geezer wasn't going to go to the hospital voluntarily so the forms were completed and signed and they put this mad geezer in the rear of the mental health officer's car. He took the wheel and Stanley sat in the front passenger seat, intending to run him up to Friern Barnet Psychiatric Hospital. So off they went, they'd got Highgate behind them and then suddenly the mad geezer apparently leapt forward and grabbed the steering wheel.'

'Oh, no,' Ingram groaned.

'Oh, yes, oh, yes, oh, yes . . . and his action, in grabbing the wheel, caused the car to crash. The patient was killed outright, the mental health officer sustained severe and permanent brain damage and Stanley Kinross was off work for the best part of a year. He recovered as much as he was going to recover but was left with a pronounced limp. The Metropolitan Police tried to retire him with some paltry, next-to-nothing package because he had only had three years' service in at that point, but the Police Federation fought his corner and he was allowed to return to work, though he was told that it could not ever be front-line policing.'

'Fair enough,' Ingram uttered. 'I mean, if you're a copper then you've got to look the part and act the part – you can't walk your beat or chase after felons with a bad limp. It just wouldn't do . . . it just wouldn't cut the mustard.'

'Reckon so.' Mundy nodded gently in agreement. 'So that's Stanley Kinross. He's been in the stores – or Criminal Records

– ever since. He gets moved every so often to stop him gathering dust, and right now he's in CR. So the career that might have been his, well, he just didn't get. He'll retire as a constable . . . a full increment, on a full-service pension, but a constable's pension is a lot less than might have been the case . . . inspector or chief inspector or whatever he might have risen to, so that could so easily have been me in that car. If I had called "heads" instead of "tails", and the richest thing is that the relationship with the female officer came to nought . . .'

'By the Grace of God, as you say.' Ingram slowed at the approach to a traffic roundabout. 'But the mental health officer must have been travelling.'

'Yes.' Mundy nodded, this time vigorously so. 'That's the issue, the whole issue. I mean, instant death, permanent brain damage and a badly smashed-up leg . . . you don't get injuries like that if you crash at thirty mph, and for quite a long time afterwards Stanley was angry with the mental health officer for speeding. He blames himself for not saying something to make the geezer slow down but the accident took place in a sixty mph zone and the MHO was not over the speed limit. On the limit, perhaps, but not over it. And Stanley is a deferential sort of bloke and he also credited the mental health officer with professional knowledge which he – Stanley, that is – didn't possess, and he assumed the mental health officer knew what he was doing in getting the patient to the hospital as quickly as possible. In the event, the speed just increased the level of stress and tension within the confines of the car with a geezer in the back seat who believed he had special powers anyway . . . and it seems that it provoked him to react in the way he did. A nice, gentle drive up to the hospital at thirty mph would have taken twice as long but with little tension within the car, and at thirty mph any injuries in a crash would have been relatively minor.' Mundy paused. 'So I go and have a chat with Stanley when I can . . . I dare say I am suffering survivor guilt.'

'He doesn't resent you?' Ingram asked.

'No, not Stanley, and he wouldn't swap my life for his.' Mundy glanced to his left. 'Outside the job his life is overflowing with fortune. He has a hugely successful marriage and two children at university – one studying law, the other studying to become a doctor. Me . . . no wife and an empty house to go home to . . . And my pension isn't a great deal more than his is going to be . . . so, no, there is no ill will. We also go for a beer occasionally.'

'That's good to hear . . . unfortunate story, though,' Ingram commented.

'Yes, but he also hasn't been badly affected by the job. Police work can make you a hard, cold sort of personality and he's avoided that being out of frontline policing – only ever dealing with colleagues, or distraught relatives of the suddenly deceased, never with criminals, and he's never been tied in knots in the witness box by clever defence lawyers, so he's not become hardened by it all. He is a very pleasant, gentle soul. That's no mean compensation.'

'Who really?' Ingram pressed after a short pause. 'Who . . . really?'

'Sorry?' Mundy turned and looked at him. 'What do you mean?'

'You said "who really" just now when I asked you what your visit to CR was for,' Ingram explained. 'It suggests something other than a chat with your mate who had his leg smashed instead of you having your leg smashed.'

'Oh, yes . . . just a case, just wanted to check something, get a detail or two.' Mundy looked away from Ingram. 'A case I was involved in a long time ago. It bothers me a little.'

Tom Ingram remained silent for a few moments, then said, 'Just take care, Maurice. You're retired and you're in the Cold Case Review Team so just stay within the rules – don't go playing the private detective. For your own sake, you must not forget that. You're in your autumn, you've been given a job because of your expertise . . . we both are and we both have . . . there's just no room for either of us to pursue a hidden agenda. Don't use your membership of CCRT to access records of cases not allocated to us. Don't step outside the box you're in.'

'I won't. Thanks for the advice, Tom,' Mundy replied, 'but I won't.'

'All right, I won't mention it again. Right, let's go and read this file. What was her name?'

'Janet Laws,' Mundy replied. 'Her name was Janet Laws. She was the fourth victim – that is if, and only if, there is a serial killer out there, but we are only interested in the link, if any, with the murder of Oliver Walwyn.'

Ingram smiled at Mundy. 'Pleased you said that, Maurice. Let's keep it focused. That's the ticket.'

Tom Ingram knocked loudly but reverentially on the black-painted door of the house. It was answered promptly by a short, thin man with a mop of ginger hair. He was casually dressed and held a tabloid newspaper, folded up, in his left hand.

'Police.' Ingram showed his warrant card. 'We're sorry to call unannounced in this manner. We'd like to ask you a few questions, if we may . . .'

'What about?' The man had a high-pitched voice. 'The police don't call like this . . . out of the blue . . . unless there is some sort of emergency.'

'There is no emergency, sir.' Ingram spoke with a gentle, reassuring tone. 'Please, don't be alarmed . . . no need to worry.'

'That's a relief . . . so what is it about?' The householder relaxed his muscle tone. 'It must be something important.'

'Janet Laws,' Mundy advised. 'A young woman called Janet Laws.'

'Janet Laws . . . Janet Laws.' The man looked momentarily beyond Ingram and Mundy at the street behind them and then at the officers. 'That name . . . it's a name that rings bells . . . I've heard that name before . . . just can't place it. But it rings a bell all right.'

'She was murdered some ten years ago. Her body was dumped beside the road . . . quite a remote road,' Ingram explained. 'We have been re-reading the file at Chelmsford Police Station and we saw that you gave some information.'

'Oh, yes, the street girl . . . poor lass,' the man replied. 'A sex worker but you can't hold that against her – so many of those girls are dreadful victims of circumstance but yes, I know who you mean. Now I remember. How can I help? I told the police all I could, all I knew, but it came to nothing. No one was arrested, not that I heard about anyway.'

'We know, hence a reappraisal,' Ingram explained. 'Can we go over the information you gave?'

'If you wish . . . please come in.' The man stepped aside and the two officers entered the house. Mundy walked into the hall and turned to his right as the householder had asked him to do and entered a very neatly kept room with a television of a modest size set upon a low shelf beside the gas fire. A narrow alcove housed six shelves, each holding books of varying sizes. Mundy and Ingram sat upon being invited to do so. As he sat, Maurice Mundy took out his notepad and then took a ballpoint pen from the inside pocket of his jacket.

'So you're Mr Golightly,' Mundy confirmed. 'Mr David Golightly?'

'Yes, that is me.' Golightly sat in an armchair. 'You know, I don't think I can add anything. In fact, I think I will have forgotten some of the details.'

'Even so . . . even so . . .' Mundy glanced to his left and right. He found the living room to be cramped as is the case, he had observed, in many new-build houses. 'Can we go over it again? What did you see?'

'Well, it was a dark night . . . it was raining heavily, coming down in stair rods, as is the expression. I saw a grey car being driven at speed down a cul-de-sac.'

'At speed down a cul-de-sac . . .' Mundy confirmed.

'Yes, I was walking home that night; well, I was walking to get a bus to take me home. I'd had a beer or two but I was still clear-headed. I was not a heavy drinker, I'm still not. I took a shortcut I knew down a narrow street which had no pavement on either side and runs between two industrial units . . . The road leads into the industrial estate . . . and during the night the estate is shut down. No traffic goes into it.'

'All right,' Mundy grunted. 'We understand.'

'So I am walking down the narrow passageway, the road at the bottom goes left and right . . . the right leads to the industrial estate while the left leads into Chelmsford . . . and I see car headlights approach from the left.'

'So from Chelmsford – the car was coming from Chelmsford?' Mundy confirmed.

'Yes. So I am suddenly thinking that I'm in trouble here

because the car has to turn right, up the narrow road I'm in, because if he goes straight on all he's going to do is enter the industrial estate and that's a dead end, a cul-de-sac. So I am frightened because I can see myself getting crushed against the wall. I might be quite small but even if I flatten myself against the wall a car will still catch me. This is what I am thinking, and I am not happy, not a happy camper at all. I am thinking strongly that I'm going to be done a real injury and there is no time to run back the way I had come to avoid getting crushed.'

'I see.' Mundy listened intently. He was finding David Golightly to be a credible personality. He noticed that Tom Ingram was also listening intently.

'And I am more frightened because the boy at the wheel is not dragging his feet, he's coming on at a fast pace. I expected him to slow to turn into the road I was walking down, then once the corner is turned to pick up speed again. I'm frightened now because I'm wearing blue waterproof clothing . . . a coat and leggings. They don't reflect car headlights; the boy will not see me. This is what I am thinking. The next day after that I bought a pair of yellow waterproof leggings because they reflect car headlights.'

'Yes, I know.' Mundy smiled.

'So . . . I am getting more and more frightened by the second and then he only drives right past the narrow passage I am in.'

'Into the industrial estate?' Mundy said.

'Yes. So I think he's giving me a chance to run to the road he has gone down because that road has a pavement and there I'll be safe. He's missed his turning—'

'His turning being the narrow passage that you were in?' Mundy asked.

'Exactly.' Golightly nodded his head. 'So I can get out of the narrow passage before he turns round and comes back and turns into the passage.'

'OK.' Mundy wrote on his notepad. 'Please, go on.'

'So I get to the end of the passage and I am safe and I see him coming back at high speed and he drives past me, past the narrow passage and goes back the way he came.'

'Back into Chelmsford?' Mundy tapped the ballpoint pen on his notepad.

'Yes, so I thought that means that he's a stranger, because a local person would know that there was no road through the industrial estate . . . and, like I said, he was going at speed as well. He was in a hurry driving at speed into a cul-de-sac . . . definitely a stranger . . . deffo . . . as my son would say . . . deffo a stranger.'

'Fair observation,' Ingram commented.

'I was going to turn into the industrial estate myself because there is a pathway which leads out of the estate but it's for pedestrians only . . . wide enough for motorcycles but there's a concrete bollard at either end to stop them from using it. There's no exit for cars. None at all. So, like I said . . . he was a stranger and he was a stranger in a hurry. But I told the police that at the time, yes I did, I deffo told the police that.'

'Yes, it is in the file . . . they did note it down.' Mundy smiled. 'They were listening to you. Did you recognize the make of car?'

'A Saab,' Golightly replied confidently. 'A Saab 90.'

'You seem certain?' Mundy observed, looking at David Golightly. 'Are you sure of that?'

'I used to own one,' Golightly replied smugly, 'so I ought to be able to recognize one when I see one. They don't make them any more . . . more's the pity. Wrap around windscreen, aircraft-like controls. You know all is well if all the needles on the dials are parallel, so you just needed to run your eye across the instruments. But if one needle is well out of parallel with the others you know something is amiss. I also liked the ignition key being situated between the front seats, just in front of the handbrake . . . a very nice touch that, so I thought, anyway. The car had a nice, stable ride, solid feel. It was a bit complicated, though – everything happened on the front wheels . . . drive, handbrake, everything – and that was why I parted company with my Saab. It was way too complicated, things kept going wrong . . . I swapped it for a Volvo and then I got reliability through simple, straightforward design. "Keep it simple, Simon" . . . the KISS principle, you see. The less there is to go wrong the less will go wrong.' Golightly paused.

'Yes, I confess that I grew to appreciate the reliability of the Volvo but I missed the sparky nature of the Saab.'

'I get the picture . . . it was a Saab and you definitely know your Swedish cars. So, if you say it was a Saab, then it was a Saab,' Mundy replied dryly. 'In your statement you said that two men were in the car as it drove past you that night?'

'Yes.' Golightly replied with continued confidence. 'It was a dark, rainy night but I was so close to the car as it went past that you couldn't get another person between me and it. I was just inches away. I remember thinking that they seemed a bit like Laurel and Hardy.'

'One big and one small?' Mundy asked. 'Is that what you mean?'

'Yes, that's exactly what I mean . . . with the little guy, the Stanley Laurel of the two being the driver and the heavy guy in the back seat.' Golightly reclined in his armchair. 'I thought nothing of it at the time but when I heard on the radio that a girl had been found just outside Chelmsford later the following day . . . naked . . . I contacted the police and gave them a description of the car.'

'So why did you make a connection with the car and the murdered girl?' Ingram asked.

'Two reasons,' Golightly replied. 'The car was coming from the area in Chelmsford where the working girls stand but especially because the big guy in the back seemed to be struggling with something or someone.'

'Really?' Mundy's jaw dropped slightly. 'That is interesting.'

'It is in the gentleman's statement, Maurice.' Tom Ingram turned to Mundy.

'Ah . . . sorry.' Mundy smiled sheepishly. 'I must have missed that.'

'Well, yes,' Golightly continued, 'he seemed to be holding something down in this manner,' Golightly leaned forward and extended both arms between his knees and towards the floor, 'as if he was pressing down on someone who was struggling to get up. The car went by in a flash and, as I say, it was dark and raining heavily, but I'm certain of what I saw.'

'Did either of the men see you as they drove by?' Ingram asked.

'I don't think so,' Golightly replied quickly. 'The geezer in the back didn't see me and the driver didn't glance at me . . . the waterproof clothing I am wearing, remember, does not reflect in car headlights.'

'Ah, yes . . . you said,' Mundy replied.

'So I told the police everything, including the description of the car.' Golightly sat back in his chair.

'Does that mean that there was something unique about it?' Mundy glanced at Golightly.

'Yes,' Golightly replied, 'it had a new side door which was of a darker colour to the rest of the car.'

'Really?' Ingram sat forward. 'That would narrow the field down considerably.'

'It would.' Golightly spoke with clear certainty. 'The car seemed to be of a greyish colour . . . possibly a light shade of blue but the door was darker, like a red or a brown . . . or a black. It was as if the original door had been damaged somehow and the owner had obtained a replacement door from an identical car but of a different colour and he wasn't at all bothered about the mismatching colours. Oh, and there was no light over the rear number plate. I noticed that because I once got a fixed penalty notice for not having a light over my rear number plate. I was annoyed at the time – I thought the police must have better things to do – but I was just eighteen and driving a real wreck of a car that probably looked a bit iffy, so the coppers pulled me over and gave me notice to present my documents at the police station within five days. Dare say I would have done the same if I was a police officer and saw a youth driving a car without proper lights showing. Driving without insurance is not big and it's not clever, yet the youth do it all the time.'

'Indeed.' Ingram smiled. 'Indeed.'

'But you know, I still see that car from time to time,' Golightly added quietly.

'You do!' Mundy gasped. 'Is that really the case?'

'Yes, very rarely, but yes, I do,' Golightly replied. 'Very, very rarely.'

'You didn't report it to the police?' Mundy raised his voice slightly.

'Not the first time . . .' Golightly replied calmly.

'Why not?' Ingram asked.

'Because the first time I saw the car again I saw the near side and noticed a brown door on a pale blue Saab and I thought another owner of a Saab has had one of his doors replaced. I thought that because the driver was a blonde-haired woman, so I thought it was a different car. Then, later – weeks later – I realized that the owner of the Saab had had both doors replaced and that he had subsequently sold the car . . . or was letting a female friend or relative have use of it.'

'Fair enough.' Mundy slowly tapped his notepad with his ballpoint. 'You say that you have seen it on other occasions?'

'Very rarely, but yes, I have . . . it's a solid old car, still going strong.' Golightly beamed. 'It's a winner, all right. Some cars are. They just go on for ever. Others are Friday afternoon jobs but that Saab is a clear winner.'

'Where do you see it?' Ingram asked.

'All over . . . all over East Anglia,' Golightly replied. 'I'm a salesman. You see, I sell agricultural fertiliser and animal feed so I get all over East Anglia. I'm winding down now though, I'll be pushing ye pen soon . . . The company says it's a reward for many years of loyal service. Taking me off the road is a reward, but that's all so much codswallop.'

'You think?' Ingram smiled briefly.

'Of course it is. You see, if you're a salesman you have to look the part, you've got to have the right appearance and part of that required appearance is youth. People just won't buy things from an old man, especially when the old man is tired and worn out and the young man is full of enthusiasm, so desk job, here I come.' Golightly smiled and shrugged his shoulders. 'Mind you, it suits me. Frankly, I am getting a bit jaded with it all, which is why you have caught me at home. I've phoned in sick . . . I am "throwing a sickie", as my brother in Australia would say. He emigrated there when he was a young man. He did all right, got a good standard of living, but I wouldn't settle in Australia . . . too much sun for me.'

'So, tell us . . . where exactly have you seen the Saab with the odd-coloured doors?' Mundy pressed.

'Where? Well . . . the first time was in Harlow New Town. I saw it when it was parked in a car park. It caught my eye as I drove past. The second time was up in King's Lynn . . . that's a damn weird town if you ask me, but then they all are up there in north Norfolk. You know, when I'm up that way I always get the same feeling that I get whenever I have visited small towns in the Irish Republic – it's like all the locals know something that strangers and visitors are not permitted to be privy to. It's all the same up there, and Fakenham . . . that is one odd little town. I mean, where else would you get planning permission to build a cinema in the middle of a traffic roundabout? It's madness . . . sheer madness—'

'All right, all right,' Mundy held up his hand, 'we'll take your word for it, Mr Golightly. So, Janet Laws was murdered ten years ago and since then you might possibly have seen the car in question twice, once in Harlow and then later in King's Lynn?'

'Yes. It was in King's Lynn that I saw a young blonde woman behind the wheel and I also saw that the driver's side door was brown . . . and there might have been a third sighting in Newmarket.'

'So the car has been seen widely over East Anglia?' Mundy observed.

'Yes . . . but once a car achieves classic status buyers will come from far and wide to look at it and possibly purchase it,' Golightly explained. 'And folk want Saabs now . . . they don't make them any more, like I said, so folk want good, used models. They're an investment now. A good Saab 90 is worth hanging on to.'

'Yes.' Mundy once again held up his hand. 'Let's keep this focused, if we can. So the last sighting was in Newmarket. How long ago was that?'

'Quite recently. It is November now, so . . . I'd say about this time last year.'

'Quite recent?' Mundy pursed his lips. 'Was it being driven by the blonde woman?'

'No,' Golightly smiled, 'it wasn't being driven at all, it was on a ramp in a garage – that is to say a service station, rather than petrol filling station – having its exhaust welded up. I had a close look at it and saw that I was right about the doors . . . both were brown on a car which was pale blue . . . if it was the same car.'

'Do you recall the name of the garage?' Mundy asked.

'The Swinton Garage . . . I was driving past with a recently blown exhaust. I stopped and asked if they could get me out of trouble. All I wanted was a quick weld to get me back on the road. They said yes, just as soon as we've welded up the Saab's exhaust we'll put your car on the ramp and weld your exhaust.'

'The Swinton Garage,' Mundy wrote on his notepad.

'Yes,' Golightly confirmed, 'the Swinton Garage in Newmarket.'

Walking away from Golightly's house, Mundy asked, 'Do you mind if we go to Newmarket tomorrow?'

'No, but we have time today, though.' Ingram fished in his coat pocket for his car keys. 'Still plenty of daylight left.'

'Yes, but there's something I need to do,' Mundy pleaded. 'It's really quite important.'

'If you like. Ten years on . . .' Ingram shrugged, '. . . I dare say that half a day isn't going to make a huge deal of difference. We're not under any time pressure.'

'Thanks, I appreciate it.' Mundy smiled. 'I owe you one, Tom.'

THREE

'So you're not a proper copper?' Joshua Derbyshire smiled briefly. 'Sort of part-time and keeping your old hand in sort of copper . . .?'

'Part-time, keeping my hand in? Yes . . . yes, you could say that.' Mundy nodded. 'But a proper copper all right, Joshua. Once a copper always a copper. That's just the way of it. So, I am a proper copper, which is why we are in here, not the visiting area. It's like . . .' Mundy glanced up at the white-tiled walls. 'It's a bit like that I have been taken off the active service list but I'm still on the team . . . look at it that way.'

'OK, I can understand that.' Joshua Derbyshire was a softly spoken man, so Mundy found, slightly built, and Mundy was interested in an alertness he noticed in his eyes. 'I was a bit lost but I can understand that,' Derbyshire added.

'You'll be wondering why I'm here.' Mundy held eye contact with the man, who was dressed in a blue striped shirt and blue denims.

'Yes . . . sort of curious.' Derbyshire nodded. 'Sort of.'

Mundy had to concede that Derbyshire looked very young and healthy for his forty-five years but that, he thought, is prison life, especially twenty-eight years of it. 'It's about your conviction. The elderly lady you murdered.'

'No, I didn't.' Derbyshire remained calm. 'I have always said that and I'll always say it. I'll do my little three score and ten before I will admit to something I didn't do. I mean, if I did it, I'd admit it. I might even be out by now . . . if I had admitted it.'

'You're in denial of murder.' Mundy continued to hold eye contact with Derbyshire.

'Yes. And I always will be.' Derbyshire continued to smile. 'I always will be.'

'You admitted it,' Mundy pressed. 'You confessed to the murder.'

'I was tired. I was confused. I was seventeen years old. The solicitor I had wasn't interested,' Derbyshire replied defensively. 'It was like he wanted to go home as soon as he could. He told me that if I pleaded guilty it would be easier for me – easier for him, more like. So I pleaded guilty then decided not to.'

'It still reads like a solid case. I read it just this morning.' Mundy leaned forward and folded his arms in front of him. 'You were obsessed with your victim. You had photographs of her in your flat. You visited her on a daily basis, entering and leaving her home at will.'

'And . . .? What does that prove?' Derbyshire also leaned forward. 'I carried her shopping for her, I did odd jobs for her . . . worked on her garden . . . worked on her car . . . I took out the refuse bags . . . all that sort of thing I did for her.'

'So why the obsession?' Mundy asked. 'What did you find special about her?'

'Because she treated me like I was a human being. Simple as that,' Derbyshire replied. 'It's as plain and simple as that. I am not very bright. I went to a special school but I have a brain . . . I do . . . a bit of a brain. I have three O-levels . . . I took them in here. I went to classes here in "the villa" and I got three O-levels. And I read. *Treasure Island* by Robert Louis Stephenson.'

'Good story.' Mundy smiled. 'A good adventure story. I read it myself many years ago.'

'I started to read it at school,' Derbyshire explained. 'I was making progress with it, I was getting there, and then a teacher took it from me. She said, "You can't possibly read that, Joshua, so stop pretending you can", and took it from me and gave me an Enid Blyton book to read.'

Mundy groaned. 'How old were you when that happened?'

'Fifteen or sixteen,' Derbyshire replied. 'Something like that, but I got hold of a copy here in the prison library and read it. I managed one chapter a day and I got through it. I read of Long John Silver and his parrot Captain Flint and Ben Gunn . . . He got fed up with it.'

'Who?'

'The author – he got fed up with the book,' Derbyshire argued. 'It reads like he did anyway.'

Mundy smiled approvingly. 'Why do you say that, Josh?'

'He begins two paragraphs in the last chapter with the word "well" like he's anxious to get to the end of the tale. Long John Silver takes his share of the dosh. He steals his fair share and vanishes into the night . . . like a thief in the night. Ben Gunn loses his share of the treasure within three days of returning to Bristol but we never know what the other folk did with their share . . . Jim Hawkins and the doctor . . . and how did they manage to hire a crew in the West Indies to sail the Hispaniola back to England without the crew finding out the ship was full of treasure? Especially since Long John Silver had broken down the bulkhead to get to where the treasure was stored, leaving the rest of the treasure in plain sight. I mean, the treasure was there for the taking, wasn't it? They would have taken over the ship and kept the treasure.'

'Good point.' Mundy nodded. 'I don't recall seeing that issue . . . well spotted.'

'I reckon he should have taken a week's holiday . . . even two weeks . . . then written the last chapter.' Derbyshire spoke with a strong London accent. 'But, see, Miss Tweedale, she wouldn't have done that. If Miss Tweedale saw me reading *Treasure Island* she would have encouraged me to carry on reading it. She wouldn't have taken it from me and given me a book for a five-year-old. Not Miss Tweedale . . .'

'No, that was bad,' Mundy said quietly. 'That should not have happened to you. That was very bad of the teacher to do that . . . very bad . . . but I can well believe what you say – schoolteachers can be like that.'

'Yes,' Joshua Derbyshire nodded briefly, 'and when I went to the special school the other kids would laugh at me, call me "soft Josh". That was my name, my nickname – "soft in the head Joshua" or "Joshie the softy".'

Mundy glanced up at the massive slab of opaque glass set high in the wall which was the room's only source of natural light. 'That shouldn't have happened either but children can be like that. I'm afraid that that is life . . . that is the way of it, sadly. Often the only thing that children learn in their secondary school is their survival techniques, so you probably didn't miss much.'

'I'll never know, will I?' Joshua Derbyshire forced a weak smile. 'But Miss Tweedale, she was good to me. She knew who I was because we lived in the same street, and she knew what the other children were doing. One day she stopped her car and picked me up because she saw I was walking towards a gang of thugs who were going to bully and tease me . . . so she stopped and picked me up. She had a lovely old Rolls-Royce and she stopped, took me into it and drove past them as she drove me home.'

'Is that how you met?' Mundy smiled. He was warming to Joshua Derbyshire.

'I reckon it was. We knew each other to see each other . . . if you know what I mean, but we never spoke to each other until the day she stopped and picked me up.'

'By sight?' Mundy assisted. 'You knew each other by sight?'

'Yes, by sight . . . I remember that day . . . and it happened again. She stopped and gave me a lift past the gang of boys, and then she said to call round on her on Saturday because she might have a job for me. So I went round the next Saturday morning and she gave me a shopping list. I went to the shops for her and I got everything on the list.'

'Good for you,' Maurice Mundy said approvingly.

'I didn't miss anything . . . and I went round again and I washed the lovely old car. It was built in 1957, so she told me. Inside it smelled lovely . . . all that leather . . . and I dug her garden, weeded it, and I mowed her lawn. We'd sit and talk and she told me all about herself. She'd been an actress and she gave me a photograph of herself when she was younger. I got my big sister to look Miss Tweedale up on the computer and copy all the photographs of her . . . and when I got my own little flat I put her pictures on the wall.' Derbyshire paused. 'She was really good to me. I liked her so much. I liked her a whole lot. I couldn't get a job so I'd go round to her house and be a good boy for her. Anything she wanted me to do, I'd do it. She was like a mum to me. I wouldn't hurt her . . . no way . . . I couldn't . . . I just couldn't hurt her.'

'But the jewellery that was stolen was found in the drawer

of your bedside cabinet in your little council flat. The murder weapon with Miss Tweedale's blood on it was also found in your flat.' Mundy slowly leaned backwards in his chair. 'And her blood on your clothing in the wicker laundry basket in your bathroom. You must admit, Joshua, it looked bad . . . it still does, in fact. It still reads like a safe conviction.'

'You know a lot about it all?' Derbyshire replied.

'I read your file earlier today,' Mundy advised. 'I told you . . . remember?'

'Why, though?' Derbyshire pressed. 'Why the interest?'

Mundy paused. 'Let's just leave it that I am interested. Let's just say that for now. Fair enough?'

'OK.' Derbyshire shrugged his shoulders. 'If you say so.'

'Is your family keeping in touch?'

'Just my sisters . . . one more than the other, it's mainly our Jane . . . good old Jane. It was Jane that used her computer to copy photographs of Miss Tweedale for me. She always used to stand up for me, even when I was little, and she stood by me all this time. I get a letter from her each week. She sends a postcard to me when she goes away from home and she visits when she can, but it's the weekly letter which keeps me going. Every Sunday evening she sits down and writes me a letter and I receive it every Tuesday. It always arrives . . . every Tuesday for twenty-eight years. I have kept them all . . . over a thousand now, and also the postcards. I saved everything she sent me.' Derbyshire smiled. 'Our Jane, she never believed I did it. She never believed I murdered Miss Tweedale. Never. Not ever. She's golden, my sister Jane. She's pure gold.'

'What about your parents?' Mundy asked.

'My dad died when I was ten. I remember him but never really knew him.' Joshua Derbyshire glanced to his left. 'My mum . . . well, she never had no time for me. She only ever wanted girls, did my mum . . . like she had some sort of downer on males. I was her third, I was. She wanted three girls but got a boy. She always told me that I was "stupid and always will be stupid . . . no girl would ever be as stupid as you" but my sisters stood up for me, particularly our Jane.

My mum didn't even come to my trial but both my sisters did. They both stood by me.'

'And Jane in particular?' Mundy commented. 'She sounds golden, as you say.'

'Yes. Golden.' Joshua Derbyshire looked downwards at the tabletop. 'Golden. She married a schoolteacher and she lives up in Nottingham – Robin Hood country. It's a day's trip for her to visit me but she visits when she can.'

'That's interesting.' Mundy sat back in his chair.

'What's interesting?' Derbyshire asked with a worried tone. 'It's interesting that she visits me? What's wrong with that?'

'It's interesting that in your file your sister is given as living in Burnt Oak,' Mundy explained.

'That was the address of our house when I was arrested,' Derbyshire explained. 'She's moved on with her life, and so has Sarah, my other sister. She lives in Clacton, a lot closer than Jane, but she doesn't visit or write as much. They gave up our tenancy when my mum died. She never wrote to me or visited me once . . . not once, my mum didn't.'

'I'd like to visit your sister.' Mundy held eye contact with Derbyshire. 'Both really, but preferably Jane in Nottingham. She sounds like a useful person to talk to. Can you let me have her name and address?'

'She's Jane Weekes now. She has two children,' Derbyshire advised. 'Why do you want to visit her?'

'For the same reason I am visiting you,' Mundy replied. 'Out of interest.'

'What . . . to laugh at me . . . "soft Josh"?' Derbyshire's tone of voice hardened.

'No . . . not at all. Am I laughing?' Mundy also spoke with a hardened tone. 'Have I laughed once since I have been here?'

'Why then?' Derbyshire demanded. 'What do you want with me?'

'Because I think you're innocent,' Mundy replied softly.

The ensuing silence lasted for a full fifteen seconds, during which both men continued to hold eye contact.

'I think you're innocent,' Mundy repeated, breaking the silence. 'That's why I am here.'

'You do?' Derbyshire gasped. 'You believe me . . .?'

'Yes,' Mundy spoke calmly, 'I do.'

'Why . . . I mean . . . why does a copper think I am innocent all of a sudden?' Derbyshire whispered. 'After twenty-eight years . . . not just my sister Jane but now a copper thinks I am innocent. Why?'

'It's not a sudden thing,' Mundy explained. 'Not a sudden thing for me, anyway. I have had my doubts about the safety of your conviction for quite some time now.'

'I appealed against my conviction,' Derbyshire once again looked down at the tabletop, 'for all the good it did. I lost the appeal.'

'I know you did.' Mundy nodded. 'The evidence was damning. I can see why you lost the appeal.'

'I got beaten up in here,' Derbyshire announced. 'It happened quite often.'

'I'm sorry to hear that,' Mundy replied. 'But again, that's the way of it. Murdering old ladies is not an acceptable crime. Crimes against children, crimes against the elderly . . . it makes you a "nonce" – you are not part of the criminal fraternity and so every now and then you get a kicking.'

'I know.' Derbyshire forced a smile. 'I found out . . . I found out the hard way but I get left alone now. I've got the years in, you see, and I know my place. I know how it works. If someone . . . if one of the top lags takes food from my plate I let him have it, and I give my tobacco allowance to a big geezer who watches my back in return but only so long as I don't annoy anyone – only if I don't make someone upset. Nobody picks on me but if I upset someone, well, then I take what's coming to me. I have to. So I avoid looking at other cons and let them take my food. I don't speak unless they speak to me and I don't speak to the prison staff, the screws . . . I don't speak to them at all. That's how I get by. I haven't had a kicking for about five years now,' Derbyshire added with a clear note of pride in his voice.

'I'm pleased you are surviving.' Mundy smiled. 'So what is your sister's address in Nottingham?'

'Appledore Crescent.' Derbyshire spelled the name for him.

Mundy committed the street name to memory.

'Number twenty-three,' Derbyshire added.

'Twenty-three.' Again, Mundy committed the house number to memory.

'You're not writing it down?' Derbyshire observed. 'You must have a good memory.'

'I have.' Mundy grinned. 'It comes with being a police officer all my working life. Well, pretty much all . . . and the number is easy to remember. They're consecutive numbers, you see: twelve, one two and forty-five . . . four five . . . and so on, so twenty-three . . . two three is easy to remember. So,' Mundy asked, 'does your sister Jane work – is she employed?'

'No, she's not employed. She's a housewife but that's work enough.'

'Yes, I know. I know just how hard housework can be.'

'You do your own?' Derbyshire asked.

'Yes, I have to.' Mundy shrugged. 'There's no one else to do it.'

'I found out how hard it was when I cleaned for Miss Tweedale,' Derbyshire reflected.

'You did her housework?' Mundy was surprised. 'That's a girly thing to do, isn't it?'

'Not her housework.' Derbyshire shook his head. 'I didn't do the dusting but I cleaned her brass. I didn't mind doing that – it was interesting. It didn't seem like it was a girl's job. She had a collection of brass shells.'

'Shells?' Mundy queried. 'Brass ornamental seashells?'

'No, from guns, you know . . . round brass things,' Derbyshire clarified.

'Ah,' Mundy patted the tabletop, 'you mean artillery shell casings. I know what you mean. They used to be popular ornaments in people's houses. You don't see them so often these days . . . sometimes you still see them in pubs.'

'I've never been in a pub.' Derbyshire looked crestfallen. 'Miss Tweedale said she'd do that, said that she would take me into a pub and buy me a pint of beer on my eighteenth birthday but I was arrested before that happened. I've been banged up in prison since I was seventeen. Youth custody until I was twenty-one then I was brought to the adult prison.'

Mundy looked aside. He felt deeply uncomfortable. Deeply ashamed.

'But the shells,' Derbyshire continued, 'we'd sit and polish them together . . . in the summer we'd take them into the garden and polish them in the sunshine. She had thirty-seven of them.'

'That's a lot,' Mundy commented. 'I've only ever seen a couple or so on the sideboard of folks houses, but thirty-seven . . .'

'Yes, thirty-seven,' Derbyshire repeated, 'not all on show. Some she kept up in the attic but all were kept well-polished. We would sit in the back garden and polish them and chat away as the bees buzzed around the flowerbeds. She would tell me about her life on the stage. She was on stage in London and had a brief spell in Hollywood making films. She made a bit of money but returned to England to work in theatre because she loved the stage. She acted in London and she also toured round the UK playing in theatres. She was a lovely lady and she called me her "own dear boy". Nobody had treated me like that before. Nobody. She called herself a "second-division actress". I remember that clearly. She said that she had shown flashes of first-division performances now and then but couldn't sustain it so she was a second-divisioner and never got the top female parts, so she used to say. But she had a nice house, full of her memories. What's it like now? Burnt Oak, I mean,' Derbyshire clarified, 'not her house . . .'

'I don't know.' Mundy smiled. 'I've never been to Burnt Oak.'

'It's on the Northern Line,' Derbyshire advised.

'Yes,' Mundy continued to smile, 'I know where it is, I've just never been there. I've never had occasion to set foot in Burnt Oak . . . and me a born and lifelong resident of London. So, you'd left home by the time you were arrested?'

'Yes, I had. Independent living, the social workers called it.' Derbyshire rolled his eyes.

'Where was that?' Mundy asked.

'In Colindale. It was a council-owned house . . . not council built but they owned it.'

'A miscellaneous property.' Mundy pursed his lips. 'Yes, I know the type.'

'It was built in Victorian times for a family,' Derbyshire continued, 'then it was divided into two separate flats. I had the upstairs one. I was quite happy there.' Joshua Derbyshire smiled to himself. 'Yes, I was . . . I used to go up to Miss Tweedale's house each Saturday and help her out any way she wanted . . . shopping, car cleaning, gardening, polishing the brass. I used to walk to her house from my little flat because she wanted me to walk. She said it was good exercise for me. I'd walk there and back.'

'She evidently liked you a lot.' Mundy scratched the back of his left hand.

'Yes, she was good to me. It was like having a mother for the first time. I really felt cared for. Because of Miss Tweedale I know what it means to have a proper mother. She said that I had more about me than a special school pupil. She said I could have coped with mainstream education. I might not be the star pupil, she said, but I didn't need the special school label stuck on my forehead.' Derbyshire spoke with a note of anger in his voice.

'Well, you've proved her right,' Mundy observed approvingly. 'You've got three O-levels . . . that's brainy enough.'

'Not all at once, though – just one a year, like I said. I mean, there's geezers in here who have got five, six, seven O-levels all in one sitting. There's even geezers in here who study for degrees.' Derbyshire paused. 'I could have had four O-levels but I failed history.'

'No shame there.' Mundy smiled. 'History is a difficult subject to get a pass in. It's very popular so they can set a high pass mark.'

'I'd like to have another shot at it.' Joshua Derbyshire set his jaw firm. 'I'd like to do it for Miss Tweedale. I got the other three for her, and when I found it was getting hard I thought of Miss Tweedale and carried on. I can get history for her.'

'Good for you, Joshua, that's determination.' Mundy eyed Joshua Derbyshire with warmth. 'That's what I like to hear . . . I like that attitude. I like it a lot.'

'It also helps to pass the time in here,' Derbyshire replied quietly. 'But mostly I want to do it for Miss Tweedale. She believed in me.'

'All right.' Mundy once again relaxed back in the chair. 'So tell me more about her – about Miss Tweedale. Was she all alone in the world?'

'She lived alone.' Derbyshire also relaxed in his chair. 'She said she liked it that way but she had relatives . . . in London and the south, I think she said.'

'Was she close to them?' Mundy asked. 'Do you know?'

'Miles away, I think,' Derbyshire replied.

'No . . . I meant emotionally speaking,' Mundy clarified.

'I don't know. She had a sister but never talked about her,' Derbyshire continued. 'She often mentioned a couple of cousins that she had. I think she liked them more than she liked her sister in the south. And she had nephews but she didn't like them. Once she said, "They're just waiting for the old girl to die. That's family for you, Josh, like a pack of circling vultures . . . any wonder I didn't want to get married? It would be like falling into a pond full of piranhas." She kept calling the family piranhas but I don't know what a piranha is . . .'

'A flesh-eating fish,' Mundy told him. 'It lives in the Amazon. It's apparently not as fearsome as it is reported to be but I wouldn't want to test it. Local people are not frightened of it, so I believe.'

'So, she had some money,' Derbyshire confirmed. 'I mean, that old Rolls-Royce must have been worth a penny or two. She also had a lot of oil paintings hanging on the walls of her home but she never flashed money around and she didn't have any expensive jewellery . . . not that I saw. Her home had a very strong feel. I liked her home. I think of it a lot.'

'Strong?' Mundy repeated. 'How so . . . strong? What do you mean?'

'I mean . . .' Derbyshire paused as if searching for the correct words, '. . . nothing cheap or tacky . . . nothing flimsy like it was about to fall apart any minute.'

'Solid furnishings?' Mundy suggested.

'Yes, I suppose that's a better way of putting it. I like that way of putting it. Yes, it was a solid old house to be in.' Derbyshire nodded gently. 'Heavy furniture.'

'Did Miss Tweedale have any friends that you knew of?' Mundy asked.

'She had a good neighbour . . . the couple next door – to the right if you looked at her house – Mr and Mrs Baxendale.'

'Baxendale,' Mundy repeated.

'Miss Tweedale said . . . she used to say, "we are the Dales", like the Yorkshire Dales, "but these Dales are in North London",' Derbyshire explained. 'I've never been out of London so I don't know but Miss Tweedale said that there is no such place as Tweedale and no such place as Baxendale.'

'I see.' Mundy stroked his chin.

'But Miss Tweedale and Mr and Mrs Baxendale were really good mates. I thought so anyway.' Joshua Derbyshire rested his hands on the tabletop.

Mundy saw they were long and narrow. An artist's hands, he thought. Derbyshire looked intently at Maurice Mundy and asked, 'So why do you think I am innocent, Mr Mundy?'

Mundy took a deep breath and exhaled slowly. 'How shall I put this . . .? Well, to be frank I don't think you smell like a murderer, Joshua, especially one who would chop an elderly lady up and steal her money. You don't smell at all like someone who would make a real bloodbath of the crime scene. That's why.'

'Murderers have their own smell?' Joshua Derbyshire gasped. 'Is that right? There are murderers in here and they don't smell any different to any other cons . . . not to me they don't.'

'Yes, but I don't mean that murderers really have their own smell,' Mundy replied. 'I don't mean that literally . . . I mean it figuratively . . . I mean that—'

'I know what literally and figuratively mean.' Derbyshire smiled. 'I have an O-level in English language, so I know what you mean.'

'Very well . . . you just don't smell like a murderer,' Mundy continued. 'You don't now and to be honest you didn't then.'

'You were there?' Derbyshire's eyes narrowed. 'You were there?'

'Yes,' Mundy glanced away from Derbyshire, 'I arrested you.'

'No . . . no . . .' Derbyshire held up his narrow hand. 'I remember it was a copper called Spate, he arrested me. I would have recognized you if you had made my arrest. I'll never forget Spate; he was a hard old geezer. Hard and bad.'

'He arrested you,' Mundy agreed. 'He said, "Joshua Derbyshire, I am arresting you in connection with the murder of Anne Florence Margaret Tweedale. You are not obliged to say anything but it will harm your defence if you do not mention when questioned anything you may rely on in court." He said that.'

Joshua Derbyshire glanced up at the high ceiling of the agent's room. 'I'll never forget those words, and he said them with his hand really gripping my left shoulder. It was like he put it in a vice.' Derbyshire put his right hand up to his left shoulder.

'Yes. So then what happened?' Mundy pressed.

'He pushed me towards two uniform cops who put handcuffs on me and they took me to the police station in a van. One drove and one sat next to me in the back of the van.'

'And you still don't recognize me?' Mundy smiled. 'I dare say you were a bit bewildered by it all. I was the constable who sat next to you in the van. My right wrist was handcuffed to your left wrist. I sat nearest the back door of the van as I was obliged to, in case you tried to jump out and make a bid for freedom.'

'You.' Derbyshire's jaw dropped. 'You were that copper?'

'Yes, that was me,' Mundy confirmed. 'Twenty-eight years ago we rode in the back of a police van, you and me. I thought then that you were guilty. I thought we had you bang to rights. I really did and I didn't like you. I thought Spate had arrested the right man, and you confessed to it. Then you retracted your confession, but you had confessed. The evidence against you seemed solid. I was new in the job then, but over the years, when I was in plain clothes and in the detective branch, I have been part of many teams which have investigated a murder and you develop a sense of someone being guilty. I began to look back at your arrest and you never smelled correctly. Eventually, in my mind, I could never see you as a murderer. Like I said, you just didn't "smell" correctly.'

'You took your time, you didn't half take your own sweet time.' Derbyshire's voice once more had a hint of anger. 'I am liable for parole in two years and only now do you come and tell me you believe I am innocent . . . and I thought I was slow at things.'

Mundy put his hand to his forehead. 'You've got the right to be angry, Josh, the very real right, but it took years in the police before I developed a nose for a guilty person and you have to allow for that. I was, as you say, a "proper copper" until a few days ago. I couldn't conduct my own investigation, but now I have a bit more room to manoeuvre. Look, Josh, do me a favour . . . do yourself a favour . . .'

'Yes, what?' Derbyshire growled.

'Don't tell anyone the reason I have visited you . . . no one, no one at all. If anyone asks, tell them I wanted information about another case, another investigation, a cold case of some years ago, and say that you couldn't help me.'

'OK.' Joshua Derbyshire nodded. 'OK, I'll do that.'

'And,' Mundy held up a cautious finger, 'this is vital . . .'

'And?' Derbyshire looked keenly at Mundy. 'What?'

'And don't get your hopes up,' Mundy spoke sternly. 'I mean that. It's important . . . don't pin your hopes on this because nothing might come of it. It still may be the case that you'll have to wait until you are paroled . . . if you're paroled, and it still may be the case that you'll die of old age in the prison hospital. This is just a ray of hope – a very small ray of hope on the horizon. Nothing more.'

'All right, I understand . . . a ray of hope on the horizon,' Joshua Derbyshire repeated as he lowered his head. 'What will you do, Mr Mundy? I mean, what are you going to do now?'

'Me . . .? Me? I'll go and talk to a few people. I must get to know as much about Anne Tweedale as I can.' Maurice Mundy stood up. 'And I'll take a trip to Nottingham – Robin Hood country, as you call it. I must visit your sister Jane . . . I'll do that . . . I'll do those things. But remember, Joshua . . . this is just a little ray of hope on the horizon, and it's a distant horizon, nothing more than that.' Mundy tapped twice on the door of the agent's room and heard a bunch of keys rattle in response.

*   *   *

'He would have been so really, really proud of them.' Janet
Thackery reached slowly and gracefully for her knife and fork
as the youthful waiter withdrew after inviting her and Maurice
Mundy to enjoy their meal. 'So really, very proud.'

'Yes,' Mundy also slowly unwrapped his knife and fork
from the neatly folded paper napkin, 'and so you must be also
. . . one is a probation officer and the other is set to fly high
in hospital administration. Not bad, not bad at all. Good careers
and safe jobs.' Mundy sank his knife into his beef pie. 'So
what about you, Janet? Will you retire when you can – is that
what your future holds?'

'I don't think so.' Janet Thackery poured thick, rich gravy
over her chips and her pie. 'They'll have to carry me out,
that's my attitude. I can work until I'm past sixty . . . women
can these days. And do you know, I think I will. I couldn't
fill my days otherwise. Is that why you've carried on after you
turned fifty-five, Maurice?'

'Yes . . . yes, I dare say it is.' Mundy glanced out of the
window behind Janet Thackery and enjoyed the late autumn
colours on the shrubs offset here and there by the evergreens.
'I too would find it difficult to fill my days, especially in the
winter months, like now, when you can't go for a turn in
the park to clear the tubes. I never was much of a reader or
a doer of crosswords and there's really only so much daytime
television you can watch. All those wretched mind-numbing
reality TV shows . . . you can keep them.'

'You would have found something to do, Maurice.' Janet
Thackery eyed him warmly. 'I know you . . . you would not
allow yourself to vegetate.'

'Dare say I would, but I like being active . . . and the Cold
Case Review Team suits me very well. You're not expected to
put in a full working week, only one job at a time, and there's
no one breathing down your neck and pressuring you for
results.' Mundy took a mouthful of food, swallowed it, and
then added, 'It's a very civilized form of police work.'

'Yes, I can imagine it would be.' Janet Thackery fell silent
and then she said, 'George wanted it kept quiet.'

'Sorry?' Mundy glanced at her. 'George wanted what kept
quiet?'

'George wanted it that way,' Janet Thackery explained. 'He wanted it kept quiet that he had gone into a hospice.'

'Oh, yes . . . I see.' Mundy smiled. 'I see. Sorry, I was a bit slow on the uptake there.'

'He didn't even want the boys to visit him . . . just myself, but I felt it was important for the boys to do so.' Janet Thackery poked at her food. 'Dying is a natural process . . . it comes to us all. The boys wanted to visit and I think that they made a better adjustment to his death because they visited him when he was dying . . . they were part of the process.'

'I can understand that,' Mundy replied softly. 'It makes a lot of sense. As you say, it made them feel included. I think I would have wanted the same.'

'Well, I just wanted you to know that that was why you were not told until after he had died. None of his friends were told, not one . . . nobody knew apart from me and the boys. We were also able to keep it quiet because it all happened very quickly. He came home feeling ill . . . had stomach pains and went to see the doctor. He was squeezed into their evening surgery. He was given a quick examination and painkillers, and he was admitted to the hospice the very next day. He was told then that he had just six weeks . . . and that is what he did have. He died six weeks to the day that he was admitted.' Janet Thackery paused. 'His brother and sister were told but even they were asked not to visit . . . even my mother wasn't told, and although she's very frail now she still has it all upstairs. It was how he wanted it.'

'Thank you for telling me.' Mundy nodded. 'It's probably a good job I wasn't told. I would probably have visited full of ebullience, trying to jolly things along.'

'Which is what George would not have wanted,' Janet Thackery replied firmly.

'Yes, yes . . . I fully understand.' Mundy put his hand to his forehead. 'It would not have been appropriate. People need to be left alone sometimes; they need space to think and prepare themselves.'

'I think he would have been upset by your visiting and also quite envious of you. It would have made the unfairness of a relatively early death seem all the more unfair. I mean, you being just two days older than him, you were born within forty-eight hours of each other. Him dying . . . and you living and healthy.' Janet Thackery wore a blue summer dress. She had auburn shoulder-length hair and Mundy thought her to be very young looking for her fifty-four years. She had, he noticed, pleasingly angular features, with high cheekbones and an appealing sparkle in her eyes. He found her very fetching. Very fetching indeed.

'Yes . . .' Mundy poured the tea. 'I feel – well, to be perfectly honest I don't know what I feel. Cancer is such a cruel disease. I live in such constant fear of it.'

'There are much worse things than cancer, much, much worse . . . arthritis, for one. Arthritis is just as painful but unlike cancer it doesn't kill you, it keeps you alive . . . that *is* a cruel disease. Cancer is merciful by comparison to arthritis.' Janet Thackery sat back a little as Mundy poured her tea. 'The nurses in the hospice were truly excellent. One nurse told him that having a good father figure for the first seventeen years of your life is much better than having a bad father who plagues you and blights your life well into your adulthood. That was what George wanted to hear because he was a very good father figure to the twins. He loved them and they loved him. I was left a real fishing widow when they were growing up. They'd leave at the crack of dawn, the three of them, and come back in the late evening with a straw basket full of trout.' Janet Thackery smiled at the memory. 'I used to complain at the time but now . . . now I'd relive those days like a shot if I could.'

'You have good memories, though.' Mundy smiled broadly. 'That's something to treasure . . . golden memories.'

'Yes, I suppose.' Janet Thackery inclined her head to one side. 'You know, you should have got married, Maurice.'

'No one would have me.' Maurice Mundy shrugged slightly.

'That I cannot believe.' She smiled warmly at him. 'I can't believe that at all.'

'True . . . it's true.' Mundy once more shrugged his left shoulder. 'I'm afraid it's true.'

'There must have been one or two near misses, surely?' Janet Thackery persisted.

'A few,' this time Mundy shrugged both his shoulders, 'but none of them took the bait. I suppose they were sensible or they were just more cautious than they were hungry.'

'Still, you missed out, Maurice.' Janet Thackery sipped her tea.

'Perhaps. Mind you, I did enjoy your wedding; it was the best wedding I attended in those years when our generation was getting married. People arrived in one's and two's on the Friday and we drank all the booze that was intended for the reception. We were pitching tents in George's back garden and the booze kept disappearing. The following morning we woke up to what we had done. So that geezer . . . I hadn't met him before . . . Tom somebody . . .'

'Tom Yorke?' Janet Thackery replied with a smile. 'Tom Yorke.'

'Yes, that's his name, Tom Yorke,' Mundy repeated. 'He had an estate car but he was still legless with a bad hangover so we pinched his car keys, drove his car into the village, bought out the off-licence and replaced all the booze we had drunk the previous day. Then we did your wedding and drank it all afterwards.'

'So we heard, afterwards,' Janet Thackery chuckled, 'but it was a trifle silly of us to leave you lot with such a mountain of booze. It was just asking for trouble. We were guilty of contributory negligence.'

'So . . .' After a short pause Mundy spoke slowly and quietly with a serious tone of voice. 'Five years. Five years now. How has it been?'

'I've made the adjustment,' Janet Thackery replied solemnly. 'Late forties, I was a bit young to be a widow, but I have a satisfying job and two lovely boys.'

'You haven't changed since you got married,' Mundy observed with a warm smile which caused Janet Thackery to look down and grin. 'It's true what they say,' Mundy continued. 'A woman's face doesn't really change, and you still have a figure many women would kill for. A size ten, I'd say.'

'All those skiing holidays.' Janet Thackery continued to keep her head lowered. 'They really keep you fit. And yes, size ten. I don't complain.'

'I can imagine. You know, I do enjoy the meals with you once a month or so, but . . .' Mundy paused. 'Well, I wonder if we could also do other things together, you and me. Go to the theatre . . . watch a film . . . go for a long walk to get out of the city . . . I mean, only if you'd like to.'

'Yes.' Janet Thackery raised her head and held eye contact with Maurice Mundy. 'Yes,' she repeated, 'I would like that. I'd like that hugely. I confess that sometimes the evenings get a bit difficult to fill. It is most especially in the evenings that I could use some company . . .'

'Good.' Mundy smiled. 'I'll see what's on and phone you.'

'Thank you.' Janet Thackery lowered her head. 'So how's the Cold Case Review Team?' she asked. 'How are you finding it?'

'It is interesting . . . less pressured than pre-retirement police work, as I said, and it's very interesting to look back at old cases.'

'Can you talk about your cases?' Janet Thackery asked.

'Yes, but not in detail,' Mundy replied. 'I . . . we have to be discreet.'

'Of course.' Janet Thackery ate her meal.

'But yes, we can, broadly speaking,' Mundy continued. 'We have just been handed a ten-year-old case of a young boy who was murdered and his body found floating in the fishing pond in the middle of his village.'

'Oh . . .' Janet Thackery momentarily pointed her fork towards Mundy. 'You know, I think I remember that murder. It got a lot of media coverage . . . if it is the one I am thinking of. He was found by the milkman, wasn't he? Strangled?'

'The postman, in fact, but yes. He wasn't strangled, though. His skull was fractured. He was just twelve years old.'

'Oh.' Janet Thackery sighed. 'Such a tragedy . . . his parents . . .'

'Yes, it was a bit of a bad case. It still is,' Mundy commented.

'I remember George saying that that was a local case. He was sipping beer before our evening meal and watching the news and he said, "Local . . . the person who did that lives locally. You can bet your life on it".'

'It seems that way, even ten years on. It seems a very local crime.' Mundy sliced into his steak pie. 'The village is remote, well remote for that part of England, not on any route from somewhere to somewhere else. You can't see the pond from the road so the culprit most probably knew it was there. It all speaks loudly of local knowledge but there was no motive that could be identified. The family lived quietly, they had no enemies, and it seemed the whole village turned out to look for him despite the fact that it was apparently a filthy night.'

'I see . . .' Janet Thackery inclined her head. 'So no leads . . . no suspect or suspects?'

'None,' Mundy replied. 'It became a cold case but it now transpires that a woman was murdered in Chelmsford on the same night.'

'Oh?' Janet Thackery looked interested. 'A connection, do you think?'

'We don't know. It's most likely to be a coincidence but it's the only lead we have,' Mundy explained. 'No connection between the two murders was made at the time, and they, the Essex Police, were probably right about that. But, like I said, right now it's the only lead.'

'I see. So tell me,' Janet Thackery asked with genuine interest, 'what's the rule if you do uncover fresh evidence?'

'Oh, in that case we have got to notify the proper coppers.' Mundy grinned.

'The proper coppers,' Janet Thackery repeated with a soft laugh. 'Is that what you call them?'

'No . . . no . . .' Mundy also laughed softly, 'that's just a term that someone used this morning. I visited him in Pentonville Prison and he used that term, the "proper coppers".'

'I see. Is he part of the cold case?' Janet Thackery put her knife and fork down and sipped her tea.

'No. No, he's not; I am pursuing my own agenda there,' Mundy admitted.

'Is that allowed?' A note of alarm crept into Janet Thackery's voice.

'Nope.' Mundy smiled. 'It isn't allowed. It's a definite no-no . . . a very big no-no. We can only look into allocated cases but I still have a warrant card so I can access our records and I can call on someone in prison and see him in the agent's

room without writing to him and asking him to send me a
visiting order.'

'Maurice,' Janet Thackery sighed with disapproval, 'you're
going to get your fingers burned.'

'Maybe, but I'm doing it anyway,' Mundy replied
defensively.

'You know George always said that about you . . .' Janet
Thackery looked at Mundy.

'No, I don't – what did he always say about me?' Mundy
smiled. 'What did he say?'

'That you were a maverick . . . a wild card . . . a loose
cannon,' Janet Thackery reported, 'and he said you'd get your
fingers burned one day . . . burned good and proper.'

'And it did happen, so George was quite correct,' Mundy
replied in a resigned tone of voice. 'It is why George and I
started out together. Both probationary constables, we left the
police college together and he rose to become a detective chief
inspector while I never got beyond the rank of detective
constable. It was all because of my "cavalier attitude", so I
was told.'

'Well . . .' Janet Thackery poured the last of the gravy over
her chips. 'I dare say you can't change your personality . . .
not at your age.'

'That's very tactful of you.' Mundy grinned. 'Very tactful
indeed. But even George distanced himself from me at work.'

'Oh, I never knew that.' Janet Thackery spoke with a clear
note of unease. 'You visited our home . . . you and George
went for a beer together now and then . . . we always spon-
taneously exchanged cards at Christmas. He never said
anything to me about it. Not one word, ever.'

'He was sensible and I understood why he had to do that.
The golden rule is the golden rule . . . which is never associate
with a failure,' Mundy explained. 'It's the golden rule in any
organization and the police force is no exception, it's no
different at all. We were mates outside work, as you say, but
he'd never be seen sitting with me in the canteen or chatting
to me in the corridor.'

'I'm sorry. I feel so . . . embarrassed.' Janet Thackery looked
away from Maurice Mundy. 'Really, that's news to me.'

'Don't be embarrassed,' Mundy reassured Janet Thackery. 'George was career-minded, I fully understood that, but I was always impatient with paperwork and I had a cocky attitude towards authority figures, especially if they were younger than me . . . which in the end they all were, of course, but that attitude did not go down well. Not well at all. I was never really anti-authority as such – I just had the tendency to treat everyone as though we were equals. "Over familiarity" I think is the term . . . I just put obstacles in my own career path. I was my own worst enemy.'

'I see. Well, thank you for telling me that, Maurice. I appreciate it.' Janet Thackery paused and then asked, 'So tell me about the unofficial case you are working on . . . if you can.'

'It's a geezer that George and I arrested,' Mundy began. 'Well, that's to say we didn't arrest him – a senior CID officer, now retired, actually arrested him, but it was me and George who took him to the police station. We were both constables at the time.'

'So . . . some time ago?' Janet Thackery observed.

'Twenty-eight years ago to be precise.' Mundy ate a slice of his meat pie.

'And he's the person you visited in Pentonville?' Janet Thackery confirmed.

'Yes.' Mundy nodded.

'He's still in prison after twenty-eight years?' Janet Thackery gasped. 'Is he serving a full-tariff life sentence?'

'No,' Mundy explained. 'He collected life and the judge set a minimum term of thirty years before parole could be considered.'

'It must have been an awful murder.' Janet Thackery finished her meal and placed her knife and fork centrally on her plate.

'He hacked an elderly lady to pieces after she had befriended him,' Mundy told her. 'The crime scene was a real bloodbath. I never knew eight pints of blood could be so messy. The evidence against him seemed utterly compelling. When he was sentenced to life with a thirty-year minimum I said "goal" and celebrated with the other officers involved in the case. We had a bit of a drink the evening of the day that he went down.'

'So why visit him?' Janet Thackery asked. 'A new development?'

'I don't know really . . . it just doesn't feel right. Looking back, it hasn't felt right for a long time.' Mundy glanced at his watch. 'Sorry, but I have to go now. I'm driving up to Chelmsford this afternoon on the young boy case . . . that being the official cold case.' He reached for his wallet.

'Of course.' Janet Thackery began to search her handbag for her car keys.

'So, if I were to phone you,' Mundy suggested, 'early next week, perhaps once I see what is showing where . . .?'

'Yes,' Janet Thackery beamed warmly, 'please do. And thank you for lunch, it was lovely. Next time I'll buy the meal.'

'Last year?' The proprietor of the Swinton Garage in Newmarket revealed himself to be a slightly built man who wore a brown smock over ordinary city clothes. He had clearly, thought Mundy, progressed well beyond the point where he had to crawl underneath motorcars for his living. Even his office was elevated above the shop floor which seemed to Mundy to be healthily full of cars and with a workforce all fully occupied. The garage clearly had an excellent reputation.

'Sometime between October and December . . . beginning of and end of,' Tom Ingram advised. 'We don't expect you to recall it but we assume you keep records.'

'Indeed we do but, as you suggest and expect, I don't remember the vehicle. One-off jobs all seem to merge into one another and you can't put them in date order in your mind.' Eric Redmond stood and excused himself, then returned a moment later with a box file which he laid on his desktop as he resumed his seat. 'The regular customers, of which we have many, we know their cars, but owners who drive in looking for running repairs . . . Offhand, I can't place a blue Saab with mismatching doors. Perhaps one of the crew might but it will be in here.' Redmond opened the file. 'The motor trade has a dodgy reputation, as I am sure you'll know. What's the phrase . . . it is "a conduit to crime", as is the antiques business. There are many reputable antiques traders but there are also those who will buy proceeds from burglaries, keep them out of sight for a few years and then slowly drip-feed them back on to the antiques market. It's like that with the motor trade . . . there are clean garages and there are dodgy ones. This is one of the clean ones. We keep an invoice for every job done and I mean every job. It does you well to keep the taxman happy and no good to annoy him.'

'Good for you.' Ingram smiled approvingly. 'That's the right attitude.'

'It is the way of it; all the boys down there will know where all the chop shops are in Newmarket.' Redmond indicated over his shoulder to the garage floor behind and beneath him. 'None of them is into anything naughty, not that I am aware of, but they'll all know someone who is.'

'Yes,' Ingram growled.

'Well . . . who can help it? Fitters' network . . . police officers' network . . . lawyers' network . . . it's a way of life. But nothing naughty happens here.' Redmond picked up the file and rotated it and handed it to Tom Ingram. 'You are welcome to sift through the invoices until you find the car you are seeking, gentlemen. The invoices are in date order. That is to say reverse date order by financial year. So the invoices at the top are from March/April this year, and the invoices at the bottom are from March/April last year. So . . . October last year, the invoices from that date onwards will be about halfway down. You can use the office next door if you like. There's usually a typist in there but she phoned in sick this morning. She hasn't phoned in sick for three weeks, which is not bad for her, then this morning she decided she has a migraine. That'll be her for a day or two.'

'Why do you put up with that attitude?' Mundy smiled as he stood up.

'Ah . . .' Redmond waved his hands in the air. 'Because there's never any urgent typing work. There is never anything that can't wait a day or two. Few women want to work in a dirty, oily garage; few women want to work in an all-male environment. Most like clean offices. Then there's the bother of advertising and interviewing the few applicants that will be

prepared to work here. So, better the devil you know is what
I say . . .'

'That's generous-minded of you.' Ingram also stood up.
'Anyway, next door office, you say?'

'Yes.' Redmond pointed to his left. 'Small office, through
there.'

Ingram and Mundy sat down at the desk in the adjacent
office and opened the box file. Ingram handed all the invoices
for October of the previous year to Mundy while he looked
at the November invoices. 'We'll share the December
invoices,' he added with a grin. The two officers then fell
silent as they carefully looked at one invoice after another
until Ingram said, 'Here it is . . . one Saab 90 "weld exhaust
tailpiece".'

'Is the registration number of the car given?' Mundy asked.

'Yes.' Ingram nodded. 'It is.'

'Breakthrough . . .' Mundy sat back in the chair he occupied.
'That is a real breakthrough. With that we can use the Met's
computer to trace the owner of the car on the day that both
Janet Laws was abducted and murdered and Oliver Walwyn
was murdered. This is a breakthrough.'

'How far do we take this?' Ingram glanced at Mundy. 'You
know the rules of the game.'

'As far as we can,' Mundy replied with a broad smile. 'As
far as we can . . . right up to the point of arrest.'

Ingram held up his hand. 'Steady, Maurice. Steady on. You
know the rules, like I say. We are obliged to report any developments and this is a development . . . you have just said so
yourself.'

'All right, I'll write a memo to the Chelmsford police that
will keep them happy.' Mundy continued to smile. 'And it will
cover us.'

'I don't like it, Maurice.' Ingram raised his voice. 'I don't
like it at all. Our case is the murder of Oliver Walwyn. The
murder of Janet Laws is a hot case and it's not ours to meddle
in. That's been made very plain.'

'Let's just see how far we get, shall we? Let's just take it
one old step at a time.' Mundy paused. 'We're still groping
in the dark; there may be nothing in this lead, nothing at all.

When we have hard facts, then . . . then we'll notify the people in other boxes. That's what we'll do.'
    'I still don't like it.' Ingram sighed. 'I'm not happy that that's correct.'
    The two officers returned to London in an awkward and strained silence.

    The man entered his house, sank wearily on to the ancient settee and used the remote control to switch on the small television. He watched the early evening news and then the local news, both with little interest. He remained seated in front of the television set, feeling drained of energy, until eight p.m., when he stood and walked into the narrow, dimly lit hallway of his house and put on a long raincoat and a scarf, both of which he had bought in a charity shop, and then screwed his brown fedora on to his head. He opened his front door and walked the few paces from the door to the pavement of Lidyard Road, N19, and then he turned to his left. He strolled the short walk to the pub which stood on the corner of Lidyard Road and Archway Road.
    The man remained in the pub for two hours enjoying a chat with the publican until the pub became busy, then he drank alone. Occasionally he would catch a glimpse of himself in the mirror behind the bar and would see a gaunt-looking, thin-faced man with grey hair cut severely short in a crew-cut style, whose clothing made him look 'genteel shabby' in terms of his appearance. When nearing the end of what he knew would be his final beer of the evening, he took a handful of coins from his trouser pocket and placed them in the British Legion Remembrance Day Poppy Appeal can. He took a poppy and a pin and affixed the poppy to the left hand lapel of his sports jacket. He raised a hand in a gesture of parting to the publican who said a cheery 'goodnight' in reply. The man stepped out of the pub on to Archway Road, buttoned up his coat against the steady drizzle which had by then begun to fall vertically on London town and walked slowly home. He entered the narrow hallway of his house, peeled off the wet coat and hung it dripping on a peg behind the door, then placed his damp fedora on the same peg over the coat. He walked to the kitchen

and took the top pizza from a pile of six which were stacked in the fridge, unwrapped the cellophane and placed it in the oven at the prescribed temperature for the correct length of time. He ate the pizza while sitting on the settee in his living room, keeping a still-uninterested eye on the television while he did so. Upon completing the meal he carried the plate to the kitchen and placed it amid the pile of washing-up in the sink. He then retired for the night.

The man was Maurice Mundy.

FOUR

'**W**ell, yes . . . yes . . . over the years. Yes, I dare say that we became quite close friends.' Felicity Baxendale revealed herself to be a portly woman of medium height with a ready smile. Upon inspecting Maurice Mundy's identity card she invited him into her house and escorted him into her living room where they sat facing each other in identical armchairs which were separated by a sheepskin rug upon a scarlet carpet. 'We met as neighbours and the friendship grew. It started as a joke . . . Tweedale and Baxendale, the "Dales" of Burnt Oak, like the Yorkshire Dales, but there is no Dale or Vale in the UK of either name, so we were amused by the coincidence of two people with similar names both seeming to be evoking a real place, and yet no such place existed in either case . . .'

'Remarkable coincidence,' Mundy commented. 'Quite remarkable.'

'Yes, but it was the joke that broke the ice and then, over time, a friendship developed despite the age gap. Anne was over twenty years older than me, you see. She had just turned sixty when she was murdered whereas I was barely forty at the time.'

'What were your feelings about that?' Mundy asked.

'My feelings about the age gap? It didn't bother me at all. As you will have found out yourself – once you're an adult, over thirty, then you're all in the same club.' Felicity Baxendale looked confused at Mundy's question.

'No.' Mundy grinned. 'Sorry, I wasn't very clear; I meant what did you feel about her murder?'

'Feel at the time? A whole rollercoaster of feelings and emotions . . . disbelief, anger, sadness for her . . . mainly anger, I think.' Felicity Baxendale glanced up towards the ceiling. 'How she took that boy into her home, how she befriended him . . . and for him to turn on her like that, carve her up with

a kitchen knife – horrible. Really, really horrible. Things like
that happen down in the East End, down in the Docklands of
Bermondsey and places like that, but it should not happen in
Burnt Oak. This is suburbia, where the professional middle
class live. Yet it did happen and the conviction was safe and
sound. So now, why the visit? What is happening after nearly
thirty years? Is it the case that the police are having doubts
about the safety of his conviction?'

Mundy pursed his lips. 'We are reviewing it, shall I put it
that way. So, leaving aside the strength of the case against
Joshua Derbyshire and the safety of his conviction . . . leaving
all that aside for a moment, can I ask what your thoughts
about him being her killer were . . . and are?'

Felicity Baxendale reclined in her armchair. Her black-and-
white cat which had been eyeing Mundy with suspicion
suddenly ran across the floor and leapt into her lap where it
curled up, yet still fixing Mundy with an unblinking stare. 'I
was shocked. Very shocked. I couldn't believe that Anne had
been murdered and I could not believe that it was the ever-
so-gentle Joshua that had killed her. I was in a terrible state
of disbelief for a long time . . . we both were.'

'We?' Mundy asked.

'My husband and I.' Felicity Baxendale began to stroke
the cat who purred loudly and contentedly. 'He has since
passed on.'

'I am sorry,' Mundy offered.

'Thank you, but it is most often the way of it. You men die
young and we women, well, we just hang on. Can't be that
much of a weaker sex, can we?'

'Fairer, I always thought.' Mundy smiled. 'I never thought
that women were necessarily weaker.'

Felicity Baxendale also smiled. 'You are diplomatic,
Mr Mundy, but it's true – men fall over often unfairly early
in life and the old creaking gate continues to creak. I dare say
I wasn't helped by being nearly fourteen years younger than
my husband, which is a significant age gap, but it left me a
widow at a relatively young age. I was in my early fifties when
my husband died.'

'I have a friend, a lady friend who is in much the same

situation. She's a relatively recent widow and she's still in her early fifties,' Mundy replied. 'She's coping well mainly due to her employment. Her job gives her something to do.'

'That's an advantage I don't have.' Felicity Baxendale looked down at her cat. 'I have no skills to bring to the workplace. I was married "from the gymslip" as the expression has it, and never did anything but manage a house and look after children. I was blissfully happy doing so. I felt totally fulfilled. I can understand why some women want a career but I was never more content than when I swapped my dolls' house for a real house and swapped my dolls for real children.' She once again looked up at the ceiling, as if recovering good memories. 'But early fifties . . . tell your friend to get married again. She might treasure her husband's memory but the marriage bed will seem very empty. She will miss going to sleep each night with a man who loves her cupping her in his arms. I missed that terribly. I still do. So give her that advice.'

'I will.' Mundy inclined his head. 'I'll tell her that . . . I see her often and will tell her that.'

'But Joshua . . . my thoughts . . . well, my thoughts were and still are that he was a most unlikely murderer.' Felicity Baxendale glanced across the living room at Maurice Mundy. 'A most unlikely murderer indeed. It would be like a lop-eared rabbit suddenly revealing a killer instinct, or a hamster or a koala or a panda . . . if you see what I mean.'

'Yes,' Mundy put his hand up to the side of his head, 'I see what you mean exactly, I can conjure the image . . . a bit like a goldfish suddenly becoming a barracuda-like flesh-eating predator, or like a sparrow suddenly swooping on a field mouse.'

'Yes . . . exactly.' Felicity Baxendale raised her forefinger. 'That's exactly what I mean.' She paused. 'You see, I am not a psychologist but I would have thought that the man who killed Anne Tweedale must have had more about him than gentle, slothful Joshua. I – we – would have seen some display of aggression, at least some form of ill temper or shortness of fuse, but we never saw anything like that, not ever.'

'So he was always very calm,' Mundy confirmed. 'Always very mild-mannered?'

'Yes,' Felicity Baxendale replied clearly. 'Always very placid, very calm, very at peace with himself . . . very head in the clouds, as if he were detached from life. I often thought that he needed a damn good shaking up. You know, I used to watch him wash Anne Tweedale's car. He would just wipe the sponge over the bodywork. He would put no effort into the job at all . . . and yes, that is the word I am looking for – effort. There was no effort in anything he did, no sense of it at all. No application. He would wash that lovely old two-tone grey Rolls-Royce of hers very slowly, quite content to move the sponge backwards and forwards, making the car wet, but when the water had evaporated the car looked no cleaner – not to me, anyway. It was more like all he had done was redistribute the dirt. He gave it no elbow grease at all.' Felicity Baxendale sighed. 'I wouldn't have had him doing odd jobs about my house. He also had the same attitude to Anne Tweedale's garden. He'd pick something up from out of the flowerbed and look about him, then stoop to pick something else up and look about him again, and when he claimed to have finished working the garden looked just the same as it did when he had started weeding it. And I'll tell you another little anecdote about Josh and the garden. Anne had a pair of shears, not an electric hedge-cutter.'

'Yes,' Mundy replied. 'Don't see many these days.'

'No. Shame, really, I think, because I quite liked the sound of the shears going *clip, clip, clip*. It was a reassuring, very Sunday afternoon summertime sound. An "all is well with the world" sort of sound . . . that's what I always felt when my late husband was trimming the hedge, but the gardener I employ these days attacks the privet with an electric hedge-trimmer. He does the job in a tenth of the time it used to take my husband but I always feel that something has been lost. The sound of an electric hedge-cutter just isn't conducive to calm . . . but Joshua, I kid you not, had to be shown how to hold the shears. When he picked them up he'd tried to cut the hedge by pointing them at the privet.'

'Oh, no.' Mundy gasped. 'That is quite pathetic.'

'Oh, yes.' Felicity Baxendale smiled. 'Isn't it just? Quite pathetic. Anne Tweedale had to take them from him and demonstrate how to lay the blades against the privet . . . that was Joshua's functioning level. Cutting a privet hedge is a man's job and she, an elderly woman, had to teach him how to use the shears, and even then it was a casual snip . . . long pause . . . snip . . . long pause . . . snip. He would say he had cut the hedge and Anne would say "Well done, Josh", and then when he had gone home she would roll up her sleeves and, damn me, if she didn't do the job herself. I really would not have tolerated him. I really wouldn't have.'

'No focus?' Mundy offered.

'None. He had no single-minded determination – none that I could ever detect,' Felicity Baxendale explained as she stroked her cat slowly and caringly. 'And it was pretty much the same inside the house as he helped her polish the brass shell casings.'

'Ah.' Mundy smiled. 'Yes, I heard about the shell casings.'

'She had quite a collection . . . all sorts of sizes, brought back from France by a relative who was over there fighting the 1914–18 war, the "war to end all wars". She had thirty-seven all told, and each one had KH scratched on the bottom, those being her relative's initials. They would sit and polish them together, her and Joshua. It was a job for a winter's day, sitting and polishing, them having a chat while they worked away in Anne's living room, but Josh's lack of elbow grease, as my father would say, meant that his version of polishing the brass was smearing the polish all over them, so Anne had to polish his shells once he had left her house. Sometimes they'd sit out in the sun and polish them but Josh's attitude was just the same. Eventually she sensibly decided on a division of labour. Josh would put the polish on the shell casing and then hand the shell to her and she would do the actual polishing. That arrangement seemed to work well – it satisfied both parties. Josh felt useful and Anne Tweedale had her collection of shell casings polished and looking resplendent. Mind you, my husband was upset about that collection, he said he couldn't help thinking that when each one of the shells was sent flying by the explosive in the casing it probably cost a young man his life or a few young men their lives in a single explosion. But Anne never thought like that. She just liked the

shiny things adorning her living room, especially since they
had been brought back by one of her relatives.'

'I see,' Mundy grunted.

'And the shopping, oh my, the shopping . . . don't ask . . .
it was just another disaster.' Felicity Baxendale put her hand
to her forehead. 'Anne Tweedale would give Josh a shopping
list and if she was lucky he'd come back with about half the
items she'd put on the list, but he was scrupulously honest,
you have to say that for him. He would hand her the exact
change . . . never a penny short. Eventually she would send
him out with more items than she wanted, so she would give
him a list of twenty items, for example, in the hope that he
would bring back the ten she really wanted.'

'She really was very accommodating of him,' Mundy
observed.

'She was very accommodating, as you say. That's the correct
word. Accommodating. Perfunctory as he was, she was very
patient and very accepting of him.' Felicity Baxendale continued
to stroke her cat, which purred contentedly, gradually losing
interest in Mundy.

'Why do you think that was?' Mundy asked. 'Why tolerate
him in that manner, to that extent, and over what sort of period
are we talking about?'

'A year, perhaps eighteen months.' Felicity Baxendale
once again looked up at the ceiling of her living room.
'Why? Well, you may ask and all I can guess is because
he might have awoken some latent mothering instinct in
her. She never married, you see. I don't think she ever
wanted to be married but I think she missed not having had
children. I think that that was a great sadness for her, and
then along came Joshua, whom she rescued from being
taunted by other children because he was a bit slow-witted.
That made him more vulnerable and therefore more
appealing to Anne Tweedale's nature. He might have been
fifteen, sixteen, seventeen or whatever age he was, but in
his head he was only about ten or twelve years old, so he
seems to have fulfilled a need she had. She also often told
me that she was certain that Josh had more about him than
people gave him credit for. She felt very strongly that he

had been dismissed too easily, too readily, and because of that belief she would engage him in conversation and encourage him to read. She tried to stimulate him, to stretch him, intellectually speaking, and you know once she said he had good eyes.'

'Good eyes,' Mundy repeated. 'He had keen eyesight, you mean?'

'No.' Felicity Baxendale shook her head vigorously. 'No, I don't mean that and Anne didn't mean that either – she meant that there was an honesty about his eyes. You know how it is said that "the eyes are the windows to the soul"?'

'Yes,' Mundy put his hand to his chin, 'yes, I have heard that and I believe it.'

'Well, that's what Anne Tweedale meant by "good eyes". She meant that Joshua had a good soul, his eyes being the window to his soul,' Felicity Baxendale explained.

'Ah . . . I understand now.' Mundy nodded slowly, lowering his hand.

'Yes. I have met people with piercing, evil eyes and have met chronic schizophrenics with the classic "glassy" eyes of people with that illness . . . a look they can't hide, whether they are unwell or whether they are just plain evil, but Josh did have an honesty about his eyes. I will go along with Anne Tweedale on that point. Readily so. I wouldn't have him in my house doing odd jobs but he did have an . . . innocence about him. He had the look of a puppy's eyes . . . sort of keen and curious but totally without a puppy's eagerness to please when it came to applying himself.' Felicity Baxendale massaged her left earlobe in a casual, subconscious manner. 'I am certainly no criminal psychologist, but I ask you, really, is that the sort of personality who could stab someone multiple times and then calmly rifle her home for valuables? I think not. Speaking for myself, I think not.'

'I can see your point,' Mundy replied, 'and I confess you do indeed paint a picture of a most unlikely murderer, a most unlikely candidate indeed.'

'And then, of course, there is the issue of Anne Tweedale's lovely valuables.' Felicity Baxendale raised an eyebrow. 'There is that issue.'

'Oh?' Mundy sat forward. 'Tell me, please, what is the issue?'

'My point is that the valuables, her jewellery, would not be of interest to Joshua – not the Joshua I knew. And Joshua would have to know where she kept them, which was upstairs in her bedroom, and it was the case that Anne Tweedale never let Josh go upstairs. Upstairs was her private space, as it is in this house. Upstairs is my bathroom, my bedroom . . . it was the same in Anne Tweedale's house.' Felicity Baxendale stroked her cat. 'These houses were built in the thirties and there is an outside toilet built into the back of the house, specifically designed for the use of the daily help. Whenever Joshua needed the toilet himself he used Anne's outside lavatory as she directed him to do.'

'Interesting . . .' Mundy murmured. 'That is interesting.'

'You see, Joshua just wouldn't have known her jewellery was there and I don't think it would have been of interest to him anyway,' Felicity Baxendale reiterated.

'What,' Mundy asked, 'would he be interested in, if anything, would you say?'

'Frankly, I can't think of anything, anything at all.' Felicity Baxendale continued to stroke her cat, which continued to purr contentedly. 'You know, Joshua didn't seem to me to be a very materialistic young man. I don't think he had any designs upon Anne Tweedale's possessions. He went there because he found acceptance and emotional warmth, encouragement and empowerment. Anne's attitude and approach to him gave him self-confidence; it empowered him to do things he otherwise wouldn't have attempted to do. She made him feel good about himself. Dragons . . .'

'Dragons?' Mundy smiled.

'Anne had a book about dragons, a book from her childhood. In it were large coloured paintings of the mythical creatures. She allowed Joshua to look at the book and he loved it. He would sit looking at the paintings and be utterly absorbed. He would return it to its place on the shelf but would always ask to see it if he was taking a rest from any tasks. If he was to take anything from Anne Tweedale's house,' Felicity Baxendale explained, 'it would be that book, and possibly photographs of Anne when she was in her prime . . . that sort of thing, not diamond rings and pearl necklaces and solid gold brooches. The only items believed to have been stolen were Anne's jewellery and the carving knife used to kill her. Nothing else was removed.'

'I see.' Mundy sat back in the armchair he occupied. 'That is a good point . . . interesting . . . very interesting.'

'For me,' Felicity Baxendale continued, 'the whole thing just does not add up – it never has. Why . . . what motive had he to kill the person who was giving him so much on an emotional level? It makes no sense, no sense at all.'

'I can see how you'd think that,' Mundy replied. Then he asked, 'Tell me, do you know if Miss Tweedale had any relations?'

'She had a sister, I do know that she had a sister, but I think they were estranged. It was some family issue, some dispute I was not privy to. The sister had sons – three sons, so Anne Tweedale had three nephews.' Felicity Baxendale put her fingertips to her forehead. 'I also think that she had cousins. Her grandmother had had a large family so she had a number of cousins, and in fact I believe her to have been closer to her cousins than she was to her own sister.'

'I can believe that,' Mundy offered. 'You don't have to live with your cousins so you don't quarrel but the blood tie is there.'

'That could very well be the reason.' Felicity Baxendale smiled approvingly. 'I never thought of that, but it could. It explains my situation, you see. I have fallen out with my own brother from time to time but never with any one of my cousins and that would explain it: we never got close enough to get into a fight. Thank you. Now I understand my own family.'

'My pleasure.' Mundy inclined his head.

'But the hostility within Anne's family was very powerful . . . it was manifest. She once told me that she believed her nephews had plans for her money but that she had made sure that they were not going to get hold of it. When she said that to me one day over elevenses she glanced at a glass cabinet which contained her silverware. I was once shown the silver collection and noticed a brown envelope with the words "the Will" written on it.'

'Oh . . .' Mundy groaned. 'She didn't lodge her will with a solicitor?'

'It seems not,' Felicity Baxendale replied with a sigh.

'That was asking for trouble,' Mundy observed. 'Really a bit silly.' He paused. 'Do you know who would have benefitted from her will?'

'I'm afraid I don't . . . no idea. It isn't really the sort of thing one would talk about with one's neighbour.'

'Of course,' Mundy replied. 'I wondered if she might have said something.'

'I do recall that her house was cleared by a removal company,' Felicity Baxendale informed him. 'Millers Removals and Storage of Burnt Oak.'

'You have a good memory,' Mundy observed with a smile.

'I'd like to think that I do have a good memory,' Felicity Baxendale replied warmly, 'especially as one's faculties tend to diminish with age. I have noticed that I have developed some difficulty remembering words these days, which worries me. My own mother lost her mind at the end and I remember the first symptoms were her inability to remember words. She'd be stringing a complicated sentence together quite happily and then, just as she was about to use a word, it would vanish from her vocabulary. So I am a little worried, but the reason I remember the name of the removal company is that it was also my maiden name. I think I made a good swap. Miller is such a dull name, I always thought, and still do. It belongs to all those other artisan names like Cooper, Potter, Wright, Farmer, Fletcher . . .'

'Oh, what's a Fletcher?' Mundy asked. 'What does that name mean?'

'An arrow maker.' Felicity Baxendale grinned. 'The feathers at the rear of an arrow are the arrows' "fletch". A fletcher was an arrow maker in medieval times.'

'I have learned something.' Mundy returned the grin.

'But I swapped dull Miller for the more prestigious-sounding Baxendale . . . and,' she held up her forefinger, '. . . I got a very good husband into the bargain. Not bad I say. Two for the price of one.'

'Not bad at all.' Mundy wrote 'Millers Removals' on his notepad. 'Not bad at all.'

'They're still in business,' Felicity Baxendale advised. 'I still see their large removal vans now and then – they are painted cream with red lettering. A bit garish for my taste but the important thing for your inquiry, I would have thought, is that they are still in existence, they're still trading. I understand that they removed the contents of the house into a storage facility pending the terms of the will being observed. The house itself was eventually sold and a very pleasant family moved in . . . very well-behaved children. The parents are still there though the children have moved on, as children do.'

'Indeed,' Mundy mumbled, 'as you say . . . as children do.'

'So that was the last of Anne Tweedale. A sad way to end one's life and a very sad way to end a good life. She wasn't that old – she could have lived for another twenty or even thirty years.' Felicity Baxendale fell silent. Then she said, 'But I still do not think Joshua could have murdered her. As I said, he didn't have any sense of ruthlessness about him. He was too considerate.'

'Considerate?' Mundy asked.

'Well, yes . . . I know a barrister. He is also a parishioner at the church at which I worship and at a church social, some years ago now, we were chatting over tea and cakes and he told me that he had been pleading in murder cases all his working life and had not defended nor prosecuted a single murderer who did not think that the sun shone just for him . . . or her. There was, he had always found, a chilling sense of self-importance about murderers, a sense of "it's all about me, the world revolves around me" – that sort of attitude, and that, he said, includes the so-called crimes of passion.'

'Now that,' Mundy replied, 'I would wholly go along with. Wholly.'

'And Joshua Derbyshire, what was he? I'll tell you . . . he was pretty feckless, pretty well inept at everything he did but he would display thoughtfulness in little ways. You see, as much as he wouldn't buy every item on the shopping list, for instance, he would sometimes use his initiative and buy things if they were on offer and if he knew that Anne Tweedale would have use of them . . . little things like that, to please her.'

'I see.' Mundy tapped his pen on his notebook. 'As you

say, not the actions of a member of the "it's all about me" brigade.'

'Yes . . . exactly,' Felicity Baxendale held eye contact with Maurice Mundy, 'that's what I thought . . . and as I have just said, that's what I still think. So I was surprised when he was convicted of her murder, but all the evidence was so solidly stacked up against him and with nothing to argue in his defence. So I assumed that I had been wrong about him and, all the while, the gentle, mild-mannered, inept, feckless Joshua Derbyshire had a very dark side that he had kept well-hidden, but my doubts about the safety of his conviction surfaced and grew over the years . . . they have grown and grown and grown.'

'So have mine.' Maurice Mundy folded his notepad and stood up. 'So have mine.'

119 Frere Way in Norwich revealed itself to be a small, council-owned property close to a single-storey primary school. It was boarded by an overgrown yellow privet hedge and the area between the road and the front door could not, in Mundy's mind, be considered a front lawn, but neither could it be called a gravelled area. It was, he and Tom Ingram saw, a mixture of both, with patches of worn grass interspersed with patches of gravel. The house shared a driveway with the house to its left as viewed from the roadway, the garages belonging to each house standing side by side at the top of the driveway, there appearing to be a clear agreement between the two householders that the driveway should never be blocked by parked cars. The house was of sixties vintage, thought Mundy, built of light-coloured and lightweight brick with a roof of concrete tiles, upon which moss was growing. The door and window frames were painted white. A narrow concrete lintel stood above the front door, supported by two circular metal columns which, like the house, were also painted in white. Lace curtains hung untidily in the single ground-floor window adjacent to the door. Ingram and Mundy walked across the gravel and grass area in front of the house, making a crunching sound as they did so. Ingram knocked on the door

with a polite yet authoritative tap. It was rapidly opened by a small, bespectacled man dressed in a clean but un-ironed blue shirt and brown corduroy trousers. Tartan-patterned carpet slippers encased his bare feet. He did not appear, to the officers, to have shaved for two or three days.

'Police,' Ingram announced as he and Maurice Mundy held up their identity cards for his inspection.

'Yes?' The man seemed to the officers to be nervous. He held the door ajar, poking his head and left side of his body round the edge of the door, between the door and the doorframe.

'Mr Cassey?' Ingram asked. 'Mr Kenneth Cassey?'

'Yes?' Cassey continued to sound nervous. Mundy thought him to be in his mid-fifties.

'Do you mind if we come in?' Mundy pressed. He was anxious to see inside Cassey's house. 'Better than talking on the doorstep in full view of your neighbours.'

'Why? What's it about?' Cassey's voice trembled.

'Did you once own a Saab 90?' Mundy asked and then quoted the registration number. 'It's about that car.'

'Yes.' Cassey suddenly sounded relieved. 'Some years ago . . . but yes, that was one of the cars I owned.'

'Grey, with red or brown doors?' Ingram asked.

'Yes, that's the one.' Cassey continued to relax. 'The previous owner replaced the doors – I bought it like that. Both had been damaged in separate accidents. He got them off a similar car but didn't have them resprayed to match. He said that the car wasn't worth the cost of the respray.' Cassey opened the door. 'Do come in . . . if you wish.'

The inside of Cassey's house was, the officers found, as plain and basic and as down-at-heel as the exterior. The floorboards were bare save for three sheets of ill-matched matting. The chairs and settee were black, inexpensive and plastic covered with thin orange cushions. A small television stood in the corner of the room resting on an equally small, flimsy-looking table. The room smelled musty and, looking beyond the room through an open doorway to the kitchen, both officers saw a large pile of accumulated washing-up in the sink. The kitchen window looked out upon an ill-kept rear garden. It was, the officers saw, the home of an unmarried, childless man. Clearly so.

'What did you do with the car?' Ingram asked.

'Sold it. Sold it on. I sold it privately . . . bought another Saab,' Cassey explained, 'then another. I had three Saabs, one after the other . . . I used to like driving them.'

'Do you run a car now?' Ingram peered out across the rear garden.

'Not any more. I got made redundant,' Cassey explained. 'I was a delivery van driver.'

'UK-wide?' Mundy asked.

'Occasionally we'd get a long drive and I'd stay in a guesthouse but usually I was home each evening. I delivered mainly round East Anglia.' Cassey spoke with a slight trace of an East Anglian accent.

'So you know East Anglia well?' Mundy asked.

'You could say that,' Cassey replied. 'Why are you interested in my old Saab?'

'We're not,' Mundy said. 'We are interested in the murder of Oliver Walwyn.'

'Who's he?' Cassey demanded with a note of fear and alarm suddenly re-entering his voice. 'I don't know anyone of that name.'

'A little boy who had his skull smashed in about ten years ago,' Mundy explained. 'You probably read about it. The story was well covered in the press and on television.'

'And his body was dumped in a fishing pond in a village green in Essex which could not be seen from the road,' Ingram added. 'I mean, the pond could not be seen from the road.'

'Indicating someone knew it was there.' Mundy spoke coldly. Then he added, 'You're quite a small, old geezer, aren't you? What are you, five six, seven?'

'So?' Cassey's voice became high-pitched. 'What's my height got to do with anything?'

'Have you got a large, well-built friend?' Ingram asked.

'I've got a few friends; they come in all shapes and sizes.' Cassey remained defensive.

'Any one large friend in particular?' Mundy pressed.

'No.' But the answer came too rapidly, too highly pitched to be believable.

'Have you got a criminal record?' Ingram asked.

'You must know that I have . . .' Cassey continued to stand his ground but his voice trembled with fear.

'Yes, we did check,' Mundy replied. 'Nothing very serious and nothing for a long time . . . all spent now. Assault, resisting arrest. All a bit violent in one way or another.'

'And you collected a few months in HM prison,' Ingram added.

'Yes. No point in denying it but that was . . .' Cassey's voice shook with fear, '. . . well, it feels like it was another lifetime. I've turned the corner. In fact, I turned the corner a long time ago. Like I said, all that is well behind me.'

'Well, good for you. But the murder of the boy,' Ingram pressed, 'what can you tell us about that?'

'Nothing.' Cassey gasped. 'I can tell you nothing about it. Nothing at all.'

'But you were the owner of a Saab 90 with ill-matching doors ten years ago,' Mundy clarified.

'Ten years? Yes, I was. I had the car for three years about ten years ago, but you'll know that if you checked with the records,' Cassey replied nervously. 'It's all on computer these days. All on those computers, wretched things that they are.'

'You don't like computers?' Mundy observed, still hearing fear in Cassey's voice. 'It sounds like you don't like them at all.'

'You can't seem to hide,' Cassey whined, 'so no . . . no . . . I don't like them. Computers and CCTV cameras on every lamppost . . . you can't hide.'

'Useful, though.' Mundy smiled. 'They're very useful to the police.'

'To you, perhaps,' Cassey sneered. 'So why question me about that boy who was murdered? Why link my old Saab with that murder? I don't see the connection.'

'You don't have to,' Mundy replied calmly. 'We have to see a connection and, when we do, we'll call back.'

'But thank you for your cooperation.' Tom Ingram smiled. 'It was very interesting to meet you.'

'Very interesting,' Maurice Mundy echoed as he felt his
shoes stick to the rug on which he stood. 'Very interesting
indeed.'

David Cole leaned forward and clasped his hands tightly
together. He took a deep breath. His face developed a ruddy
hue. 'I am . . .' he said quietly and slowly, '. . . trying to
remain very, very calm.' He glanced out of his office window
at the vista it offered of central Chelmsford, of modern, late-
twentieth-century buildings and narrow streets carrying a
heavy flow of traffic. 'I have never dealt with Cold Case
Review officers before so I confess I am not sure of my
ground. I am trying to remain calm. I will have to consult
my boss, take advice and let him decide to notify your
governor or not.'

'Fair enough,' Ingram replied.

'But I would have thought that you have jeopardized our
inquiry into the murders of those girls,' Cole continued.

'We did not mention them at all,' Ingram protested. 'We
enquired only about our case . . . Oliver Walwyn. We did not
mention any of the murdered women – not once. We were
very careful not to do that.'

'But you tipped him off that we know he used to own a
distinct car which was seen in the vicinity of the area where
Janet Laws was known to be abducted with one man driving
and another leaning over something or somebody as if in a
struggle. That's sufficient to tip them off.' Cole took a deep
breath. 'And you implied that we had a description of the two
men in the distinctive Saab . . . one short and driving, the
other large. You asked if he had a well-built friend. If it is
them then he'll be phoning his mate now. If they have collected
trophies from their victims they now have all the time in the
world to dispose of them. You've blown our case if it is Cassey
and another man.'

'We are entitled to interview people who may be connected
with the crime.' Mundy sat back in the chair which he occupied
and which stood in front of Cole's desk. He remained forcibly
calm as he spoke.

'But not suspects!' Cole then slapped his palm on the

desktop. 'Not suspects, that is clear . . . that was made clear. Not suspects! You don't interview suspects.'

'We didn't.' Mundy remained relaxed. 'We didn't know that he was a suspect until we were in his house, and then we found that he reeks of guilt.'

'Reeks of it,' Ingram echoed. 'And he's got the right profile. Single man, a low-life . . . was employed as a delivery van driver all over East Anglia and further afield on occasions, but he'll know East Anglia, he'll know it well – all the little lanes off the beaten track. He trembled with fear at the mention of his old Saab, and of his well-built mate . . . the Laurel and Hardy duo. He's your man, all right. He's the Stanley Laurel.'

'And the "Oliver Hardy" is now covering his tracks, especially since you waited twenty-four hours to tell us,' Cole growled. 'Considerate of you, I must say!'

'We had to return to Scotland Yard to check our records,' Mundy explained. 'That took time.'

'Oh, and we're in the dark ages up here in Essex, are we?' Cole snarled. 'We're still burning witches at the stake, are we? We've got our own computer which interfaces with the Police National Computer. Or didn't you know that?'

'Sorry.' Mundy shrugged. 'I suppose we just thought "London".'

'Typical arrogance of Met coppers, if you ask me.' Cole sighed. 'I'll talk to my boss and we'll probably arrest Cassey on suspicion, but it's likely going to be a damage limitation exercise. If he is released from custody don't go near him. Not without clearance . . . and then only about your investigation.'

'Fair enough,' Ingram replied for both he and Mundy. 'That's fair enough.'

Cole stood up. 'Just get back to London. I'll go and talk to the next floor up about this but they won't be a set of very happy campers. You can bet on that.'

The girl was black, an Afro-Caribbean, short, with heavy make-up about the eyes, brightly dressed in a red coat and a yellow scarf with multi-coloured beads around her neck. She eyed Mundy with a poorly disguised sneer at a pathetic, sad old man who was on the 'Callie' seeking a little empty-headed company. She said, 'Are you looking for a girl?'

'Yes, I am,' Mundy replied, looking down at the waif.

'So what do you want, darlin'?' the girl replied. 'And I only do safe?'

'Sensible of you,' Mundy said, 'but she's mixed race, taller than you, shorter than me and I hope she only does safe as well. She's called Roberta.'

'If you're a regular of hers you should always know where to find your girl.' The woman admonished Mundy with an air of aggression and effortless superiority for one so young that surprised him. 'Sorry, mate, I can't help you. I don't know any girl called Roberta and time is money.' She turned away and was lost in the crowd at the bottom of Caledonian Road in the gathering evening gloom.

Eventually Mundy found the girl he was looking for and took her to a cheap Italian-owned and run café. He watched with no little dismay as Roberta Loss emptied much of the contents of the sugar jar into her tea.

'You won't taste the tea,' Mundy warned. 'Not that there is a great deal of tea to taste in here but at least it's warm and wet.'

'It goes with the territory.' Roberta Loss picked up the teaspoon with slender, wasted-looking hands and stirred the concoction within the cup in front of her. 'Smackheads get to stop photosynthesis . . .' The woman shrugged. 'We develop an addiction to sugar and have to take loads of it because we can't obtain energy from the sun . . . not no more, we can't.'

'Are you still living alone?' Roberta Loss's statement about photosynthesis made no sense to Maurice Mundy and he did not comment on it.

'Yes. I like it like that.' She sipped the tea. 'It's a reaction to the way mother and him used to live, I suppose . . . knocking lumps out of each other with me cowering behind the settee, but for some reason they stayed together. I just couldn't understand them. I still can't. They're probably still doing it now under the palm trees.'

'It seems to work for some people.' Mundy also sipped his tea. 'It's like they feed off the violence, though I could never understand it either. It's like they like the violence for the peace which follows. Like banging your head on a wall because it feels good when you stop. Most people wouldn't knock their heads against the wall in the first place.'

'Headbangers.' Roberta Loss smiled. 'I know what you mean. I meet a lot of them in my line of work.'

'I imagine you do.' Mundy sighed. 'Or it's the chemistry which seems to work between small, feisty women and large, biddable men. I could never understand that either. Finally I stopped trying to understand it. If it works for them, it works for them . . . so leave them as is. I am sorry you had to see that, though.'

'Couldn't be avoided.' Roberta Loss cupped her hands around the mug of tea.

'Anyway, I'm pleased I found you,' Mundy said with a smile. 'I have thirty pounds to spare . . . I'd like you to have it.'

'I'm not happy about taking it,' Roberta Loss complained.

'I know but I'd like you to take it,' Mundy argued. 'You'll get home earlier if you do. You'll be a little safer.'

'OK.' Roberta Loss took the money and slipped it into her purse.

'Any employment?' Mundy asked, though he knew what the answer was going to be.

Roberta Loss inclined her head to the window of the shop. 'Just what's out there, just what's going at the bottom end of the Callie.'

'I don't like you doing it,' Mundy spoke calmly.

'Where else can I go but the Callie? I can't work Piccadilly, not young enough, and not good looking enough for "the Dilly Lady" . . . so it's the Callie for me . . . or King's Cross. It's the same difference, the Callie or King's Cross.'

'I don't mean I don't like you standing on the Caledonian Road,' Mundy spoke quietly. 'I don't care where you stand, the Callie or "the Dilly Lady" or King's Cross, I mean I don't like you doing it at all. I don't like you standing anywhere.'

'What else can I do?' Roberta Loss gulped her tea. 'Tell me, oh wise one, what else can I do? How else can I earn money? A girl like me. I have no qualifications . . . no work experience. I had reasonable looks before I got wasted with heroin, so I stand on the street, and I've been here ever since. It's a common enough story out there.'

'I dare say.' Mundy felt deeply uncomfortable. 'Are you still living in the same place?'

'Me old bedsit in Earls Court? The Kangaroo Canyon? Yes . . . still there.' Roberta Loss put more sugar into what remained of her tea. 'I'll let you know if I change address.'

'I'd appreciate that,' Mundy replied, 'but your tea won't absorb any more sugar.'

'I know.' Roberta Loss smiled. 'I eat the sludge these days. Like I said, I don't get anything from the sun no more. I have to eat sugar.'

'Eating sugar.' Mundy sighed. 'You can move in with me. I've told you that before. I won't take any money off you so you wouldn't have to work . . .'

'What? And you'll handcuff me to the bed so I can't leave the house to score some H?' Roberta Loss inclined her head to one side. 'Is that what you'd do?'

'If I thought it would do any good,' Mundy sighed, 'yes, I'd be prepared to do that . . .'

'I'd scream my lungs out and you'd be done for false imprisonment.'

Roberta Loss drained the last of her tea and was left with a slush of tea-soaked sugar in the bottom of her cup. She took a teaspoon and began to shovel the slush into her mouth. 'It gives me energy,' she explained. 'It's going to get cold out there tonight. You know, it's good of you to keep inviting me to move into your drum but it wouldn't work – we'd get on each other's nerves. I may take you up on it for a few days if the alternative is rough sleeping, if I get evicted. So it's good to know that I have that as a safety net. Thank you.'

'Have you had any treatment?' Mundy asked.

'I tried methadone but it didn't work for me,' Roberta Loss explained. 'At the clinic they say if you can do without it for a day, you can do without it for a week, and if you can do without it for a week, you can do without it for a month, and so on. And they told us the story of the old lady . . .'

'I don't know that one,' Mundy asked. 'What's that story?'

'Well,' Roberta Loss spooned more sugary slush into her mouth, 'it is the story of an old . . . a middle-aged lady who was told she was very ill. In fact, it was believed she was terminally ill but they didn't tell her that and her doctor arranged for a nurse to visit her and give her a daily shot of heroin to ease the pain.'

'I see.' Mundy sipped his tea, which had by then gone cold.

'So,' Roberta Loss continued, 'the doctor retired and his practice was taken over by a new doctor who reviewed all the patients and their treatments and came across the records of the middle-aged lady and her daily dose of heroin. By then she had been getting a daily shot for ten years.'

'Ten years!' Mundy gasped. 'So she wasn't terminally ill?'

'No, there had . . . what was the phrase they used?' Roberta Loss looked to her right. 'A mal . . . or a misdiagnosis, and so the doctor visited and said, "I'm sorry your treatment has taken so long but now you are cured and I am going to stop the treatment". He visited her a couple of days later expecting to find her in a dreadful mess . . . the shakes, stomach cramps, vomiting . . . the whole cold turkey number.'

'But . . .' Mundy prompted.

'But she was as right as rain. Apparently. So the story went. She said that she did have a period of influenza-like symptoms for a day or so but that soon passed. She was just pleased she was cured and could go out for a whole day without having to wait in for the nurse to call and give her an injection.' Roberta Loss scooped the last of the slush from her cup into her mouth. 'So there she was, living an addict's dream . . . a heavy hit of pharmaceutically pure heroin every day. She came off it without being eased off it and all she experienced was feeling like she had had a mild dose of influenza for a day, the point being that they say that the need for heroin is a myth . . . it's all in the head.'

'Interesting,' Mundy replied. 'That's very interesting indeed.'

'And it's true because whenever I have been in prison and couldn't get any heroin the craving wasn't as strong. In fact, on some days it wasn't there at all,' Roberta Loss explained. 'It just vanished. Vanished.'

'So why go back to it?' Mundy appealed.

'Because it's who I am . . . it's my place . . . it's my identity.' Roberta Loss looked down at the tabletop. 'I am a heroin-addicted street-worker . . . part of the underground sex industry. I'm known as that. The suppliers push H on to me. If I wasn't that what could I be? There's nothing else I could be.' Maurice Mundy felt cold anger rising in him. 'If I don't buy I'll get my face burned off with acid,' Roberta Loss added. 'So they've got you cold. No escape.' 'Animals,' Mundy hissed. 'Animals. So why don't you move to a new location? Relocate to some place where you are not known and establish yourself as a non-user.' He casually examined his tablemat which depicted a racing Ferrari in Italian Racing Red, and then he glanced at a huge photograph of St Mark's Square in Venice which hung on the wall behind Roberta Loss. 'It's the only way you'll break free. Honestly, it's the only way you'll do it. And you'll have to break free if you wish to live. It's as serious as that.'

'I know . . . I know . . . do you think I don't know? Each week we hear about a working girl getting iced. Often it doesn't make the newspapers.' Roberta Loss dropped her teaspoon into her empty cup. 'So you don't have to tell me, oh wise one. But, like I said, it's all caught up in the self-image and all the pressure on you. That old lady didn't know she was a heroin addict and she didn't have very heavy men being nice and kind to her if she bought white powder from them or threatening to break her legs, or worse, if she didn't. But I'll think about what you said . . . promise.'

'Please do. You know where I live and you have a set of keys . . .' Mundy paused. 'All right, enough of the lecture. Shall we have another cup of tea?'

'So . . .' Roberta Loss upturned the sugar jar into the second cup of tea after it was served in an off-hand manner by the olive-skinned waitress who scowled at Roberta Loss as she did so. 'Tell me, how is the new job? Good?'

'Interesting . . . it's very interesting, looking over old cases. Old, unsolved cases – "cold cases", as we call them. Better than sitting at home soaking up daytime television or sitting in the pub all afternoon making each pint last an hour.' Maurice Mundy stirred his cup of tea despite not having sweetened it.

'It gets me out. I'm up in East Anglia all this week and I'll be going to Nottingham tomorrow.'

'So you work Saturdays?' Roberta Loss sounded surprised.

'If we have to,' Mundy replied. 'Our work time is more liberal, less structured than the so-called "proper coppers". We don't have to work those long hours of endless overtime or do surveillance well into the night. It's all more civilized. Reviewing evidence, talking to witnesses who may have recalled something over the passage of time which they didn't think relevant at the time or were not asked about at the time. We're not allowed to interview suspects; we have to notify the proper cops of any new information we might uncover.'

'"Proper coppers".' Roberta Loss smiled. 'I like that term.'

'Someone used it earlier this week and I seem to have adopted it, for my sins,' Mundy explained.

'So what takes you to Nottingham?' Roberta Loss asked.

'Oh, that's just a personal agenda I am pursuing. You can join me if you like, for the journey. I can't take you to the house I have visited but we can travel up and back down together . . . have lunch, look round Nottingham. It'll be a full day.'

'No, I can't . . . I'm working tonight.' Roberta Loss looked at the window and groaned. 'And it's started to rain – that'll slow things down. It'll be a late finish for me, even with the thirty pounds you have given me. I'll be working late tonight and I won't be getting out of my pit until midday . . . probably, by which time you'll be in Nottingham. What time will you get back, do you think?'

'Early evening, I should imagine. Won't be late.' Maurice Mundy sipped his tea.

'Will you get something to eat?' Roberta Loss asked in a concerned tone of voice.

'I have a pile of pizzas in the fridge; I saw that they were reduced to half price in the supermarket. They had reached their sell-by date so I grabbed all six that were on offer.' Mundy looked pleased with himself. 'I'll have an early night and I'll have all day Sunday to recover . . . then it's back to the Cold Case Review Team on Monday.'

'Why didn't you rise in the police?' Roberta Loss asked

suddenly. 'I mean, detective constable – that's not very much, is it? I've been arrested by detective sergeants who were in their twenties.'

'I can imagine. The company men . . . the so-called "young thrusters". They have the work, sleep, work, sleep, work mentality. I could never get into that mindset.' Mundy glanced at the falling rain. 'I never was that keen.'

'Is that the real reason?' Roberta Loss eyed him intently.

'It's the reason that I am giving you.' Mundy avoided her stare. 'It's part of the reason.'

'So there's another reason?' Roberta Loss smiled.

'Possibly.' Mundy smiled back. 'The whole truth is out there.'

'But you won't tell me what it is?' Roberta Loss winked at Mundy.

'Nope. So I didn't achieve greatness then, but no one in the CCRT did. Those who achieve greatness retire at fifty-five years of age with a huge pension and turn their backs on the police. The low fliers . . . well, our pensions won't run to good living and we still can keep our hand in if the pressure is kept off. It's a better deal than taking a job as a night watchman or a school-crossing warden like some retired police officers have to do. It offers a certain self-respect.' Mundy swallowed a mouthful of tea. 'It keeps me in the police, and that I like.'

'I see.' Roberta Loss emptied yet more sugar into her tea. 'So, tell me, who is up there in Nottingham?'

FIVE

'Thank you very much for the phone call, I really did appreciate it.' The woman smiled. She was tall, with neatly kept hair – elegant, Maurice Mundy thought, in a three-quarter-length dark green dress, her slender legs placed in sensible brown shoes with a small heel. 'It enabled me to ensure I was at home.'

'It was really in my interest.' Mundy reclined in the armchair, which he found soft and comfortable. The room was light coloured and airy with a large window which looked out on to Appledore Crescent, and an equally large window on the further side of the room which looked out on to the rear garden of the property which, Mundy noted, was modest in size but very carefully tended. Within, the house smelled of air freshener and furniture polish, as if it had been prepared in readiness for his visit. Prints of old Nottingham hung on the wall provided the decoration. 'It would have been a long way to come to find that you were not at home.'

'Indeed.' The woman smiled again. 'It is really the case that it is in both our interests. So, you are interested in Joshua?'

'Yes.' Mundy glanced around the room and then held eye contact with Jane Weekes. 'I am interested in Joshua . . . specifically, I am interested in the safety of his conviction.'

'Is this official police business,' Jane Weekes asked guardedly, 'or a private pursuit of justice? I note that you are but one man. I understand that plainclothes police work in pairs.'

'The latter,' Mundy confessed. 'My visit is wholly unofficial.'

'But you are a police officer?' Jane Weekes spoke in a calm, relaxed manner. Mundy noted that she had not lost her London accent.

'Technically, yes,' Mundy explained. 'I am semi-retired and with limited room to manoeuvre but not yet put out to grass.'

'I see. Joshua did not kill that woman,' Jane Weekes asserted. 'He did not kill her.'

'I don't believe he killed her either.' Mundy quickly relaxed in the presence of Mrs Weekes and felt that he was going to enjoy the visit to her home. 'I think, with growing conviction, that there has been a terrible miscarriage of justice.'

'And so little compensation that he has benefitted from prison,' Jane Weekes replied. 'It is hardly any compensation at all.'

'Benefitted?' Mundy repeated. 'How? In what sense? What do you mean?'

'In the sense that he is more alert – the rigorous regime has brightened him up and brought him down to earth. His feet are now on the ground. He lives life rather than sliding over the surface of it. He is now fully engaged with life. I think it has brought out his latent potential. He has had a bit of an education in prison. Joshua is not a highflyer, he wouldn't . . . could not manage a university correspondence course, but three O-levels meant that he could have coped with a mainstream school all along and avoided the stigma of a special school attendee.'

'I also found him more alert than I had expected, I readily confess,' Mundy replied. 'He has read *Treasure Island*, for example.'

'Has he?' Jane Weekes beamed. 'Well, good for him. Good for Joshua. That book must have a reading age of about fourteen.'

'I would think so . . . and not only had he read it but he could criticize it,' Maurice Mundy advised. 'He was able to pick holes in the plot, so he had really read it, and read it very carefully.'

'How interesting? What did he say?' Jane Weekes continued to smile broadly.

'He said . . .' Mundy glanced upwards, '. . . what did he say now? Oh, yes . . . he said that Stephenson seemed to get tired of the book by the time he wrote the final chapter and he rushed to finish it. He said that two paragraphs in the final chapter began with the word "well", like he was having a quick gossip over the garden fence with his neighbour, and he said that Stephenson should have taken a week's holiday then written the final chapter.'

'Josh said that!' Jane Weekes gasped. 'That is not special school material; he definitely could have coped in a comprehensive school – the lowest ability range, perhaps, but he could have kept his head above water.'

'I thought so too.' Mundy inclined his head. 'And he was able to pick holes in the plot, as I said, such as that it is the case that the reader never finds out what Jim Hawkins and the doctor do with their share of the treasure . . . and he asked how did they manage to conceal the treasure from the crew they hired in Jamaica to help them sail the Hispaniola back to England without the crew discovering the treasure on the ship?' Mundy raised a finger. 'Especially since Long John Silver had forced a hole in the bulkhead of the hold of the ship where the treasure was stored and taken his fair share before spiriting himself away in the night. That action of his meant that the treasure was in plain sight of the newly hired crew. Josh picked that up by himself.'

'That really is interesting.' Jane Weekes took a deep breath. 'My husband will be interested to hear that. I have talked with him about Josh, as you might imagine, and he says that it sounds like Joshua suffered from "negative Pygmalion effect".'

'You'll have to forgive me,' Maurice Mundy pleaded, 'I am not familiar with that term . . . the negative Pygmalion effect. What does it mean?'

'My husband is a schoolmaster,' Mrs Weekes explained, 'and a damn good one too. He is a strong advocate of the Pygmalion effect. He says that people, but especially children, will believe what is said about them if they are told it often enough. If you tell a girl she is plain and unprepossessing, she will be plain and unprepossessing . . . but if you tell that self-same girl she is beautiful and attractive, she will become beautiful and attractive. If you tell a boy he's a team player, he will become a team player, but if you tell him he's better off on his own, he will grow up to be better off on his own.'

'Ah, yes,' Mundy smiled, 'I understand. I have come across that attitude. I just didn't know it was called the Pygmalion effect.'

'Yes,' Mrs Weekes continued, 'my husband is an idealist and he started teaching at a struggling comprehensive, not by then labelled as a failing school but well on its way there. The children just wouldn't cooperate in the form he was given, which was a notoriously difficult form. They would get up and walk round the classroom in the middle of lessons, sometimes even walk out of the classroom in the middle of a lesson . . . you know, the sort of thing that they'd be shot for in an earlier era. But my husband let them know how much he enjoyed teaching that form because they were intelligent and hardworking. He didn't lay it on with a trowel but he'd say that to that particular form once a week and they began to settle down, became interested and they began to work. Eventually he got good results from them.'

'Good for him.' Mundy smiled. 'Well done him.'

'Yes . . . my husband took his attitude to the staff room; he told his colleagues what he was doing and they followed suit. Within a few months the whole school had been turned round – utterly transformed. It was a huge success story. It is now a very successful inner-city comprehensive and my husband has risen to become the head of history. He was offered a headship but he doesn't want to leave the classroom to manage a school.'

'You know, that rather explains now why I didn't work at school,' Mundy growled. 'I failed my eleven-plus and was sent to a secondary modern because someone has to drive the buses and build the brick walls . . .'

'And stack supermarket shelves.' Mrs Weekes also growled with disapproval. 'Yes, I know all about the evils of the eleven-plus system being an eleven-plus failure myself. But those days are gone . . . thank goodness. It's all comprehensive now.'

'Thankfully.' Mundy nodded in agreement. 'Thankfully.'

'But I mention the Pygmalion effect to explain Joshua,' Mrs Weekes continued. 'I think my mother had some issue with her father which wasn't talked about like such things might be today, and I don't think there was a great deal of passion in my parents' marriage. I think my mother got married to have daughters. She got two, wanted a third but got a son instead – a son for whom she had no time. Poor Josh, he just couldn't do anything right. He was our mother's victim from day one. That was bad enough, and then he turned out to be a bit slow.

So then what was he but "stupid" – every day he was told that he was stupid. So he became stupid because it was expected of him. He went to the special school and became "soft Joshua" – a target for the local bullies . . . but Anne Tweedale rescued him. She saw potential in him and showed him warmth and acceptance. She mothered him and he responded with loyalty and doing what he could to please her. Then he stabs her multiple times and steals her valuables? I don't think so. It is just not credible. I don't believe that he did that.'

'Neither do I.' Mundy sighed. 'Neither do I.'

'So what is your interest in my brother?' Jane Weekes asked after a slight lull in the conversation.

'I arrested him.' Mundy held eye contact with Jane Weekes and watched as her jaw sagged and the colour drained from her face. After a second brief pause, Mrs Weekes said, 'I am not sure that I am happy . . . I am not very comfortable with your presence in my house, Mr Mundy.'

'Please hear me out. I understand how you might feel, but please let me explain.' Mundy held up his hand, palm facing outwards towards Jane Weekes. 'I was a junior constable then, still in uniform, and I didn't arrest him as such – it would be more accurate to say that I was present when a senior officer arrested Joshua and myself and another constable escorted him into custody.'

'I see,' Jane Weekes replied cautiously. 'And it's taken you twenty-eight years to express your concern about the safety of his conviction? Not a man in a hurry, are you, Mr Mundy? Not a man to run for the bus, it might seem.'

'It's taken me a few months really.' Mundy defended himself. 'You see, I never achieved high rank in the police, and anyway, someone has to investigate the theft of the lawnmower from the cricket club's garden shed, but I have also been part of murder inquiry teams. I may have only been a "pit pony", kept largely in the dark and the sort pulling loads no one else wanted to pull, but despite that I have been close enough to the action to see things, and over the years I have learned that murderers have a distinct personality trait.'

'Oh . . .?' Mrs Weekes replied with a look of alertness in her eyes.

'Yes.' Mundy spoke softly but firmly. 'It was described to me very recently as believing that the sun shines just for them, and often they subscribe to the belief that it's always somebody else's fault . . .'

'As, for example . . .' Jane Weekes' voice became a little warmer.

'As a case I recall when a man's wife walked out on him and went to live in a woman's refuge. The man was so full of self-importance that he couldn't cope with his wife leaving and he persuaded a friend who worked for British Telecom to provide him with the address of the refuge, which his friend could do because his job allowed him to access the address of the ex-directory numbers. He said that he wanted to talk to his wife to try to rescue their marriage . . . or so he explained to his friend, and like an idiot his friend agreed and furnished him with the address of the refuge.'

'Oh . . . no . . .' Jane Weekes put her hand up to her mouth. 'Oh, no . . .'

'Oh, yes.' Mundy raised his eyebrows, 'I'm afraid so. This man's idea of rescuing his marriage was to go round to the hostel with cold premeditation, armed with a carving knife, and he ran his wife through for walking out on him – "nobody walks out on me" being his attitude . . . and he was totally without remorse when we arrested him. He was not at all bothered that his friend lost his very good job and was not likely to get another – not one that was worth having, anyway . . . He was not in any way bothered that his wife lost her life when still less than halfway through her expected lifespan. He said that it was all her fault for leaving him because he was a little bit violent at times, and that wasn't his fault either – it was the beer that made him like that.'

'That is not Joshua, that is not Joshua at all,' Jane Weekes replied indignantly. 'He would never, never, ever think like that. Never!'

'I know, but it took me many years of arresting real murderers before I could look back on Joshua Derbyshire's arrest and say, "that young man is not a murderer", but even then I could not say anything until I retired from mainstream policing.'

'I see.' Jane Weekes spoke softly. 'That is interesting. I am less uncomfortable now. So how can I help you, Mr Mundy?'

'Could you tell me who Joshua's legal team were?' Mundy asked. 'I might be able to talk to them, even after this length of time.'

'You might well . . . His solicitor was a young man called Greenall.'

Maurice Mundy took his notebook from his pocket. 'Greenall,' he repeated.

'He might still be with us even after this length of time,' Jane Weekes added. 'He was employed by a firm of solicitors called Pope and Steadman.'

'Pope and Steadman.' Mundy wrote in his pad.

'Of Burnt Oak,' Jane Weekes advised. 'He seemed to be genuinely unconvinced of Joshua's guilt. His barrister was an elderly man who hadn't taken silk so he was not a star player, and he put up a very perfunctory performance at Josh's trial. He brought only one character witness as his defence package. He didn't sum up the defence argument and declined to address the jury at the close of the trial which, of course, only served to make Joshua look guilty. He was a man called Levy. Oh, and he also declined to put Josh in the witness box; that also made him look guilty . . .'

'Yes.' Mundy looked around the home, built in the sixties, he guessed, and he found it cold within. A single gas fire, turned down low, served to take the edge off the cold but didn't warm the room. 'That indeed would make Joshua look guilty, as you say. Can I ask if you knew Miss Tweedale?'

'I knew her quite well. Josh made no secret of his going to her house. He was only about fourteen or fifteen, probably nearer fifteen, when he met her and so she would run him home on dark nights or I would collect him from Miss Tweedale's house. He still needed looking after and protecting even at that age, because we genuinely thought he had a functioning level of about ten years of age,' Jane Weekes explained.

'I understand.' Maurice Mundy smiled.

'She was a very nice lady and Josh became devoted to her. As I said, he got from Miss Tweedale what he didn't get from our own mother.'

'Yes, it all sounds to have been very difficult for Josh,' Mundy commented. 'Do you know if Miss Tweedale had any relatives?'

'She had a sister,' Jane Weekes advised. 'She did mention her once but other than that I'm afraid I don't know. Mrs Baxendale is the person to ask. She is . . . she was Miss Tweedale's neighbour.'

'Yes, I have met her . . . a very nice lady,' Mundy replied.

'She must be getting on now?' Jane Weekes commented. 'She was a bit less accepting of Joshua than Anne Tweedale was but, nevertheless, I remember her being a very pleasant lady, as you say.'

'She is, and she is still healthy, though sadly she has lost her husband.' Mundy shivered slightly. He hoped it wasn't noticeable. 'I might return and revisit her; I'd like to know more about Miss Tweedale's family.'

'Miss Tweedale would have told Mrs Baxendale if she told anyone,' Jane Weekes replied. 'She certainly did not and would not divulge anything like that to me; I was barely out of school myself in those days.'

'Well.' Mundy closed his notebook. 'Thank you for the information, Mrs Weekes. I appreciate it.' Mundy stood up. 'It's been very helpful.'

'Not as much as I appreciate it, Mr Mundy. I now have renewed hope.' Mrs Weekes also stood up. 'It's a long way for you to come for a face-to-face; we could have easily talked on the phone.'

'Not true.' Mundy smiled. 'A stranger phoning you . . . about your brother? I could have been anyone. You would have been reluctant to talk and it's always good to put a face to a name.'

'Well, thank you, anyway.' Mrs Weekes shook Mundy's hand. 'You'll let me know of any developments?'

'Of course.' Mundy picked up his hat. 'Of course.'

Upon his return home to his house in Archway, the journey from Mrs Weekes' house to his taking four hours door to door, Maurice Mundy, opening his front door, was assailed by a strong smell of house-cleaning materials and noticed that his home had been tidied. In the living room he found a hand-written note trapped under the clock on the mantelpiece. It read:

> *Wise one . . . your house is a mess. Even for you it's a real pigsty. Anyway, there's a pre-cooked lasagne in the oven for you. You just need to heat it for an hour at gas mark 5. Better than a pizza after a long journey . . .*
> *Love,*
> *Roberta*

Mrs Felicity Baxendale opened her front door widely and beamed at Maurice Mundy.

'Are you sure you don't mind me calling on Sunday?' Mundy swept off his fedora. 'As I explained on the phone, it's really for my convenience.'

'No bother at all, Mr Mundy, no bother at all. I find Sunday afternoons difficult to occupy so your company is most welcome. Do please come in.'

'That's very kind of you.' Maurice Mundy stepped over the threshold of Felicity Baxendale's house.

Once seated, over a more-than-welcome cup of tea and with notebook and pen to hand, Maurice Mundy opened the interview by saying, 'I am really interested in Miss Tweedale's relatives. I believe she had a sister . . .?'

'Yes, as in fact I told you when you visited me on the last occasion,' Felicity Baxendale replied. 'Her sister is called Phyllis and she has three sons. I also told you that there was ill feeling in their family . . . some issue . . .'

'But you don't know what?' Mundy inquired.

'You know, perhaps I just might. After you left the other day I did recall an incident or a comment, more like. She had received a postcard from her sister, sent from some cheap resort like Benidorm . . . in fact, I think it was Benidorm, and which she looked at with distaste and said, "She'll be asking me to bail her out again. She always does within a few weeks of sending me a postcard but I won't . . . not any more. She made her bed; she must lie in it. Father warned her what he'd do if she married that man . . . and he did it, he kept his word, so hell mend her. I feel that I have to honour my father's wishes".'

'She was disinherited?' Mundy observed. 'The sister, I mean?'

'It would appear so,' Felicity Baxendale mused. 'There is that suggestion. She lived – probably still lives – south of the river. I met her just the one time. We . . . that is, a group of neighbours, were having strawberries and ice cream in Anne Tweedale's garden one blisteringly hot July afternoon and a strange woman called. She walked round the side of the house into Anne Tweedale's back garden, bold as brass, calm as you please, saw the group of us and looked crestfallen. Anne introduced her to us and she gave her sister a bowl of strawberries and ice cream. You could tell that they were sisters . . . they looked similar. Anyway, an awkward silence fell on our little gathering and the sister, Phyllis, gobbled up her strawberries and ice cream, made her excuses and left. After she had gone, Anne said that she was probably seeking some money. It was the only reason Phyllis ever called on her, she told us – borrowing money she had no intention of paying back. But, you know, I think that the only person who might help you there is Anne Tweedale's cousin.'

'Cousin?' Mundy replied in a saddened, disappointed tone. 'If he's her cousin, he or she . . .'

'He . . .'

'He will be in Anne Tweedale's age group . . . elderly, and that is only if he's still with us.'

'Probably still with us,' Felicity Baxendale replied with a ready smile. 'It appears that Anne Tweedale's grandmother was a woman who enjoyed or was cursed with a certain fecundity depending on how you view such things, and as a girl Anne apparently had many uncles and aunts spanning quite an age range, so she told me. And the youngest of her cousins was really some twenty years Anne's junior so now he'll be a man in his sixties. He is her uncle's son . . . Anne's paternal uncle's son, so he will also be a Tweedale.' Felicity Baxendale put her hand to her forehead. 'She used to refer to him as "H" and said that he had brought shame on the family. He served a prison sentence, you see.'

'Oh,' Mundy smiled gently, 'that is quite useful. You see, if that is the case it means that we can trace him. An H. Tweedale, possibly now in his sixties – that's all I need.'

'Yes, but I did know his name . . . "H" . . . but he wasn't a career criminal, you understand. He apparently made a mistake, just one mistake, and it ruined his life. Apparently he gambled away a shedload of money that wasn't his to gamble. Anne blamed the person who gave him the money to take to the bank, knowing that her cousin was a gambling addict. She said it was like giving a bottle of whiskey to an alcoholic.'

'The temptation, you mean?' Mundy tapped his pen on his notepad close to where he had written H. Tweedale.

'That's what Anne meant. It was too much of a temptation for him. Horace . . .' Felicity Baxendale smiled broadly. 'That was it . . . that was his name. Horace Tweedale. I remember now . . . Horace Tweedale.'

'Horace.' Mundy wrote the name on his notepad.

'Anne was angrier for him than with him,' Felicity Baxendale explained. 'She wrote to him regularly when he was in prison and she also helped him out financially when he was released.'

'Thank you . . . I will trace him.' Mundy smiled with gratitude.

'He'll be able to help you much more than I can when it comes to the goings-on in Anne's family,' Felicity Baxendale advised. 'Much more.'

SIX

'They were very unhappy.' DCI Pickering clasped his hands together and rested them on the surface of his desk. He glanced away from Mundy and Ingram in a clear gesture of disapproval while they sat motionless, occupying a chair each in front of Pickering's desk. 'Seriously unhappy.'

'I can't see why they should be so upset,' Mundy replied calmly. 'We have provided them with a suspect. They were getting nowhere fast; we're in the case and within a few days we provide them with a suspect.'

'A damn good suspect as well,' Ingram added. 'Damn good. They should be taking a long, hard look at that man Cassey. A long, damn hard look.'

'They were not getting anywhere, anywhere at all, like I said,' Mundy continued. 'It had all stagnated, and what do we do? Me and Tom . . . we make two home visits and hey presto, we hand them a very likely suspect. But they're unhappy. What planet are they on?'

Pickering took a deep breath. He once again glanced out of his office window at the buildings on the south bank of the Thames. He was a large, muscular man, even for a police officer. Mundy thought him to be a particularly large man. 'You interviewed a suspect. CCRT officers do not interview suspects and they don't interview anyone in respect of any inquiries not allocated to them. I made that perfectly clear to both of you.'

'We did neither.' Mundy remained calm. 'Let me remind you, sir, with respect, that we did neither.'

'We called on him in connection with a motor vehicle he once owned,' Ingram reasoned, 'and we did not mention any one of those murdered women that the Essex Police were investigating. We said we were investigating the murder of Oliver Walwyn. We made that crystal clear.'

'Was the car seen in respect of the murder of Oliver Walwyn?' Pickering asked. 'That's the issue.'

'No,' Mundy conceded. 'No, it wasn't.'

'It was, though, was it not, seen in connection with the murder of Janet Laws?' Pickering argued.

'Possibly,' Ingram replied. 'Only possibly.'

'Possibly,' Pickering repeated, 'and that possibility means that you have tipped Cassey off that he is a prime suspect in a series of murders. His car is a loose connection to the murders of those women. It's loose . . . very loose, I grant you, but it's a connection all the same.' Pickering paused. Then he continued, 'You're getting to be a loose cannon, Maurice . . .' Pickering paused, then he addressed Tom Ingram. 'Tom, I'm sorry but could you wait outside, please?'

'Yes, boss.' Ingram stood and left the room.

'A loose cannon,' Pickering repeated when Ingram had closed the door of Pickering's office. 'I was puzzled as to why you never made it beyond detective constable. Now I know.'

'The Tracy Black inquiry.'

'Yes.' Pickering sat slowly back in his chair. 'You blew that, and you'll blow the East Anglia murders inquiry if you're not careful. If you can't play with the team you'll have to go . . .'

'Yes, sir,' Mundy replied softly.

'It is just the way of it, Maurice. If you – if anyone – does not play with the team, they play against it.' Pickering picked up a rubber band and began stretching it, relaxing it and stretching it again in an absentminded manner. 'I don't mean that you, or anyone, will deliberately oppose the team. I don't mean that, you know I don't, but if you are not a team player then you don't pull your weight, or if you pull in the wrong direction or jump the gun, or if you tread on toes . . .'

'Yes, sir.' Mundy shifted awkwardly in his seat.

'Anyway, the Essex boys at Chelmsford have brought Cassey in for questioning,' Pickering spoke softly, 'so their anger is tempered with not a little gratitude . . .'

'Ah.' Mundy smiled. 'I am gratified.'

'Yes,' Pickering wound the rubber band around his fleshy wrist, 'There is that compensation.'

'Is he talking?' Mundy asked.

'No, not to them.' Pickering snapped the rubber band. 'He's insisting on talking to you.'

'To me!' Mundy gasped. 'Why so?'

'Yes, to you. Why, I don't know. To both you and Tom Ingram, so you might be interviewing a suspect after all.'

'I see.' Mundy took a deep breath. 'I see . . . I see.'

'The Chelmsford police think he's playing games so they won't be giving in to his demands . . . not easily. But if it's the only way forward, they might agree. They have not charged him yet so the clock isn't ticking. He's apparently making no demands to be allowed to leave the police station – while he is there on a voluntary basis the Chelmsford boys are milking it for all it's worth. He seems to like the attention – Cassey, that is, so they're letting him have a lot of it, but it may be that they will ask you and Tom to return if they don't think that they are making progress.'

'Yes, boss.' Mundy smiled his satisfaction. 'I understand.'

'What plans have you for today, Maurice?' Pickering asked in a less angry tone.

'None.' Mundy leaned forward. 'We seem to have come to the end of the road with the Oliver Walwyn inquiry and, as you say, Cassey now belongs to the Chelmsford crew.'

'All right.' Pickering once again snapped the rubber band against his wrist. 'Better hang fire for the rest of the day . . . catch up on your administration or something.'

'Yes, sir.' Mundy stood up. 'There is in fact something I can be doing if I may have leave?'

'All right.' Pickering nodded his assent. 'We have your mobile number if we need to contact you.'

'Yes, sir,' Mundy replied with an alertness in his voice.

'Tell Tom Ingram what's happening up in Chelmsford, if you would, please. Bring him up to speed,' Pickering added. 'He needs to know about Cassey.'

'Yes, sir.' Maurice Mundy turned and left DCI Pickering's office. 'I'll certainly do that. Leave it with me.'

Maurice Mundy walked to the canteen in New Scotland Yard and, it being yet mid-morning, he found that there was only a short queue at the counter. He bought a cup of tea and a toasted teacake and carried his tray to an unoccupied table against the far wall, not having sufficient status as a serving police officer to sit in the centre of the room. He had eaten the teacake and was sipping the remains of his tea when an officer, unknown to him, placed his hand on the back of the chair opposite his. Maurice Mundy did not like the man. He felt a strong and an instant dislike of him. Mundy saw cold, steely blue eyes. He saw great cruelty in those eyes. He saw a man dressed to perfection and with an unhealthy small knot in his tie. He smelled clouds of aftershave from the man. The man was clearly a police officer, but he was, Mundy was certain, the sort of police officer who, if he wasn't a law enforcer, would be a law breaker. Such officers, Mundy knew, exist in all police forces the world over. Mundy guessed the ice man's age to be late twenties.

'Do you mind if I join you?' the young man asked in a distinct London accent, without a smile or a trace of warmth in either his manner or his voice.

'Not at all,' Mundy replied, but by then his new companion had already pulled the chair out from under the table and was seated opposite him, leaning forward and smiling a thin, cruel-looking smile.

'You're DC Mundy?' the man asked. 'Is that right? Do I have the right man?'

'Am I?' Mundy felt apprehensive. 'What makes you think that is my name?'

'Yes, I believe you are.' The youthful detective smiled. 'I think I have the right man.'

'Well, you might very well be correct.' Mundy also leaned forward. He was determined not to be cowed by the man or allow himself to be intimidated. 'It really depends on who you are?'

'Spate,' the man said, 'Detective constable. Same rank as you,' he added with a sneer. 'So far, but I am going places.'

'Spate,' Mundy echoed, 'Spate . . . you wouldn't be any relation to Duncan Spate?'

'Son,' Spate replied. 'I am Christopher, the number three son. I have two older brothers – we are all serving police officers, though I am the only one in the Metropolitan Police. My eldest brother is with the Kent Constabulary and my other brother is with the Greater Manchester force.'

'Quite a dynasty,' Mundy observed dryly.

'You could say that.' Christopher Spate continued to smile a thin and – to Mundy's eyes – a very insincere smile. 'As you say, quite a dynasty.'

'How is your father?' Mundy asked. 'I remember him well.'

'He's still with us. He's pushing eighty now,' Spate replied.

'He would be.' Mundy sipped his tea. 'Heavens, none of us are getting any younger.'

'So I have noticed,' Spate replied with a hint of sarcasm. 'It makes you determined to use your life well and to the full, don't you think?'

Mundy did not reply.

'But yes,' Spate continued, 'the old man is still with us, though he's beginning to lose his mind. It's not unusual for men of his age to get confused.'

'I am sorry to hear that,' Mundy offered, 'but, as you say, men and women of his age tend to lose their faculties.'

'It happens,' Spate replied, 'but the old boy has had a good innings. He enjoyed his retirement. He had a very good pension. He and my mother bought a villa in Spain.'

'Nice,' Mundy growled. 'All that sun.'

'They went there for the winter,' Spate explained, 'to escape the English weather, you see.'

'Oh.' Mundy put his cup back into the saucer. 'So he didn't retire there?'

'Oh, good Lord no . . . no. He bought a house in Wimbledon and upon his retirement he splits his time between London and Spain.'

'Very nice,' Mundy replied. 'Very, very nice.'

'Yes. I grew up there – it is a rambling old Victorian house. He did retire with a senior rank, of course . . . received a lump sum and then went straight into an inflation-proof pension. He put his money into property. He said, "Buy land – they don't make it any more".' Spate paused and then added, 'I see you have done the same – that's quite a neat little house at Archway you have there. Quite neat and compact.'

Mundy scowled. 'You have been busy.'

'It wasn't difficult . . . one copper to another.' Spate grinned menacingly. 'It wasn't difficult at all.'

'So how can I help you?' Mundy spoke coldly.

'I am just a little curious,' Spate replied, still smiling insincerely.

'About?' Mundy asked quietly. 'What are you curious about?'

'About why you should want to access the file on Joshua Derbyshire all of a sudden?' Spate replied. 'A twenty-eight-year-old case . . .'

Maurice Mundy sat back in his chair. 'It's not all of a sudden. It's something that has been nagging away at me for a while.'

'Oh, and what might that be?' Spate pressed. 'I would be interested to know.'

'Probably nothing. I'm probably worrying about nothing at all.' Mundy sat forward and hung his head. 'I've done that before . . . worry about nothing.'

'You can try me,' Spate encouraged. 'Can't hurt, can it?'

'Why? Do you know the case?' Mundy asked, speaking slowly. He was by now feeling deeply curious and cautious.

'I know of it. It was the last major conviction my father won before he retired,' Spate explained.

'To Wimbledon,' Mundy added.

'And to Spain. With extended angling holidays in Ireland, he really made full use of his retirement.'

'Seems so,' Mundy growled. 'It certainly sounds as though he did.'

'Well, he had the money.' Spate smiled.

'Yes, his pension,' Mundy replied. 'You said.'

'So what worries you about the conviction of Joshua Derbyshire?' Spate pressed. 'It was a very safe conviction. It still is.'

'Yes. Going by the evidence it does read safe,' Mundy conceded. 'It reads to be as safe as houses.'

'So why the interest? What's nagging you?' Spate continued to press Mundy.

'I don't know. I can't put my finger on the reason,' Mundy

replied determinedly, 'but do you think your father would agree to see me?'

'I can ask, but remember his mind isn't what it used to be. He forgets words and has a poor short-term memory.'

'So he'll remember the Joshua Derbyshire case?' Mundy asked hopefully. 'If his long-term memory is still healthy.'

'Very clearly.' Spate reached into his jacket pocket for his mobile phone. 'He still mentions it from time to time. I'll see if he is at home.' Spate keyed in a number in his mobile phone and pressed the 'call' button. Mundy heard as Spate said, 'Hello, Father . . . Chris here . . . yes, I have found Mr Mundy. He says he's asking if he can call and see you about the Joshua Derbyshire case. OK, I'll ask him.' Spate took the mobile phone from his ear. 'How about this evening . . . early doors?'

'Ideal.' Mundy smiled. 'That's ideal.'

'It's a goer,' Spate spoke into the mobile phone. 'OK . . . yes.' He switched the phone off and looked at Mundy. 'Between six and seven . . . suit you?'

'Ideal,' Mundy repeated. 'Just ideal.'

'Good. I'll let you have the address,' Christopher Spate advised coldly. 'Have you got a notepad handy? It'll have to be early because he gets tired easily these days.'

'Understood.' Mundy smiled. 'I'll be there as soon after six as I can.'

'This is twice in as many days.' Stanley Kinross turned and limped towards Maurice Mundy, who stood at the reception desk in the Criminal Records department. 'Good to see you again, Maurice.' The two men shook hands warmly. 'So what can I do for you?'

'I've just had an interesting conversation,' Mundy replied. 'A very interesting little chat.'

'Oh?' Kinross raised his left eyebrow.

'Up in the canteen about half an hour ago,' Mundy explained. 'I waited for a while until the other geezer had gone before coming down here. I suddenly have the sense of being followed.'

'Oh?' Kinross repeated. 'That is interesting. It's also a bit worrying. How can I help, Maurice?'

'Tell me,' Mundy began, 'how would an officer in "the Yard" find out where another officer lives?'

'By phoning the personnel section,' Kinross explained. 'If the call came from within the building and was not an outside line, and if the person seeking the information had a friend in the personnel section, they could very easily, and if he was asking on the QT . . . Quite against the rules, of course, but very easily done.'

'Yes.' Mundy nodded thoughtfully. 'I had assumed that that would be the answer. So, Stanley, the next question is how would someone know that I had read a particular file?'

'If some other officer is recorded as being an interested officer,' Kinross explained. 'I entered your accessing that file the other day into the log, as I had to do – a computerized log . . .'

'I see,' Mundy replied. 'Again, I had assumed that that would be the case.'

'And the computer would automatically send a signal to any officer nominated as an "interested officer" in that case,' Kinross explained. 'These machines . . . I am not of the computer generation but apparently it follows the Yorkshire Ripper investigation in the eighties when they did the post-mortem on the investigation.'

'Which was a mess,' Mundy sighed.

'Indeed . . . one mistake after another.' Kinross also sighed. 'But when they did the post-mortem on the whole sorry affair they found out that quite a few officers were interested in Sutcliffe and were all reading the file they had on him but each officer was doing so unknown to the others.'

'Ah . . . I see where you are going.' Mundy nodded.

'Yes, so if they each knew about the other officers' interest they would have conferenced Sutcliffe and shared their suspicions. It might have led to an earlier arrest and the prevention of one or two murders,' Kinross explained. 'So now any "interested officer" is automatically notified if another officer accesses any file with a said "interested officer".'

'So how does a copper become an interested officer?' Mundy asked.

'Quite simply by requesting myself or any other person

working down here in Criminal Records to be entered on to any file as an interested officer. It's all quite simple and painless,' Kinross advised. 'It just takes a matter of seconds.'

'Upon his own initiative and without the approval of a senior officer?' Mundy drummed his fingertips on the surface of the desktop. 'It's that easy?'

'Upon his own initiative,' Kinross confirmed, 'and yes, without the approval of a senior officer. Like I said, it's all very simple and painless.'

'Interesting.' Maurice Mundy smiled. 'OK, thanks. Look, we really will have that beer sometime soon. But that's very interesting, Stan, thank you.'

'Look forward to it.' Kinross returned the smile. 'Take care, me old mate, and be careful to watch your back. No one else will.'

'I confess I was hugely disappointed in our counsel's performance. I was very saddened. I felt he had let us all down.' Thomas Greenall's office was lined with law books – none of which, by the absence of creasing down their spines, appeared to Maurice Mundy to have been read, but their shiny blue leather binding did, he felt obliged to concede, look impressive. Greenall's desk, Mundy noticed, was surprisingly clear of clutter. Greenall's office building was a thirties semi-detached house on Greencourt Road in Burnt Oak. His office was the room designated to be the front bedroom of the house and his secretary, Mundy had found, occupied the ground-floor front room immediately beneath Greenall's office. The front lawn of the home, like many on Greencourt Road, had been paved over and, in Thomas Greenall's case, it accommodated a black Audi with tinted windows which indicated to Mundy that, despite the absence of paperwork on Greenall's desk, he was nonetheless clearly making a handsome living. Greenall himself, who sat with his back to the bay window, was a tall but slightly built individual, dressed in a dark blue three-piece suit. He had a drawn face and very closely cut silver hair, and he spoke with Received Pronunciation. 'I thought – I still think,' he said, 'that he could have worked a lot harder for Joshua than he did . . . a lot harder. He could have worked harder to put doubt into the jury's mind. You know, it's cases like that which make me so envy the Scots with their third verdict of not proven, but as you know, in England and Wales and Ulster, juries can only return a verdict of guilty or not guilty.'

'Indeed.' Mundy nodded.

'But the Scots, lucky them,' Thomas Greenall continued, 'can return a verdict of not proven which means just that. It means that the accused might indeed have committed the crime in question but the Crown has simply failed to prove its case. And a counsel with more fire in his belly could easily have achieved a not proven verdict in Joshua's trial had the case been heard north of the border. Down here he could still have worked to a not guilty verdict by default by so weakening the Crown's case that the jury would have been made to feel that a guilty verdict was unsafe. There was no motive. The murder . . . the act of extreme violence was out of character. It was wholly out of character for Joshua to commit an act of violence. He had no motivation, and Joshua's unquestioning devotion to Miss Tweedale was hardly mentioned. Also, our man refused to put Joshua in the witness box, which always makes an accused look guilty.'

'Yes.' Mundy glanced at the sky behind Greenall and noticed it beginning to cloud over, with the clouds appearing to move northwards. Rain, he felt, would by then be falling steadily on central London. 'Perhaps that was a sensible thing to do, though,' Mundy pointed out. 'I have met Joshua. He would not have been able to stand up to aggressive questioning by a Crown barrister out for his blood.'

'Perhaps . . . but with a courtroom full of police officers all staring at the jury, no strong defence argument and I think a weak jury,' Greenall opened his right palm, 'a guilty verdict ought not to have been a surprise, and frankly it wasn't. The jury was intimidated, I think. It was then compounded by the fact that Joshua went in front of Mr Justice de Vere, who was also known as the "Hanging Judge". He is no longer with us and our counsel's refusal to address the jury at the conclusion of the trial also served to make Joshua look guilty.'

'Why engage such a poorly performing barrister in the first place?' Mundy asked. 'Who was he anyway . . . Levy, I think?'

'Yes, an old boy called Daniel Levy. The sad, burnt-out old case that he was, we simply couldn't find anyone else. It's as straightforward as that. I was with Pope and Steadman then and our clerk worked hard but no defence barrister worth anything wanted the case. The evidence weighed so much against Joshua that the barristers our clerk approached would only take the case if Joshua pleaded guilty, and so they could argue in mitigation of sentence, but Joshua insisted on going NG and, of course, we had to take his instruction. All we could get was bumbling old Daniel Levy, also no longer with us so, all in all . . . A high level of sympathy for the victim – such a violent crime, including the betrayal of the victim's trust in Joshua, taking him into her home – a courtroom full of uniformed police officers all staring at the jury, like I said . . .'

'I didn't know about that,' Mundy remarked. 'About the police, I mean.'

'Oh, yes.' Greenall nodded. 'The police fielded the full squad all right and, as I also said, probably a weak jury.' He paused for a moment. 'You know the old story about the graffiti on a wall in the cells beneath the Old Bailey which reads, "I have just been convicted by twelve people who are all too stupid to avoid jury service" is probably apocryphal.'

Mundy smiled. He had indeed heard the story. Many times.

'But it is quite true that the professional, well-educated people we really very badly need to make up our juries are the ones most adept at avoiding jury service. The ones we do get are the bored housewives and the chronically unemployed men who are only too pleased to do jury service to provide an escape from their dull routine.'

'That's probably quite cynical but also probably quite true.' Mundy observed rain beginning to fall. 'You appealed, I believe?'

'Yes, yes, we did. We appealed against the conviction but there were no new grounds to make the original verdict unsafe and so it stood, as did the life sentence with the thirty-year tariff.' Greenall shrugged. 'Like I said, and like I keep saying, de Vere was a hanging judge. The sentence brought gasps of surprise when it was announced. A minimum of thirty years for a seventeen-year-old, and a seventeen-year-old who was borderline diminished responsibility. We could have appealed against the sentence but if we had done that we would have had to change Josh's plea to one of guilty, and Joshua would have none of that. So . . . the conviction stood, as did the sentence. He'll be approaching the tariff now.'

'Two more years,' Mundy advised, 'then he will have done the thirty.'

'Thirty years.' Greenall shook his head slowly from side to side. 'I still can't help feeling that some terrible injustice has been done. I can't help feeling that I failed him somehow. But we have to take clients' instructions and work with what material we have been provided with. We can't do anything else . . . and you feel the same, you say?'

'About the lack of safety about the conviction,' Mundy replied quietly. 'Yes, yes, I do.'

'Despite being involved in the investigation?' Greenall smiled.

'Only on the periphery. I was a "penguin",' Mundy explained. 'I was right on the edge.'

'A "penguin"?' Greenall queried. 'What on earth is that?'

'It's a term of abuse within the police force.' Mundy glanced at the rain now falling heavily over suburban Burnt Oak. 'The plainclothes officers refer to uniformed officers as "penguins".'

'Ah . . .' Greenall nodded his head. 'I see. That's a new one on me.'

'"Woodentop" is also another term of abuse and also means the same thing,' Mundy continued. 'Though the uniformed officers don't have any term of abuse for the plainclothes officers because they all want to be one.'

'I see . . . interesting. I live and learn,' Greenall smiled. '"Woodentops" and "penguins" . . . indeed.'

'So what do you think happened?' Mundy asked. 'That is, just between you and me and the gatepost? What is your theory?'

'Pleased you said that.' Again, Greenall's expression became solemn. 'I won't be going on record about this. I must make that quite clear . . . perfectly clear.'

'Accepted,' Mundy replied. 'I have the same attitude. I am reluctant to go on record or make wild allegations.'

'Good, good . . . well, on that understanding . . .' Greenall glanced to his left out of the bay window, '. . . oh, rain. Anyway, on that understanding I think that the evidence against Joshua was planted.'

Mundy smiled. 'So do I. I think that very strongly.'

'It really is the only explanation,' Greenall continued, 'but thereafter it is open to speculation as to the motive for the planting of said evidence. For myself, I think the evidence was not so much planted to wilfully implicate an innocent man, nor to convict a local oddball or misfit for a high-profile murder to "solve" the crime . . . but, speaking for myself, and speaking for myself only, I see it as the police being genuinely convinced of Joshua's guilt that they were determined to use any means they could devise to ensure his conviction. That's how I saw it and that's how I still see it. In their own eyes they were furthering the ends of justice. That happens a lot and it is quite different from fitting up a man the police know to be innocent. That also does happen but less so.'

'Yes, I know,' Mundy replied. 'And yes, I know that also.'

'And that is an issue a barrister with a bit more lead in his pencil might have raised and exploited but sad old Daniel Levy, burnt out, never took silk, felt himself a failure . . . The wreck of a human being that he was, he just didn't have the energy.'

'So much more could have been said in Joshua's defence,' Mundy groaned.

'Yes . . . yes.' Greenall turned again to look at the rain. 'Better than drought.'

'What?' Mundy glanced at Greenall. 'Sorry, what's better than drought?'

'Rain,' Greenall explained. 'We might complain about it but it's better than drought. Rain is life-giving . . .'

'Oh, I see.' Mundy stroked his chin. 'Yes, as you say, better than drought and life-giving . . .'

'But I saw Joshua at his appeal,' Greenall continued, 'and he said that he was enjoying prison.'

'Enjoying it!' Mundy gasped. 'What did he mean?'

'Yes . . . granted he'd rather be out than inside doing bird, but he knew that he was innocent and he explained that that was carrying him through. He had occupied the moral high ground, you see. He had been attacked by the other prisoners but by the time his appeal was heard he had found his place and had developed his survival techniques. Anyway, his attitude made me even more convinced that a great injustice has been done. I think if I was in his shoes I would also enjoy prison.'

'Knowing that you had been wrongfully convicted, you mean?' Mundy clarified.

'Yes . . . yes, that's exactly what I mean. It is exactly what I mean.' Greenall shifted his position in his chair. 'If I had been rightfully convicted it would destroy me. I would feel that I had betrayed my family and my friends, and my enemies would gloat. Knowing myself, I would be suicidal with the guilt and the shame of it all. But if I knew I was innocent, wholly innocent and not just innocent because of a technicality . . .'

'Yes.' Mundy nodded his head vigorously. 'Yes, I understand . . . I think I would feel the same.'

'But were I wholly innocent, then I too would enjoy prison. I would also relish the smugness of knowing I occupied the moral high ground. So yes, I knew what Joshua meant.' Thomas Greenall glanced up at the ceiling of his office. 'I fully understood him and I think that is really quite impressive thinking for a boy who attended a special school.'

'Yes, he was probably ill-served there as well,' Mundy growled.

'Oh?' Greenall raised his eyebrows. 'What do you mean?'

'That's another story. Tell me, did the family live close to here?' Mundy asked.

'Yes. The Derbyshires lived in the council estate on the other side of Burnt Oak Broadway, on the delightful-sounding Silkstream Avenue, though it is much less delightful to walk down. And Miss Tweedale lived up the hill, as befits a moneyed lady with a Rolls-Royce. She lived on Penshurst Gardens, just beyond Edgware tube station. She owned a very nice property.'

'I have visited her neighbours,' Mundy explained. 'As you

say, a very nice property, but I really was curious as to the whereabouts of the Derbyshire house.'

'Silkstream Avenue,' Greenall repeated. 'Council property, as I said. It would take about half an hour to walk between the two houses, especially if you took the back road up Deans Lane and down Deans Way. So what are you going to do now, Mr Mundy? Where do you go from here?'

'I have an appointment with the officer who led the investigation . . . one Mr Spate.'

'Oh, yes, I remember him,' Greenall replied sourly. 'Do I remember him. It was in fact his attitude which convinced me that the police were determined to have Joshua convicted. Very zealous – overzealous, I thought. A man of closed-minded determination to ensure Joshua's conviction. You ought to be careful if you are interviewing him and the issue of planted evidence has been raised. Tread carefully, Mr Mundy. Tread very, very carefully.'

'I will,' Mundy breathed deeply, 'I will. I will be completely discreet, as you suggest. Fully discreet. In fact, I met his son this morning and he put me well on edge. His son is now a police officer with the Met, you see.'

Greenall paused. 'They could make things difficult for you,' he said quietly. 'Very difficult, if not dangerous.'

'I know. He took the opportunity to let me know that he knows where I live,' Mundy replied, equally softly. 'Like I said, I was well on edge.'

'Oh . . .' Greenall groaned. 'Do you think you need protection?'

'Not yet.' Mundy placed his hand up to his mouth. 'I have not played my hand yet, largely because I have no hand to play . . . yet.'

'If they have something to hide they won't wait for you to play your hand – they'll make a pre-emptive strike,' Greenall cautioned. 'You'll disappear, or your body will be found – something like that.'

'That hadn't occurred to me,' Mundy glanced to his left, 'and me a lifelong copper. That had just not occurred to me.'

'Well, if it's any use, I will remember this conversation,' Greenall offered, 'and if I read of your disappearance or death,

I will contact the anti-corruption people at Scotland Yard. What is the department called?'

'A10,' Mundy replied. 'It's called A10. Thank you. I would appreciate that.'

'A10,' Greenall repeated. 'I can remember that. And what you should also do is write your suspicions down and post them to me, here, at this office. If something does happen to you I'll post it on to A10. We can't be too careful.'

'As you say,' Mundy replied quietly. 'I suddenly feel that I am getting into deep water.'

'And it's full of crocodiles,' Greenall added. 'Just be careful and keep your cards close to your chest, Mr Mundy. Very close. It might be best if you act the bumbling idiot. That will encourage them to underestimate you . . . make things a little safer for you.'

'Yes. Yes . . . I'll do that.' Mundy looked out of the window behind Greenall at the rain which by then was falling steadily. 'The bumbling idiot, but not too far from the truth, idiot that I am,' he mumbled. 'Idiot, indeed.'

'Did Josh or his family ever mention a young woman called Chisholm?' Greenall asked quite suddenly. 'Geraldine Chisholm?'

'No.' Mundy shook his head slowly. 'I have never heard that name. Why? Who is she?'

Greenall reached into his desk drawer and extracted a small card index file. 'I still have her number here . . .' He began to sift through the cards.

'Who is she?' Mundy repeated.

'A journalist,' Greenall explained. 'Sorry, she's a reporter. A young, enthusiastic crusader. Well, she was back then. Nothing as grand as Fleet Street but she too wasn't at all happy with Joshua's conviction. She made enquiries and was hoping for an exposé which would launch her career as an investigative reporter but she must . . . Yes, here it is. Yes, she must have come up against a brick wall . . . or she might have met a dead end because nothing was written. Nothing was ever published anyway. Have you got a notepad there? This is her number. She might be worth a visit. It might be worth picking her brains. Just a thought . . . you know. Just a suggestion.'

The two men stood and shook hands. Strangely, Mundy thought, Greenall held on to his hand at the moment Mundy expected it to be relinquished. 'You know, Maurice – you don't mind if I call you Maurice?'

'Not at all,' Mundy replied with a note of curiosity in his voice. 'Not at all.'

'The Cold Case Review Team – I have come across that team before. Your days of mainstream police work are behind you . . . retirement beckons.' Greenall then released Mundy's hand.

'Yes.' Mundy became curious. 'Yes, it beckons.'

'Well, I ask because I have need of a private investigator. It won't be anything glamorous,' Greenall explained. 'You won't be in my employment – not officially but not illegally either. I'll pay cash in hand . . . a reasonable rate, plus expenses. Just checking the validity of evidence, that sort of thing. If the police say they have a witness who saw the assault take place at the bus stop when he was putting out his empty milk bottles on his front door step, then you would, for example, take a trip out there and verify that the bus stop and the witness's front door are intervisible. If the police say that my client perpetrated a crime at a certain time and place but independent witnesses or CCTV put my client at a different place about an hour earlier, for example, you would travel between the two locations and verify that the journey can be done within that time frame. It's not glamorous, as I say, and you'll be working for the defence rather than the Crown Prosecution Service. But you will be working in the interests of justice and you seem to me to be like the sort of man who values fair play.'

'Thank you.' Mundy held eye contact with Greenall. 'I will give your offer real consideration. Real consideration.'

'Please do, Maurice.' Greenall also held eye contact with Mundy. 'You have my phone number.'

'I feel uplifted, so uplifted,' Maurice Mundy commented as he and Janet Thackery walked away from the church and down towards Trafalgar Square. As they walked their shoulders occasionally brushed against each other's. 'Lunchtime recitals of

Baroque music . . . I am so pleased you suggested it. Search as I might, I couldn't find anything which seemed suitable . . . thank you.'

'It's not always Baroque,' Janet Thackery replied, 'but there is a recital there at that church each weekday.'

'I will remember that.' Mundy glanced up at the sky. It was still mostly grey but with occasional patches of blue making an appearance, and the rain had stopped. Life-giving as it may be in Thomas Greenall's view, Mundy couldn't help feeling thankful that the rain had stopped.

'Do you have time for lunch?' Janet Thackery looked at her watch. 'It'll be a late lunch but it would be nice to get off these greasy pavements.'

'Yes, let's do that.' Mundy also glanced at his watch. 'I have to be in Wimbledon for six p.m. but yes, I have time for lunch.'

In a small café behind St Martin-in-the-Fields, Janet Thackery asked over her quiche, 'So tell me, Maurice . . . if you can. I have no right to know but I am curious. In fact, I am burning up with curiosity . . . Can you tell me what it was that you and George quarrelled about?'

'Yes, I can tell you, and it's good of George that he didn't tell you . . . good man that he was, but we didn't quarrel at all. You have a right to know the story.' Maurice ate a mouthful of his spaghetti Bolognese before continuing. 'It was during the investigation into one Tracy Black.'

'Who is she?' Janet Thackery asked. 'Female villains are very rare.'

'Was . . . and it was he,' Mundy explained. 'She's a he.'

'What do you mean?' Janet Thackery put her fork down on her plate. 'Was he a transvestite?'

'No. He was all male, one hundred per cent testosterone. He was a real East London street turk. The story apparently was that his father, in some twisted version of child psychology, gave him a girl's name so the children at school would tease him and he would have to learn to stick up for himself. He'd have to learn how to handle himself in a skirmish and he did that all right – he became a gangster with a chip on his shoulder. Tracy could easily have called himself by a boy's name – you know, changed his name once he was an adult – but he didn't out of some odd sense of loyalty to his old man.'

'George never mentioned him,' Janet Thackery replied, 'but he never mentioned any of his work. He left it all at the Yard.'

'That was very caring of him.' Mundy toyed with his food. 'I have known marriages fail because police officers come home and dump on their wives, emotionally speaking, making their wives carry the stress of their job. That sort of number. Very unfair of them.'

'Yes, I have also heard of that.' Janet Thackery glanced out of the window of the café. 'But George never did that – never.'

'Good for him.' Mundy forked food into his mouth. 'But Tracy Black, he became a crime lord. He grew through the ranks of East London gangsterism and established his own empire.'

'I never heard the name,' Janet Thackery repeated.

'No one ever has – no one outside the police, that is,' Mundy explained. 'He was never convicted, ever . . . not of anything. He was the exception to the rule that you don't get accepted in gangland unless you've got some prison time under your belt. Tracy Black never even attracted so much as a parking ticket – he was Mr Clean. He was also Mr Downright Evil, but in terms of his record he was Mr Squeaky Clean.'

'Really?' Janet Thackery picked at her meal. 'So he was quite a big fish?'

'Oh, yes. One to hook and bring into the keep net.' Mundy glanced casually at two middle-aged women who came to sit at the adjacent table; they each carried bulging shopping bags and began to talk to each other in a foreign language. German, he thought, or possibly Dutch. He turned again to Janet Thackery. 'Tracy Black . . . well, he . . . he was into everything: hard drugs, people smuggling, extortion, money laundering, contract murder . . . you name it, his paw prints would be on it. He had his snout in every unlawful trough there was, and the more money there was to be made then his snout was in all the deeper.'

'I get the picture.' Janet Thackery also looked at the two

female overseas visitors. She then turned her attention back to Maurice Mundy.

'Yes,' Mundy continued, 'the police wanted him badly and we were building up a case against him for the murder of a low-life called "Micky the Grass" Hopper.'

'Grass Hopper.' Janet Thackery smiled. 'The names they call each other.'

'Yes.' Mundy returned the smile. 'Michael "Micky the Grass" Hopper got his nickname not only because of his surname but also and mainly because he was an informant. He was a grass. He'd grassed somebody up to save his own skin.'

'Oh,' Janet Thackery groaned, 'not a clever thing to do. Very public spirited, but if you are a member of the underworld that is seen as a form of treason, isn't it?'

'Yes. Yes, it is.' Mundy nodded gently. 'It's treasonable in terms of gangland values, and according to their code to grass on someone is a term of high treason. And once a grass always a grass. Over the years Micky Hopper grassed up quite a few people. Eventually Tracy Black realized he had a grass in his outfit, found out who it was and ordered him to be iced. He was iced, quite horribly. I won't go into details . . .'

'Thank you.' Janet Thackery grinned. 'Especially over lunch.'

'Yes. Anyway, the investigation was kept at a low key . . . a need-to-know basis only because information travels in both directions and it was believed that Tracy Black had a few police officers in his pocket.'

'Oh, really?' Janet Thackery looked alarmed. 'That is bad.'

'Yes. It continually seemed that he was always one step ahead of any investigation, as though a police officer was making a phone call from a public call box to an agreed number and tipping him off.' Mundy finished his meal and placed his fork centrally in the oval plate. 'Hence the importance of keeping the Hopper investigation very hush hush, and George and I were posted to it.'

'They must have thought highly of both of you.' Janet Thackery beamed at Mundy.

'It would be nice to think that that was the case,' Mundy

wiped his mouth with the napkin, 'but the truth was that we had served our time as "woodentops" and had recently joined the plainclothes boys, so were both thought unlikely to be corrupt. We were known not to be in anyone's pocket.'

'Oh . . . well, but at least you were in the CID,' Janet Thackery said warmly. 'It was promotion – a step up the ladder.'

'Yes.' Mundy nodded. 'Anyway, the investigation was proceeding well and we were closing down very nicely on Tracy Black. The case was building well and . . . and . . .' Mundy glanced out of the window of the café. 'Sorry, this is difficult, but . . .'

'In your own time,' Janet Thackery replied. 'And remember, you don't have to . . .'

'No, I do have to . . . I want you to know. Well . . . in a nutshell . . .' Mundy forced the words, '. . . in a nutshell I blew the whole investigation.'

'Oh, no.' Janet Thackery groaned. 'I am so sorry, Maurice.'

'Oh, yes, I'm afraid so. I brought Tracy Black in for questioning about the Micky Grass Hopper murder, and interestingly enough that was the one and only time Tracy Black had been inside a police station so I scored a certain point there, but, of course, it only served to tip him off that we were closing in on him. Alibis were arranged and potential witnesses disappeared . . .'

'So you feel that you have blood on your hands?' Janet Thackery offered in a sympathetic voice. 'Not comfortable for you.'

'Yes . . . and you know I think that that is the real issue.' Mundy looked at his empty plate. 'They might have been felons but they still had a right to life. For the police, for the top floor, though, the issue ruined the whole investigation. Anyway, Tracy Black lived out his life living in luxury in a huge villa in Spain, surrounded by ex-dancing girls who dutifully attended to his every need, and he died peacefully in his sleep when he was in his seventies.' Maurice Mundy paused. 'The top floor were baying for my blood and wanted me back in uniform helping old ladies across the road, but the Police Federation stepped in and helped me fight my corner. At the disciplinary hearing they argued that I had acted in an over-eager manner and that I was an inexperienced young officer who should have been more closely supervised, and by doing that the Police Federation managed to spread the responsibility. They managed to shift some of the blame on to the senior officers in the investigation. Anyway . . . the upshot was that I received an official reprimand which was to remain on my file for five years.'

'Ouch.' Janet Thackery grimaced. 'But you acted with all good intentions.'

'I know, I know, but to continue . . . I was taking the lift after the disciplinary hearing and a member of the disciplinary panel stepped into the lift with me. On the way down he explained to me that the decision of the hearing was really an invitation for me to resign. He told me that my cards had been well and truly marked and that if I wanted to do something with my life I should leave the police and become a probation officer or some such occupation. But if I stayed, I'd retire as a detective constable.'

'But you stayed in,' Janet Thackery observed.

'Yes, it was all I could do, all I ever wanted to do,' Mundy explained. 'I left home at sixteen to join the army as an escape from a bit of a difficult family life. After two years as a boy soldier I joined the Royal Army Catering Corps. Can you credit it . . . I learned how to cook but live on pizzas from the supermarket.'

'Oh, I'll cook you a meal.' Janet Thackery smiled broadly. 'My cooking probably won't impress an army chef but it sounds like you could use a bit of home cooking.'

'Yes, I'd like that.' Mundy raised his head and smiled across the table at her. 'And I'm hardly an army chef. I didn't even do the sergeants' mess cooking course. But I can boil potatoes in large quantities, so I'd like that, a bit of home cooking, yes. Thank you.'

'OK, we'll arrange a date for you to come and eat.' Janet Thackery smiled warmly.

'Thank you, but after two years in the Catering Corps I transferred to the Military Police. I didn't get into the Special Investigation Branch – I dare say that I wasn't good enough

– and spent my time arresting drunken squaddies, but I developed a taste for police work. I left the army with an exemplary service record and an honourable discharge and joined the Metropolitan Police. I met your late husband and my good friend at the police training college. But . . .' Mundy paused, '. . . because of my little error of judgement, I remained a bottom feeder and George steadily rose, so that's the story. George and I never quarrelled but I became *persona non grata* . . . a failure . . . and if you want to rise you must never associate with a failure. Because of that George could not afford to be seen sitting with me in the canteen. Keep your desktop neat and tidy and be very careful who you are seen with, if you want to rise . . . that's the rule. It's the golden rule.'

'I see. I'm sorry.' Janet Thackery looked away from Mundy. 'I feel awkward. George should not have rejected you like that. I am surprised to hear that of him. I feel a bit disappointed in him as well.'

'I was not offended. We still saw each other when we were off duty and I was made welcome in your home, but at work . . . at work . . .' Mundy spoke softly. 'At work he had a game to play and he played it well. He rose quite rapidly and I investigated the theft of lawnmowers from garden sheds.'

'So is that why you joined the CCRT?' Janet Thackery asked. 'To investigate higher levels of crime?'

'Partly,' Mundy replied, 'and partly because I can't survive on a detective constable's pension. I'm still paying off my mortgage, for one thing. A pensioner with a mortgage . . . how sad is that? How bad is that?'

'Oh, that's not funny.' Janet Thackery looked uncomfortable.

'Yes, that explains why I'm a little threadbare.' Mundy forced a smile. 'I get my clothes from the charity shops.'

'Well, I must get this meal,' Janet Thackery insisted. 'Let me get this.'

'I wouldn't hear of it,' Mundy protested.

'Yes, I want to. It was my idea to have something to eat anyway so it's only fair,' Janet Thackery reached for her handbag, 'and it's been a long time. I have not had male company for a meal for a few years until we met up the other day. And I did enjoy it. Thank you for telling me the story. I'll buy this meal.'

'All right,' Mundy smiled his thanks, 'but only if I can buy the next one.'

'The next meal out.' Janet Thackery continued to smile. 'Because, remember, the next meal is going to be at my house. I do a seafood casserole to die for. Suit you?'

'It sounds wonderful,' Mundy replied warmly. 'Just ideal.'

Maurice Mundy looked curiously at the house on Lambourne Avenue, SW19. He saw a low, white-painted wall, beyond which was a stand of thick, evergreen shrubs, perhaps ten feet high or so, he estimated. The entrance to the property was set halfway along the wall and was composed of two black-painted wrought-iron gates, which were hung on tall brick gateposts and which opened on to a wide gravelled-over area. The house itself seemed to Mundy to be of thirties vintage, and was, like all the houses on the cul-de-sac that was Lambourne Avenue, detached. Two bay windows stood on either side of a large, white-painted door set in an open porch, the roof of which was supported by pillars. The upper floor of the house also had bay windows above the windows on the ground floor and a large window of stained glass above the door. Maurice Mundy, in fading light, was looking at the home of Detective Chief Inspector Spate (retired).

Mundy opened the gate and crunched over the gravel towards the front door, causing two large-sounding dogs to begin barking at the sound of his footfall. He walked confidently up to the front door, took hold of the highly polished brass knocker and rapped it twice, causing the two dogs to bark more loudly, more excitedly. The door was opened by an elderly woman in a dark dress who glanced at him but did not speak. The two dogs continued to bark but remained unseen.

'I am Maurice Mundy,' Mundy announced, 'here to see Mr Spate. I think I am expected?'

'Yes.' The woman gave little away and Mundy instantly thought her to be cold-hearted. 'Please come in, Mr . . . er . . .?'

'Mundy.' Maurice Mundy smiled his reply, though he felt

the woman's apparent forgetting of his name was deliberate and intended to offend.

'Yes . . . Mundy. Well, please come in.' The woman moved aside.

'Thank you.' Mundy stepped over the threshold, sweeping off his hat and wiping the soles of his shoes on the mat as he did so.

'I'll let my husband know that you are here.' Mrs Spate closed the door behind Mundy. 'If you'd care to wait in here, please.' She opened the door to a living room to the right of the hallway just inside the house.

'Thank you,' Mundy repeated, and smelled air freshener and furniture polish and noted a very neatly kept hallway. The Spates clearly had domestic help, he reasoned.

Mundy stepped into the room and was similarly met with a heavy odour of air freshener and furniture polish. The room itself was, he observed, a sitting room with a three-piece suite, bookcases, a small television and a coffee table. His eye was immediately caught by a line of brass artillery shell casings of various sizes which stood on a shelf beside the bookcase. Upon the door being closed behind him, Mundy strode silently across the deep-pile carpet, picked up one of the smaller shell casings and examined it. On the base of the shell casing the initials KH were clearly visible, scratched deeply into the brass.

Maurice Mundy went cold.

Hearing the noise of movement in the entrance hall, Mundy carefully replaced the shell casing and walked silently back to the centre of the room. The door opened widely and Duncan Spate entered the room, accompanied by two black Labradors, both of which barked at Mundy until Spate said, 'Hush!' The dogs fell silent but fixed Mundy with a steadfast gaze.

'What can I do for you?' Duncan Spate was, Mundy noted, much drawn about the face. He had a liver-spotted complexion and his hands seemed to Mundy to be twisted with arthritis which, he reasoned, probably caused the man a lot of discomfort. He was but a shadow of the man Mundy recalled, and Mundy hoped the look of surprise which he felt upon seeing him did not show.

'It's about the conviction of Joshua Derbyshire,' Mundy explained.

'Who?' Spate demanded in a cracked voice.

'Joshua Derbyshire,' Mundy repeated.

'Joshua Derbyshire?' Spate lowered his head. 'Is he here?'

'No, he's not here,' Mundy replied in a soft voice. 'He's in prison.'

'Who did you say you were?' Spate demanded. 'Who are you?'

'Mundy, sir. You probably won't remember me but I was a constable at the time that you arrested Joshua Derbyshire for the murder of Miss Anne Tweedale.'

'Tweedale,' Spate repeated. 'Where is that? In Yorkshire? Up north somewhere?'

'It's the name of a murder victim, sir,' Mundy advised.

'Murder . . .' Spate responded to the word. 'Who's been murdered?'

The door opened and Mrs Spate entered the room. She had a stern look about her eyes and face. 'I'm sorry, mister . . . whatever your name is,' she said. 'I must ask you to leave this house. My husband is unwell. He gets confused and tired easily. He really doesn't know who you are. I doubt he can be of help . . . whatever it is you want.'

'Yes, I can see that, Mrs Spate.' Mundy nodded. 'I am very sorry to have bothered you.' He edged towards the door and left the house, anxious to reach the safety of the public highway. He hoped that his taking leave of the house did not seem to be as unduly urgent as he felt it to be.

SEVEN

'We've obtained a search warrant. We were able to convince the magistrates that we had reasonable grounds for suspicion and it turns out that he has been a very busy little squirrel has our Mr Cassey.' DCI David Cole glanced at Maurice Mundy and then at Tom Ingram. 'Quite a busy little squirrel indeed.'

'Oh?' Ingram raised his eyebrows. 'Really?'

'Yes, really. His garage and his loft were full of stolen items . . . a whole treasure trove of goodies taken during burglaries in this general area and also further afield. We are still drawing up the inventory, so I dare say we owe you one for that.' Cole smiled and nodded approvingly. 'I confess I was sceptical of the usefulness of the Cold Case Review Team but I am now forced to revise my opinion.'

'Pleased to be of service.' Mundy returned the smile. 'The pleasure was ours.'

'Anyway, when we questioned him about the murder of Janet Laws and the other young women he became a "no comment" merchant,' Cole advised. 'He knows how to defend himself.'

'Which always means they are guilty,' Ingram offered as he glanced out of Cole's office window at central Chelmsford and pondered that it was not a town he would be happy to live in. It was, he thought, all too new. It had little perceptible history that he could detect.

'Of course it does,' Cole replied coldly. 'We all know that . . . don't we all know that, but it does not help us any. We know they are guilty, and the "no comment" cowboys know that we know that they are guilty, but it doesn't get us any nearer to the charge bar, still less any nearer to a conviction. But in Cassey's case we can at least hold him on the receiving of stolen goods charge. He's not going anywhere and right now he's in Blundeston Prison, having been remanded.'

'I'm pleased about that, it's progress.' Mundy sat back in his chair and crossed his legs. 'But why ask us to come up to Chelmsford? Has he said anything about the murder of Oliver Walwyn?'

'No.' Cole also sat back in his chair. 'Not at least in so many words. What he has said is that he is prepared to talk to you two gentlemen but about what he did not say, and will not say.'

'That's interesting,' Ingram replied. Then added, humorously, 'We must have made a good impression on him.'

'It's the nearest thing that we have to a breakthrough.' Cole clasped his hands behind his head. He did not respond to Ingram's attempt at humour. 'I think it's clear that we are going to get "no comment" from now on and only "no comment". So if you two gentlemen could help us, please, we would be appreciative.'

'Delighted.' Tom Ingram grinned.

'Just point us in the direction of Blundeston. I confess I have never been there.' Maurice Mundy began to stand up.

'It's close to Lowestoft,' Cole advised, 'to the north of here, less than an hour's drive. It's only a Category C prison but it's secure enough to hold Mr Cassey. If you two gentlemen can please see what you see, find out what you find out.'

'Yes, it's a fairly new prison, as you can see,' the tall, silver-haired prison officer commented as he escorted Ingram and Mundy to the agent's room, 'and it's already earmarked for closure. I'll be redeployed, which worries me a bit because I quite like living in this part of the world. And I'll also be sorry to see it closed. We have had some interesting guests. Here we are – I'll let you two gentlemen use this room.' The prison officer unlocked the door with a rattle of a bunch of keys which were attached to his waist with a long silver chain. 'Make yourself at home. I'll have Mr Cassey brought down from the cells.'

Mundy and Ingram sat side by side at the metal desk in the agent's room. Mundy noted it to be a brightly-coloured room painted in cream and red with a floor of brown, hardwearing carpet. The ceiling was about twelve feet high, Mundy guessed, and thus prevented the room from having an oppressive feel. Natural light entered the room via a narrow window set at the top of the wall opposite the door, although the room was principally illuminated by a filament bulb concealed within a Perspex screen and fitted to the ceiling.

Outside, the officers heard a clanging of doors and a rattle of keys. The door of the agent's room opened and Kenneth Cassey entered. He was dressed in a heavy cotton shirt, white with blue stripes, a pair of denim jeans and inexpensive sports shoes. He sat, sullenly and unbidden, in the chair which stood against the table opposite Mundy and Ingram. 'Come to gloat?' he asked with a sneer as he sat down.

'Why on earth should we want to do that?' Mundy replied. 'It was you who told the Chelmsford police that you would only talk to Mr Ingram and myself.'

'We're only here because you indicated to Mr Cole that you would talk to us,' Ingram added. 'So we are here. There's no gloating going on.'

'I just thought that you might be pleased to see me like this since it was you two gentlemen who got me arrested.' Kenneth Cassey glanced around the room.

'Yes, perhaps . . .' Mundy sat forward, '. . . but you have been arrested for receiving stolen goods. We're interested in the other matter.'

'The little boy?' Cassey replied calmly. 'You're interested in him?' A silence descended on the small room.

'Yes.' Mundy spoke calmly. 'What can you tell us about him?'

'Everything.' Kenneth Cassey looked away from the officers. 'I can tell you everything.'

'Be careful what you admit to,' Mundy warned. 'We must caution you.'

'Yes, but I am not going to sign anything, and,' Cassey held out a hand and touched the wall, 'I don't see a tape recorder set in the wall with the spools spinning and the little red light glowing to let everyone know the thing is recording every word . . . I don't see that.'

'There are two of us,' Ingram added. 'We will be able to confirm anything you say.'

'There could be two hundred of you.' Cassey smiled knowingly. 'Without a signed confession or a double recording then anything I say in here stays in here. You know that and I know that. Tell me about the boy's parents,' he asked. 'Tell me about them.'

'Only his mother is still alive. They were elderly parents when they had him. He was their world. His father died shortly after he was murdered – he never recovered. His mother battles on alone,' Ingram explained. 'I confess it is strange that women are often referred to as the "weaker sex" but not only do they live longer than men, they demonstrate more emotional strength than men. Why do you ask anyway, Kenneth? Is your conscience beginning to eat away at you?'

'Frankly, yes.' Cassey looked down at the tabletop. 'Yes, it is. It's being in here, lying on my bunk. I have only just arrived and already found that you have a lot of time to think if you're in prison.'

'So it's gnawing away at you,' Ingram prompted. 'It does that. Guilt is like that. Once the guilt sets in it never lets go, and it gets worse. Each day the guilt is worse than it was the previous day.'

'It's going to get worse?' Cassey appealed to the officers.

'Yes,' Mundy replied, 'it's going to get a lot worse; an awful lot worse. Guilt and regret are both like that – they both get worse.'

'And then you die,' Ingram added.

'So the police are closing down on us,' Cassey moaned. 'What will we get?'

'Life,' Mundy told him, 'full life tariff . . . no parole. We are talking about, what . . . six murdered women – at least six murdered women, and young women in the main – and one murdered schoolboy. He was only twelve years old. What else do you think that you can expect?'

'But I like me beer . . . I like the outdoors, especially in the summer,' Cassey whimpered.

'So did your victims,' Mundy growled. 'One of whom will never grow old enough to taste beer.'

'You've only got one possibility of being granted parole,'

Ingram suggested, 'and I won't mislead you, it's a slim possibility at best. So slim that it's hardly even a possibility.'

'Full confession,' Cassey anticipated, 'and telling you who Oliver Hardy is?'

'Yes. The full monty,' Mundy advised. 'Do not hold anything back. Anything at all.'

'They don't let you be buried on sanctified ground,' Cassey said flatly.

'Who . . . murderers?' Mundy thought Cassey looked even smaller than when he had first met him in his little house in Frere Way in Norwich.

'No . . . no, they don't. An unmarked grave in the prison grounds. That's what murderers get.' Cassey drew a deep breath. 'I'll be a "nonce". Murdering the women is one thing but a twelve-year-old boy . . . I'll get sliced up in the showers. Look at me. I can't handle myself at all and there are some rough boys in here.'

'And it's only a Cat C,' Ingram reminded him. 'The rough boys in here are nothing compared to the rough boys in the Category-A prisons where you will be going. Nothing. Believe me.'

Cassey made a low wailing sound and folded his arms across his chest.

'Time to start working for yourself, Kenneth.' Mundy cleared his throat as the strong odour of the disinfectant in the agent's room reached him. 'It's the old story . . . you can work for yourself or you can work against yourself.'

'I don't know what to do for the best,' Cassey whined.

'Come clean,' Ingram retorted. 'It's always the best thing to do.'

'I lie awake at night in here,' Cassey whispered. 'I'm so glad I don't have any family – no one close enough to be shamed by all this anyway, just some very distant cousins with different surnames.' Cassey seemed to Ingram and Mundy to be talking more to himself than to them. 'No one to get hurt over all this.'

'So tell us about Oliver Hardy,' Mundy suggested. 'You know you want to.'

'Oh, a fine mess I'll be getting him into.' Cassey smiled at his own joke.

'Making less of a mess for yourself, though, Kenneth,' Ingram replied encouragingly.

After a pause, Cassey said, 'It was him who killed the boy.' A further silence descended on the room.

'So what happened?' Mundy asked softly after a few seconds had elapsed following Cassey's disclosure.

'Off the record, remember?' Cassey looked at both Mundy and Ingram. 'This is all off the record. I won't sign anything.'

'Understood,' Ingram replied. 'All off the record.'

'OK . . . you know that I feel better already. So we topped the brass . . . Oliver strangled her in the back of the car as I was driving. It was him that killed them all. So we did what we did, what we always did: grab a brass, top her in the car and then drive her out into the country and leave her to be found. I took the back roads out to Chelmsford and we found ourselves out in the country. It was dark, a really dark, rainy night. Not too late but dark . . . We found ourselves on a dark road with a smaller road leading off it like a farm track. Oliver was positioning the body against a gateway, then he said, "You've seen too much". I didn't know what he meant at first, then I saw him stride over to a little lad who was just standing there in the rain. Neither of us had seen him approach and Oliver had a spade in his hand. He just strode over to the boy, who didn't move – it was like he was rooted to the spot. If he'd have run away he'd be alive. We couldn't have caught him, but he didn't run . . . he was frozen . . . and Oliver Hardy brought the spade down on his head, then he brought it down on his head once again just to make sure, but I think the first blow probably killed him outright. So Oliver picked up the brass and put her back into the car, and picked up the boy and put him in the car on top of the brass, and we drove back the way we had come. We got to a village looking for a place to drop the boy so he wouldn't be found quickly. We drove round this huge green and Oliver Hardy sees a sign – No Fishing or Private Fishing or something like that.'

'Yes,' Mundy said, 'Private Fishing. The sign is still there. Probably been re-painted since you murdered the little boy but that's what it says. Still, carry on . . . you're doing well. You're helping yourself.'

'OK . . . anyway, Oliver sees it and tells me to stop and put the car's headlights on full beam to blind anyone coming from our front, and he pulls the boy's body out of the car and carries it into the dark. I hear a bit of a splash and then he returns and we drive off. Oliver said we had to dump the brass's body a long way off so the police wouldn't connect the two murders – which we did and they didn't. Until a couple of days ago.' Cassey paused. 'So that's what happened and that's why I asked to talk to you. You got there and you're easier to talk to, not like those younger Chelmsford coppers, shouting into both my ears at the same time. All that made me do was say "no comment" to all their stupid questions. I was only storing them for a few weeks.'

'What?' Ingram asked. 'Storing what?'

'The goodies taken by the burglars I know. They gave me a handy-sized wedge to let them store all that stuff for a month before they could move it to a more secure lock-up. If you'd called one week earlier . . . or three weeks later, the police wouldn't have found it all and I wouldn't have been in here lying awake all night, thinking. Lucky you, eh?'

'Lucky us,' Ingram replied. 'And you know you're on your way to making a statement on the record?'

'And we'll need Oliver Hardy's name,' Mundy added. 'If you want to help yourself you'll have to do what you said and get him into a fine mess, Stanley.'

'I know . . . I'll need to think about it.' Cassey stood and banged loudly on the door of the agent's room with the flat of his hand. 'Let me have a day or two to think about it.'

'Or a night or two,' Mundy replied. 'It seems to be the case that you do all your most useful thinking at night. But yes, we can do that, although we are obliged to notify Chelmsford police of what you have just told us.'

Cassey shrugged. 'Tell the world, because, like we all know, it's still meaningless without a signed confession.' A rattle of keys was heard and the door to the agent's room was silently opened. 'But do give my regards to the Chelmsford cops. You can tell them that you got their man . . . they didn't. You can tell them it took a couple of old, grey boys in the autumn of their lives to do in a few days what they couldn't do in ten years. You tell them that, from me. Bless their little cotton socks.'

'My . . . our grandmother, lovely, lovely lady that she was, had eight pregnancies, from which she had twenty-two grandchildren. And every last one of them turned out all right except me.'

Maurice Mundy smiled warmly at Horace Tweedale. In him, Mundy thought that he saw an honest man. He liked the look in Tweedale's eyes, he liked the softness of his voice and he liked the man's frankness.

'I am the black sheep of the Tweedale family.'

'Sorry to hear that,' Mundy replied. 'I am sorry that you feel that way.'

'Well, it helped you find me, didn't it?' Horace Tweedale shrugged. 'My criminal record?'

'Yes, it was useful. For theft, I noticed, but only one conviction and that was quite a few years ago.' Mundy read the room. He found it basic, lacking in comfort and luxury, the home of a single man on a low income. The heating was turned down, causing Mundy to shiver.

'I don't put the heating on until my breath condenses,' Horace Tweedale explained. 'I wrap up well indoors and if it gets too cold I climb into my bed . . . but yes, I have just the one conviction – sufficient to ruin my life. I found it difficult to get a job and I have been on the dole for so long now that I am unemployable. As you can see . . . my little rented flat is not much to show for my years. I'll be sixty-five soon and then I'll be a pensioner . . . I've never worked in my life. Not to speak of, anyway. The great disappointment of the once-proud Tweedale family . . .'

'You must be able to find some positives in your life,' Mundy suggested. 'It can't all be doom and gloom.'

'Oh, yes.' Tweedale nodded. Mundy saw a short, slightly built man dressed in a thick yellow pullover and brown corduroy trousers, both of which items he recognized as having 'charity shop' stamped on them. 'I have good health for my years. I get out for a walk most days; it's only very bad weather keeps me at home. Just around the area but it gets me out . . .

I did steal a few thousand pounds and that was a few thousand pounds a good few years ago. You could quadruple that to get today's equivalent value. It was enough to buy a new mid-range motor car . . . a new Volvo saloon or a new Audi . . . so it was a tidy sum, all right. Very tidy.'

'What happened?' Mundy asked. It was not the reason for his visit but he'd become curious.

'I dipped my hand in the till,' Tweedale explained matter-of-factly. 'Same old story.'

'It must have been quite a deep till,' Mundy observed.

'I was employed as a gofer by one of my other cousins,' Horace Tweedale explained. 'My cousin, Margaret. She married a man in the licensed retail trade and he was given the stewardship of a working man's club. She persuaded her husband to employ me as a gofer. You see, the Tweedale cousins, all twenty-two of us, were very close . . . more like brothers and sisters. Nothing and nobody could get between us. Tweedale brothers and sisters fall out but no Tweedale cousin ever quarrelled with any other Tweedale cousin.'

'I see. So you knew your cousin Anne very well?' Mundy clarified.

'Yes.' Horace Tweedale smiled. 'Yes, my cousin Anne was the top cousin, the one who had achieved the most in life with her acting. We were all very proud of her, although it was my cousin Sandra who became the kingpin. She keeps us all notified of any family news. Anyway . . . to cut a long story short, I had a gambling problem. I still have, in fact. Being a gambler is a bit like being an alcoholic . . . an alkie is either wet or dry but he's always an alkie.'

'Yes, so I believe,' Mundy replied.

'And a gambler is either active or inactive but he's still a gambler,' Horace Tweedale explained. 'A dry alcoholic can't take a single drink without starting to drink again and an inactive gambler can't walk into a betting shop without starting to gamble heavily again. It is just the way of it.'

'Again, so I believe.' Mundy glanced at the double-decker bus as it drove slowly past the building in which Horace Tweedale rented a flat.

'So, my sad tale,' Horace Tweedale continued, 'was that

each weekday morning I took the previous night's takings to the bank and paid it in.'

'You held a position of trust?' Mundy observed.

'Yes.' Horace Tweedale sighed. 'But I was family and I wasn't going to steal from family, or my cousin's husband, Roy. He and I hit it off together . . . I really got to like Roy.'

'I see,' Mundy replied.

'Anyway, I'd been doing that for a few years,' Horace Tweedale took a deep breath before he continued, 'and the walk took me past a betting shop.'

'Oh, no . . .' Mundy put his hand to his head. 'I think I can see where this is going.'

'Yes.' Horace Tweedale glanced out of the window. 'Anyway, on that fateful day two or three things happened. The first is that it was, by coincidence, just sheer coincidence, my birthday and I was well out of sorts. I was really down in the dumps because I felt I had not done anything with my life. I had no trade or skill to offer on the job market. I had won and then lost a lot of money through gambling. I hadn't had a serious long-term girlfriend in my life. The same depressed attitude that can lead a man to drink can also lead a man to gamble.'

'Yes,' Mundy offered by way of condolence, 'I can understand that.'

'So, anyway . . . the next thing was that that morning was the first working day after a four-day weekend, so I had four nights' bar takings to pay in instead of the usual one night, or three nights in the case of Monday mornings, and the final nail in the coffin was that there was a delay in making up the bag that day.' Again Horace Tweedale paused to take a deep breath. 'So when I walked past the betting shop, which was normally closed when I passed it, the wretched thing had opened for the day's business.'

'The temptation was too great,' Mundy anticipated.

'Yes. If it had been open and I was feeling better about myself I probably wouldn't have gone in to it . . . but in I went.' Horace Tweedale hung his head. 'And all the gamblers' logic just clicked in, all that self-delusion . . . I'm only borrowing it . . . I'll make a profit and pay back what I borrowed so no one will notice . . . And you know, the rich thing was that I did that – just that. I turned a profit, not much, sufficient for a night in the pub . . . but I got greedy.'

'Fatal.' Mundy nodded.

'You don't have to tell me . . . almost quite literally fatal.' Horace Tweedale spoke in a low voice. 'I was suicidal at the end of it, but . . . I was greedy. I wanted more and I bet and began to lose. But I had tasted a win so I started chasing it . . . and the upshot was that by the end of the day I had only some loose coins left so I jumped on a bus, went north to the river and put them into slot machines in a Soho amusement arcade. I had just ten pence left in my pocket when I went into Tottenham Court Road Police Station to give myself up.'

'Have you gambled since?' Mundy thought it a very sad tale.

'No. I was sentenced to six months in prison, ordered to attend Gamblers' Anonymous and to pay the money back,' Tweedale explained.

'Have you,' Mundy asked, 'paid the money back?'

'Oh, yes . . . like how?' Tweedale appealed to Mundy. 'The words blood and stone spring to mind. No, the money was never recovered. Roy lost the stewardship of the working men's club and the whole business . . . well, it put a terrible strain on their marriage. But they pulled through and Roy obtained another stewardship.'

'Fortunate,' Mundy commented. 'He was lucky.'

'Yes.' Tweedale nodded. 'But he could argue he hadn't done anything criminal, that the practice of allowing me to carry the money to the bank had worked well for years and he'd learned a valuable lesson – that being if you want something done properly, do it yourself.'

'Yes.' Mundy sat back in his chair. 'It's often good advice.'

'And the post he was offered was difficult to fill – a rough club in a rough area – but of all the cousins it was Anne that was the most supportive.' Horace Tweedale smiled briefly. 'Good old Anne . . . and it is, of course, Anne who you want to talk about.'

'Yes, but it is interesting to hear how supportive she was to you.' Mundy once again glanced round Horace Tweedale's cell-like room in Plumstead.

'That was Anne all over.' Horace Tweedale sighed again. 'She kept telling me that I mustn't blame myself. She even offered to let me have the money to give to Margaret and Roy but I felt I couldn't accept it.'

'Noble of you,' Mundy commented.

'Possibly.' Horace Tweedale shrugged. 'But I felt I had to rescue something. We were middle church as an extended family . . . lower middle class . . . upper working class, spread about Catford and Forest Hill. The girls left school to work in banks, the boys took apprenticeships, all very self-respecting . . . and our Anne rose up above that and became a film star, in a small way, but she worked in Hollywood for a while. I was quite close to her despite a twenty-year age gap. I met the boy who murdered her on a few occasions . . . He doted on her. I couldn't believe it when he was convicted of her murder. I just could not believe it. He just wanted to please her, so it seemed to me. I thought he was very child-like in many respects.'

'Yes.' Mundy shifted his position in the chair in which he sat. 'I understand there was a rift between Anne Tweedale and her sister?'

'Anne and Phyllis . . . like I said, no two cousins ever fell out but brothers and sisters did. Anne and Phyllis quarrelled, all over Phyllis's choice of husband,' Horace Tweedale explained. 'Their father, my uncle Edward, disapproved of the match so much that he said he'd disinherit Phyllis if she married him, and she had an awful lot to lose by being disinherited. Uncle Edward was a successful businessman who saw the value of property and he built up quite a portfolio of houses, about ten or twelve, which he rented out to young, professional people. It wasn't like this shot-through-with-damp pile I have to live in which the owners rent to the chronically unemployed, but they were, in fact, good, solid houses, let to the sort of people who respected the property – mainly young, profes-sionally employed females because he believed that they would be more house-proud, and he had retained a gardener to look after the gardens.'

'Nice,' Mundy commented. 'It sounds a very safe place for his money.'

'It was. It was a nice little earner for him. The rents provided a steady income and of course he owned the houses . . . so yes, it was a nice little empire he had built up. But . . . the threat to disinherit her didn't stop my cousin Phyllis from marrying the man of her choice,' Tweedale opened his left palm, 'and my uncle Edward followed through with his threat and rewrote his will, leaving everything to Anne. He was a widower by then, you see.'

'Ah.' Mundy nodded. 'I was going to ask.'

'So the rift followed upon Uncle Edward's death. Phyllis and her husband were struggling on his salary and Phyllis asked if she – Anne – would give her and her husband a proportion of their father's estate. Anne wouldn't consider it. She explained it wasn't that she was being heartless and selfish and that she wanted it all for herself and all the rest of it, but the issue was that she had to honour her father's wishes out of respect to his memory. So Phyllis got nothing. I mean that she still got nothing while Anne kept everything. And then Anne made herself even wealthier from her acting career.' Tweedale paused. 'But that didn't spoil her. She never forgot her Forest Hill roots and she always had time for her family – it was just that she and Phyllis became estranged.'

'I see. Did you ever meet Phyllis's husband?' Mundy asked.

'Oh yes, a couple of times. I attended the wedding, in fact . . . it was a proper church do. Her father paid for it and gave her away in the traditional manner, but he still disinherited her.' Tweedale once again glanced out of the window of his small flat. 'But I did see what her father didn't like in him. Her husband had cold, hard green eyes. He was a policeman and . . . I don't know if this makes sense but I felt that if he wasn't a police officer he'd be a felon. He had that look of evil about him.'

'Oh,' Mundy raised his head, 'yes, I know what you mean . . . I know exactly what you mean. Do you recall his name?'

'Spate,' Horace Tweedale replied. 'She married a geezer called Spate.'

Mundy paused, then said, 'I knew you were going to say that. I was very afraid that you were going to say that, but at the same time I knew that you were going to.'

'Duncan Spate,' Horace Tweedale continued. 'Spate . . . like a river in flood . . . same spelling. Why? Is that significant?'

'Probably.' Mundy decided to be circumspect. 'It probably is significant but only probably. I don't want to rush any fences. I understand that Anne Tweedale had quite a collection of brass artillery shell casings from the Great War?'

'Yes, she had quite a few . . . thirty or forty of them. They had been brought back from France by a relative of our grandmother. You know, you hear stories of such bad luck from that war . . . of soldiers being killed after being at the Front for just a few hours, and the statistic that the life expectancy of a junior officer in the infantry once he had arrived in France was just ten days. But my grandmother's relative went through all the four years of it without so much as a scratch. He collected the shell casings and brought them home each time he had a period of leave. As I said, I think there were about thirty-plus all told,' Tweedale informed. 'All kept well-polished.'

'He was "KH",' Mundy asked, 'being the initials scratched on the shell casings?'

'Yes, Keith Hammond, Hammond being my grandmother's maiden name, but what relative he was to her I don't know. She inherited them and my uncle Edward inherited them from her, and when he died they became Anne Tweedale's possessions, as did the rest of Uncle Edward's estate.'

'And Anne's house was cleared and then it was sold,' Mundy continued. 'Do you know what happened to her wealth?'

'Nope.' Horace Tweedale shrugged. 'No one knew where it all went . . . her house, her savings, her possessions . . . None of the Tweedale clan saw any of it – not to my knowledge, anyway.'

'Are you in contact with your cousin, Phyllis?' Mundy asked.

'I can contact her if I need to. My cousin Sandra will be able to tell me where she lives, but Phyllis, she seems to have drifted apart. And now with respect of all the cousins it's a case of "no news is good news". If we don't hear that any of us are seriously ill or have died then it means that they're still alive and kicking somewhere . . . Cousin Sandra will know where.' Horace Tweedale forced a smile. 'That's what it has come to. The Tweedales are fading – we are such a shadow of our former selves. We are but a pale shadow of our former selves.'

'It is often the way of things, sadly.' Mundy stood up. 'Great families fade. But thank you for your information. It's been useful, very useful indeed.'

Horace Tweedale also stood up. 'Look, I don't like saying this, I don't like asking . . . but I really have run out of grub, not even a can of beans left, and I don't get my dole for a day or two.'

'Of course.' Mundy took his wallet from his pocket and gave Tweedale a twenty-pound note.

'Thanks, squire. It'll all go on food, I promise.' Tweedale smiled as he took hold of the money. 'Like I said, I didn't like to ask but you seem a good-hearted young geezer.'

'Long time since anyone has called me "young".' Mundy smiled as he replaced his wallet. 'A long, long time.'

'You're younger than me.' Tweedale held warm eye contact with Maurice Mundy. 'But thanks again. I'll spend it on food, not squander it down the bookies. You have my word.'

'It's an old family firm,' Norris Miller of Millers Removals and Storage consulted the file. 'I am fourth generation. My father and grandfather were very good – they didn't bully me into joining the family firm upon leaving school. I got a bit of further education and then travelled to Australia and New Zealand where we have relatives. In fact, they said to go and get a bit of life experience, sleep under strange stars, chew some dirt and come and join us when you're ready to join us . . . only when you are ready. They wanted me to come with enthusiasm, not resentment.'

'That sounds to have been very sensible advice.' Maurice Mundy sat with his legs crossed in front of Miller's desk in a small office overlooking a parking bay in which five large vans, of cream livery with red lettering, were parked in a neat row. Mundy noticed that two of the lorries had larger-than-normal cabs so as to provide sleeping accommodation above the driving position. The interior of Norris Miller's office was decorated with photographs of Millers Removal Vans of earlier years.

'It was very sensible. It meant I came here when I wanted to. If I was bullied into joining upon leaving school I would have grown to resent it and they clearly knew that. In the event, I was twenty-six when I came to work here. I stayed because I wanted to stay and I grew to love the work. The crew like it . . . it's mainly manly physical work and it's clean – we just handle people's household possessions – and it's safe work. There is a certain skill involved which I had not appreciated until I started here. It's just awesome watching two geezers remove furniture, negotiate tight corners without touching the walls, lifting heavy items without any apparent effort. I am well used to it now but when I started it was breathtaking to watch.' Norris Miller beamed. 'Really breathtaking.'

'I can imagine.' Mundy forced a smile.

'Anne Tweedale . . . that job was before my time – just before my time, though. North-west London is a bit moneyed and we get to do removals for a few celebrities. Anne Tweedale, the actress, was one of them. I remember my father remarking a year or two later what a sad old business that had been for them, clearing the house of a murder victim . . . of someone who should still be alive. All the crew were upset by it.' Norris Miller continued to leaf through the file. 'It's an unpleasant job to clear a house when someone has died. Natural causes is one thing but when someone's life has been taken . . . then clearing a house when the owner should still be alive . . . that's a hard old number to play.' Norris Miller was a large, broad-chested individual who seemed to Mundy to be very muscular under his plum suit, red remembrance poppy and yellow cravat. He seemed like a man who could lift a settee on to his shoulders as easily as another man would lift a rucksack. Physically speaking, he seemed to Mundy to be well suited to the removal business in addition to being the manager. 'Ah . . .' he tapped the file, '. . . here we are. Miss A. Tweedale's possessions removed and stored. She died intestate. Quite strange, really, a woman with her wealth and possessions, you would . . . well, I would have thought that she would have left a will. The only "intestates" we deal with are those who have next to nothing to leave anyway. We get them from time to time.'

'I imagine you do.' Mundy sat forward and rested his fedora on his knees. 'What did you do with Miss Tweedale's possessions?'

'Put them in our storage facility out in Hertfordshire, near Borehamwood. It sounds grand but it's really just a lot of second-hand containers in a field.' Miller grinned.

'Second-hand?' Mundy echoed in an amused tone of voice.

'Yes, we have no need to buy new containers. No need at all. After travelling round the world on ships . . . and being loaded and unloaded, sometimes not very carefully, then, after a few years, they get a bit bent and scratched and worn . . . but so long as they are watertight and can be secured they are still of interest to us to use as fixed site storage facilities. So we took Miss Tweedale's possessions from her house and stored them in container forty-three, it says here, that is fourth row, third container . . . and we kept them until she was declared intestate, upon which her next of kin, given here as being one Mrs Phyllis Spate, arrived with legal notification that she was the rightful owner of Miss Tweedale's possessions. The Court of Probate, Divorce and Admiralty which sits in an antechamber of the Houses of Parliament approved her claim to be Miss Tweedale's next of kin.' Norris Miller picked up the file, rotated it through 180 degrees and handed it to Mundy. 'I dare say I can let you have a photocopy of that document, if you wish.'

'No, thank you.' Mundy read the notification. 'That won't be necessary – not at this juncture, anyway. We may need a copy at a later date, though. So long as I can say that I have seen it, that will suffice for now.' Mundy re-rotated the file and handed it back to Miller with a smile of thanks.

'Why the police interest after all this time?' Miller asked.

'It's just a loose end I was asked to tie up,' Mundy replied. 'It's of little importance, which is why I am calling on you alone. Usually, you see, we work in pairs.'

'Yes . . . I didn't want to ask or comment but I thought a

lone officer was unusual.' Miller took the file and closed it. 'But you showed me your ID so I assume it's all right.'

'Oh, it's quite all right. And the issue of Miss Tweedale's possessions and their disposal is not important in itself. All I can say is that it impinges distantly upon another investigation.'

'Well, if Millers Removals of Burnt Oak can be of assistance then I am pleased you asked.' Norris Miller glanced at his watch. 'Which brings us neatly up to knocking-off time. I don't suppose you work nine to five?'

'No, we don't. Crime doesn't stop and neither do the police.' Mundy stood and extended his hand to Miller. 'But I work in the Cold Case Review Team now . . . it keeps my hand in until I retire on a full-time basis, so in my case, the job is less time-consuming.'

'Good.' Miller took Mundy's hand in a warm grip. 'I am looking forward to my retirement; my sons will take over from me but I'll do what my father did . . . kick them out of the UK and tell them not to come back until they want to stand in my shoes. I see the rain has begun again.' Miller glanced out of the loading bay towards the street. 'Got far to go?'

'Archway.' Mundy put on his hat.

'Across London in the rush hour.' Miller looked despairingly at Mundy. 'Rather you than me. Which way will you go?'

'A410 to Friern Barnet and down the A1,' Mundy replied. 'It ought not to be too bad. Once I pick up the A1 all the traffic will be going in the opposite direction. I should be all right.'

'Then in for the night like me?' Miller smiled. 'Home is the only place to be on a wet November evening.'

'No.' Mundy grinned. 'I've got a date with a lady. You still get them, even at my age. But thank you for your assistance. It is appreciated. Deeply so.'

Mundy sat on the settee and glanced up at the ceiling. 'Oh . . . that,' he said, 'was a most wonderful meal. Thank you so very much. I have not had home cooking in . . . well, it seems like a geological age.'

'I'm so pleased you enjoyed it.' Janet Thackery also looked

contented. 'I enjoyed cooking it. It's been long enough since I cooked a man a meal which he appreciated. We must do it again.'

'We must.' Mundy held eye contact with Janet Thackery. 'Yes, we must.' He looked around the room. 'You have redecorated,' he observed.

'This is five or six years old,' Janet Thackery explained. 'It was the last major job that George did in the house. I will, of course, keep it just as it is.'

'Of course.' Mundy yawned involuntarily. 'Sorry,' he said. 'The meal is making me sleepy.'

'So,' Janet Thackery looked warmly and approvingly at Maurice Mundy, 'will you be going up to Chelmsford again . . . on your cold case?'

'Yes, I will, as well as pursuing the other matter,' Mundy replied.

'Be careful there, Maurice.' Janet Thackery's jaw set firm. 'I really want you to be careful there. I freely confess that I don't like the sound of what you're doing. I don't like the sound of it at all. You could be treading on a lot of wrong toes, even if the cause is just.'

'I'll be careful, don't worry.' Mundy nodded thoughtfully. 'Mind you, I can't see what harm they can do to me?'

'Still . . .' Janet Thackery replied with a stern note in her voice. 'George always said, "You can never be too careful". So for me and for him, please take that advice.'

'I will . . . I will.' Mundy paused. 'I also want to do what I can for my daughter, so I have quite a full timetable. Plenty to keep me occupied.'

'Your daughter!' Janet Thackery's mouth fell open. 'Maurice, you are a dark horse. I never knew that you had any children, but all along you have a daughter. I never knew that about you.'

'I didn't know I had one either.' Mundy raised his eyebrows and inclined his head towards Janet Thackery. 'Well, that is to say I knew I had fathered a child but her mother left me shortly after her birth, taking the child with her. She wanted nothing to do with me . . . no financial support . . . nothing. She was an Afro-Caribbean woman, she was very headstrong and the relationship was brief. It was an indiscretion . . . and Roberta was the outcome.'

'Roberta . . .' Janet Thackery repeated the name. 'I like that name, I like it a lot.'

'I don't.' Mundy forced a smile. 'I wouldn't have agreed to it . . . in my opinion it belongs to those names like Freda, Wilma, Davida, Georgina, Edwina . . . couples who were wanting a boy and had decided what to call him before he was born. In the event they are blessed with a daughter so they give her a feminized version of the name they had chosen for their son. The tradition is very strong in the Hebrides, I believe. If I had had my say in it she would have been given a proper girl's name . . . such as Alison. I have always wanted a daughter called Alison, but . . . mother and daughter vanished from my life. They left me wondering over the years what had become of them . . . and just last year my long-lost and only child made contact with me. She's twenty-six years old.'

'Oh . . . married . . . a career?' Janet Thackery sat forwards with keen interest.

'No . . . no . . . she's not married.' Mundy sighed. 'She's single.'

'Plenty of time. Twenty-six is still young. Does she work?'

'Yes . . . she works.' Mundy drew a deep breath and then added, 'She's twenty-six years old, of mixed race, a heroin addict who works the streets. She sells her body to raise money to buy little packets of white powder.'

'Oh, Maurice.' Janet Thackery sighed deeply and sat back in her chair. 'I am so sorry. You must be so worried about her.'

'I am, being a police officer.' Mundy replied also with a sigh of resignation. 'I know the danger she's in. One working girl a week is murdered in the UK . . . on average. I've seen the bodies, shortly after they're found, sometimes recently deceased, sometimes in an advanced state of decomposition. I've broken bad news to relatives and taken relatives to view their daughter behind a glass screen when possible. The CCRT case up in Chelmsford impinges on a series of murders of street girls. It brings it all home . . . quite forcibly.'

'It would do, it would,' Janet Thackery repeated, 'but you can't blame yourself.'

'I don't . . . I wasn't there.' Mundy smiled briefly. 'I don't blame myself at all.'

'What happened?' Janet Thackery sat forwards.

'It's a horror story,' Mundy protested. 'It will ruin a good supper. I did love that seafood casserole.'

'Tell me. I am interested,' Janet Thackery encouraged Mundy. 'It won't ruin the meal.'

'Well,' Mundy also sat forwards, 'Roberta told me that her mother and her went to live in Southampton and when she was five her mother took up with a West Indian gentleman and they . . . that is, Roberta's mother and her boyfriend, went to live in Jamaica, leaving Roberta in their house. Just turned the key and left her alone . . . five years old.'

Janet Thackery gasped. 'That is just too bad.'

'I don't know the full story, just Roberta's version,' Mundy continued, 'but she says she was alone in the house for about three days before the police broke in and rescued her.'

'That must have been traumatizing for her.' Janet Thackery spoke quietly. 'That sort of thing will leave dreadful emotional scarring. It will lead to self-medicating through alcohol or narcotics.'

'Yes. Two things apparently saved her,' Mundy explained. 'A leaking tap in the bathroom and a letterbox which was low down in the door.'

'Yes, I know the type.' Janet Thackery smiled.

'And,' Mundy continued, 'the fact that the letterbox was free hinging; it hadn't got a spring attached to it. That helped a lot.'

'I see.' Janet Thackery nodded. 'I know the type,' she repeated.

'It is Roberta's story that the leaking tap was her source of water so she didn't get dehydrated and eventually died of thirst . . . and she was able to push small objects out of the letterbox. A sharp-witted neighbour saw the pile of small items on the step underneath the letterbox, realized their significance and notified the police . . . and Roberta's life was saved.'

'Were her mother and her mother's boyfriend traced?' Janet Thackery asked angrily.

'No, not to my knowledge,' Mundy replied. 'They were not.

They just disappeared into a new life in the Caribbean. So
Roberta was placed in care and spent the next eight or nine
years in an institution. She was mixed race . . . it is a bar to
fostering. She didn't fare well on the "P" test.'

'The what?' Janet Thackery gasped. 'What on earth is that?'

'Social workers have a P test applied to children whom they
want to see fostered or adopted . . . "pink, perfect and a pair",'
Mundy explained. 'Any of those will be an aid to placing the
child. Roberta was perfect but, being of mixed race, she was
of little interest to either white or black couples . . . and not
having a sibling meant she was an even less attractive fostering
prospect. She read her file when she was sixteen and found
she had been put in the "hard to place" list.'

'That must have done wonders for her self-esteem.' Janet
Thackery once again sat back in her chair. 'No wonder she
took to sticking hypodermic syringes in herself. I mean, no
wonder.'

'It gets worse.' Mundy spoke matter-of-factly.

'Worse!' Janet Thackery caught her breath.

'Yes . . . it transpires that when she was about thirteen or
so a couple expressed an interest in fostering her to the delight
of social services and the introductory visits went well . . . so
she was "placed" with them. No other children in the house,
just Roberta and the foster parents.' Mundy clasped his hands
together. 'Pretty soon the reason why they wanted a girl to
foster became clear.'

'Oh, no, they weren't paedophiles . . . is that what you're
going to tell me?' Janet Thackery put her hand up to her
mouth. 'I have read that those people apply to become foster
parents, but thirteen years old is a bit old, I would have thought.'

'No, it wasn't as bad as that,' Mundy sighed with relief,
'but bad enough. It was the case that she was wanted as a
domestic servant. When she came home from school she was
set to do the housework.'

'Oh, no.' Janet Thackery thumped the chair arm with her
fist. 'Didn't those wretched social workers monitor the
placement?'

'Seems not.' Mundy sighed. 'They should have done but
they seemed so pleased to have been able to place a child who

was on their "hard to place" list that they congratulated themselves, walked away and forgot about her. So it appears.'

'She could sue them,' Janet Thackery protested.

'Possibly, but it would be difficult to prove,' Mundy replied. 'Anyway, her schooling suffered because she was not allowed to address her homework until she had done all her housework, and that could be as late as nine p.m. So she was often in trouble for poor quality or non-production of homework . . . but she told me that she impressed her teachers sufficiently that they implored her foster parents to let her stay on at school to obtain qualifications, but her foster parents were adamant that she leave school at the earliest opportunity and take up employment so as to contribute to the family income . . . which is what she did.'

'So no qualifications despite having the ability?' Janet Thackery clarified. 'How deeply unfair . . . how horribly unfair.'

'Yes, that about sums it up.' Mundy put his fingertips to his forehead. 'Anyway, in the event, she didn't get a job, the housework fell on her shoulders in its entirety and her so-called "foster parents" took her dole money off her . . . also in its entirety.'

'Evil!' Janet Thackery hissed. 'That is just plain evil.'

'Yes, isn't it, evil, as you say . . . so she lived like that until she was eighteen, when a friend suggested she make a living by working King's Cross. So she did and has thus been self-employed from that day to this. I go and meet her, buy her a meal, even sometimes just a cup of tea, and I give her what money I can afford. At some point along the way some false friend offered her acceptance and emotional warmth and a wrap of white powder . . . and that is my daughter.'

'How did you find her, Maurice?' Janet Thackery leaned forward.

'I didn't . . . she found me. She knew my name from her birth certificate. Her mother once told her I was a policeman, though as I remember her mother to be, she probably described me as "the Filth". She developed an anti-police attitude in the short time we were together, which is probably why she walked out on me.' Mundy paused. 'So Roberta wrote to me. She addressed the envelope to "Police Constable Maurice Mundy, the London Police". Her letter was brief and to the point. "I am your daughter, Roberta. This is my address . . . can we meet?" The letter was opened, as all letters are, and it was passed to our personnel section who found where I was stationed and sent it to me with a compliment slip. So we met up, me and my daughter, and we still meet. I have done what I can to persuade her to move in with me, even as a halfway step to freeing herself from heroin and the street, but she is trapped in a "this is my identity" loop and can't seem to move on.'

'So who were those awful foster parents?' Janet Thackery demanded.

'Roberta won't tell me, which is probably just as well.' Mundy's jaw set firm.

'Why? Because you'll visit them carrying a pickaxe handle?' Janet Thackery spoke coldly.

'That sort of thing.' Mundy nodded slowly. 'Although I was thinking more along the lines of a sawn-off shotgun. But she has been to my drum, and now and then she lets herself in using a set of keys I let her have and leaves a cooked meal in the oven for me to come home to.'

'Nice.' Janet Thackery smiled warmly. 'That is nice of her. She must think a lot of you, Maurice.'

'Yes.' Mundy smiled. 'We rub along very well as father and daughter, I can say that, but I do fret for her welfare. She does cause me a lot of worry.'

Maurice Mundy took his leave of Janet Thackery with sincere thanks for a lovely meal and returned home. Upon reaching Archway he parked his car as close to his house as he could and walked the remainder of the journey under the street lamps. He turned into Lidyard Road and saw three male figures standing in the shadows outside his house. He approached with caution as they watched him walk towards them. One he recognized as the steely-eyed Christopher Spate. He did not recognize Spate's companions.

'Working late?' Mundy commented dryly. 'I like to see dedication in young detectives.'

'So are you.' Spate's reply was cold, cynical and sarcastic. 'So it looks like. Such dedication in an older officer is quite an inspiration.'

'I'm not working.' Mundy held eye contact with Spate. 'I've just had dinner with a friend.'

'How civilized,' Spate sneered. 'So you visited my old man?'

'Yes.' Mundy tried to sound relaxed.

'How did you find him?' Spate asked with an icy edge to his voice.

'Seems he is quite unwell,' Mundy replied calmly. 'I don't think he knew who I was. He seemed very confused.'

'Yes . . .' Christopher Spate hissed the word. 'He is very confused so there's not much profit to be had in taking your inquiry further, is there?'

'None,' Mundy replied. 'None at all.'

'Good.' Spate smiled an insincere smile. 'That is good . . . so long as we understand each other, Maurice. We'll leave it like that.' He turned and he and his two companions walked away, watched by Mundy until they were swallowed by the mist which by then was falling over London town.

EIGHT

'I just never made the grade, as simple as that.' Geraldine Chisholm forced a smile. 'It didn't happen for me. I got married instead, had three children and returned to work later in life. All those earth-stopping journalistic exposés I was going to write . . . hey ho . . . pie in the sky . . .'

'But you seem fulfilled,' Maurice Mundy observed. 'You seem to be a very contented person, if you don't mind me saying.' He replaced his ID card in his wallet.

'Not at all, of course I don't mind you saying that, and yes, I am fulfilled. I have a good marriage to a lovely man. I have three lovely children . . . all grown up now and all entered into the professions, and I have two grandchildren with more promised. So yes, on an emotional level I am fulfilled as you say, but I completed my journalism degree so I could write for the *Sunday Times* . . . and here I am . . . the *Catford Chronicle and Advertiser*. I started out here and returned here to end my working days.' Geraldine Chisholm was a large-boned, round-faced woman with big brown eyes. Her office on Brownhill Road in Catford was small and cluttered. Outside her office, Mundy heard the clatter and footfalls of a busy newspaper office. 'So how can I help the Metropolitan Police?'

'Tom Greenall.' Maurice Mundy enjoyed the musty smell of the premises of the *Catford Chronicle and Advertiser*.

'Tom Greenall?' Geraldine Chisholm inclined her head to one side. 'Tom Greenall . . . Tom Greenall. That name rings half a bell.' She spoke with a distinct south London accent.

'Joshua Derbyshire,' Mundy prompted. 'The murder of Anne Tweedale.'

'Oh . . . of course.' Geraldine Chisholm's face brightened up. 'I didn't get anywhere with that . . . that was another pie in the sky.'

'What was your interest in the case?' Mundy asked.

'A multiplicity of interests . . . not all altruistic, I confess.'

Geraldine Chisholm sighed. 'I was out for what I could get as much as anything – I'm prepared to admit to that.'

'Meaning . . .?' Mundy frowned. 'What do you mean?'

'Well,' Geraldine Chisholm paused, 'I was convinced of Joshua Derbyshire's innocence. I wanted to expose an unsafe conviction but I had intended to write a book about it, make some money for myself and also use the book to lever me into investigative journalism, to get a position as a crime reporter on a national newspaper. The case made quite a media splash and I began to look into the background of Joshua Derbyshire because initially I thought it was a safe conviction. I was looking for early signs of depravity, hoping to find a childhood friend who could tell me how Joshua Derbyshire used to torture small animals for fun . . . that sort of thing.'

'And did you?' Mundy asked.

'No.' Geraldine Chisholm shook her head vigorously. 'In the event, all I found was a great sea of puzzlement . . . so many unanswered questions, things which didn't add up and deliver. I did manage to get an interview with the lead detective on the case. What was his name? An icy character . . . he was one very cold fish.'

'Spate,' Mundy suggested.

'Yes, that was it, Duncan Spate.' Geraldine Chisholm paused. 'I found him a frightening character. He seemed utterly convinced of Joshua Derbyshire's guilt and was determined to prove it at all costs – closed-minded is just not the expression. It was like he was a police officer, judge, jury and executioner all rolled into one. I found him to be a very threatening presence.'

'I see,' Mundy replied softly.

'But by the time I interviewed Duncan Spate I was by then of the firm belief that Joshua had been wrongly convicted, because far from anyone telling me what a violent little boy he had been, how he used to torture cats and shoot birds with his air rifle, all I heard was what a big softy he had been with not the slightest indication of violence in him. He seemed to have been a boy who didn't have any application at all. He was very lazy and perfunctory, allegedly . . . just not the sort of person who would murder someone by attacking them with a knife. That takes effort – determination, I would have thought. So I put my thoughts to Duncan Spate and he said, "He's guilty, all right, he's where he belongs," and then he turned and walked away.' Geraldine Chisholm looked down and to one side and paused.

'You're going to tell me something,' Mundy suggested softly.

'Yes . . . yes, I am.' She paused. 'Give me a moment, please. The very next evening, after talking to Duncan Spate, I was walking home and I was attacked. I was grabbed by a tall, strong man and pulled into an alley. I thought this is it . . . this is the rape I've been dreading . . . this is everything I have been living in fear of. I was pushed up against the wall and punched twice in the stomach, which winded me so I couldn't scream. He knew what he was doing. The attacker then grabbed me by my hair, held my head against the wall and put his mouth up to my ear. He said . . . growled really. Holding my head in both of his paws, he growled, "Don't shove your nose where it doesn't belong . . . don't ask questions, not if you want to live . . . understand, wench?" Then he banged my head against the wall a couple of times and walked away.'

'Wench?' Mundy repeated.

'Yes.' Geraldine Chisholm nodded. 'That word . . . wench . . . becomes significant.'

'I see . . . sorry.' Mundy reclined in his chair in front of Geraldine Chisholm's desk. 'Please carry on.'

'I didn't recognize the man who attacked me,' Geraldine Chisholm continued. 'I didn't know him but I found out later that he was a young thug called Billy Tipton.'

Mundy pulled his notebook from his pocket. 'I must make a note of that name . . . Billy Tipton.'

'William Henry Tipton.' Geraldine Chisholm spoke confidently. 'If he's still in this world he'll be pushing his fiftieth birthday.'

'You're very positive about his identity,' Mundy remarked.

'I am utterly certain of it.' Geraldine Chisholm maintained a cold, serious expression. 'A week later, just a week after the attack, I was covering a sitting of Lewisham Magistrates Court for this newspaper. Lewisham Magistrates Court hears cases of crimes committed in this neck of the woods, you see. Anyone arrested for being drunk and disorderly in the street out there will appear in front of the Lewisham bench, as you probably know, being a police officer . . .'

'Yes.' Mundy nodded. 'I do know that.'

'Well, who should come up before the Lewisham beaks but a large, well-built thug called William Henry Tipton, who gave his age as being eighteen, and who spoke in the same distinct accent as the man who attacked me. He pleaded not guilty to the assault of a woman and said in his defence, "The wench slapped me so I slapped her back" . . . distinctly using the word "wench".'

'I see.' Mundy nodded slowly.

'I was sitting a few feet from where he was standing and I knew, just knew, it was the same man who had attacked me,' Geraldine Chisholm explained. 'The case unfolded and it turns out the woman slapped his face because he made a lewd suggestion and in retaliation he put her in hospital. He collected three months in prison. His victim was in hospital for longer.'

'That has happened before.' Mundy sighed. 'All too often, in fact.'

'Yes, but that very unpleasant and very distinct West Midlands accent . . . his size . . . his use of the word "wench". I made some enquiries and I found out that the use of the word "wench" is widespread in the Black Country,' Geraldine Chisholm explained, 'the area to the north-west of Birmingham centred on the town of Dudley and containing towns like Coseley and Oldbury . . . and would you know that Tipton is a common local name, also being the name of another small town up there. So that is . . . that was the man who attacked me and who warned me not to ask questions.'

'He was referring to Joshua Derbyshire?' Mundy clarified.

'Had to be,' Geraldine Chisholm replied. 'He was the only person I was asking questions about.'

'Did you report the attack?' Mundy asked.

Geraldine Chisholm shook her head. 'No. There were no witnesses . . . I was frightened . . . I wanted to live. Anyway, at his trial the bench found the case proved and before he was sentenced, the bench asked if "anything was known", meaning has he any previous convictions.'

'Yes,' Mundy groaned, 'I know that.'

'Sorry,' Geraldine Chisholm forced a smile, 'of course you'd know that. Anyway, the prosecuting police officer then read out a long list of previous convictions. As I recall it was all petty stuff really but it meant that Tipton was well known to the police. It seemed like he was in the hands of a bent copper. That's what I thought at the time. You do a little job for me and I'll make this or that investigation go away. He couldn't make the investigation into the assault on that wretched "wench" go away because he did her too much damage and he did so in front of a pub full of witnesses, including her two sisters, but I'm certain in myself that something unpleasant went away in return for him putting the frighteners on me.'

'It seems very likely.' Mundy breathed in and exhaled. 'It seems very, very likely.'

'So what did happen to Joshua Derbyshire?' Geraldine Chisholm asked.

'He's still in prison,' Mundy replied calmly.

'Still!' Geraldine Chisholm gasped. 'I assumed he would have been released on parole. It's been so long . . . thirty years. It must be thirty years now.'

'No parole.' Mundy remained calm. 'No, he's still inside, still doing bird. The judge set a thirty-year tariff and Joshua Derbyshire refuses to admit his guilt.'

'So something has happened to make the police reopen the case?' Geraldine Chisholm asked.

'No, nothing has happened. I am a police officer but this is more of a personal crusade for me,' Mundy explained.

'I see.' Geraldine Chisholm leaned forward. 'So what do you think happened? Why would Duncan Spate want to frighten me off?'

'Because . . .' Mundy opened his palm. 'Because . . .'

'Joshua didn't kill her,' Geraldine Chisholm suggested, 'because Joshua didn't kill anyone?'

'Is my thinking,' Mundy replied.

'Can you prove it?' Geraldine Chisholm's interest was manifest.

'I don't know,' Mundy replied. 'But I can already provide sufficient cause for a retrial.'

'Oh.' Geraldine Chisholm beamed at Mundy. 'How can you do that?'

'It has turned out that Duncan Spate was the brother-in-law of Anne Tweedale . . . Josh's victim.'

Geraldine Chisholm gasped. 'He shouldn't have been involved at all.'

'Nope,' Mundy replied in a soft voice. 'There was also considerable ill will between the two sisters, Mrs Spate and Miss Tweedale. All their father's estate went to Anne Tweedale and nothing to Phyllis Spate née Tweedale. Upon Anne Tweedale's death her will vanished and she was deemed to have died intestate. Her entire estate eventually passed to her sister, Mrs Spate.'

'Did nobody pick that up at the time?' Geraldine Chisholm looked shocked.

'No, apparently not,' Mundy advised. 'The intestacy procedure takes about two years, by which time the dust had settled on the murder and on the trial. Nobody who was involved in the intestacy hearing noticed that Miss Tweedale's sister had the same surname as the man who led the investigation into her murder.'

'That stinks,' Geraldine Chisholm remarked coldly. 'It smells like Billingsgate Fish Market at the end of a long summer's day.'

'I know.' Mundy smiled. 'I know. You might get a book out of this after all.'

'How can I help?' Geraldine Chisholm asked eagerly. 'Can I do anything to help?'

'By noting our conversation,' Mundy requested. 'I have already written a report detailing my concerns to Mr Greenall, should anything happen to me.'

'Why? Have you been threatened?' Geraldine Chisholm looked genuinely concerned.

'Yes,' Mundy replied, 'I have.'

'By whom?' Geraldine Chisholm queried.

'Duncan Spate's son, Christopher,' Mundy replied flatly, 'who is now also a police officer.'

'It gets worse,' Geraldine Chisholm put her hands on her head. 'It just gets worse.' She laid her hands on her desktop. 'So where is Duncan Spate now?'

'He's living in a house in Wimbledon,' Mundy told her, 'which he could not have possibly afforded on his police officer's salary, and he's pretending to be suffering from senile dementia.'

'Pretending?' Geraldine Chisholm queried.

'Well, when I called on him it seemed that he didn't know who I was and couldn't understand what I was saying, yet just a few hours earlier he had given me a precise time to call on him and, when I was there, he stopped his two dogs from barking at me,' Mundy explained. 'He also asked if Tweedale was a place in Yorkshire.'

'That is not the action of a man with dementia,' Geraldine Chisholm observed. 'My dad's got dementia. Believe me, I know dementia and that is not a man with dementia.'

'My thoughts exactly.' Mundy smiled.

'So what do you think happened?' Geraldine Chisholm asked.

'I think Duncan Spate arranged for someone to murder Miss Anne Tweedale, and that he planted, or arranged to have planted, evidence that would implicate a local misfit and have him convicted of the murder so that his wife could claim Anne Tweedale's entire estate.' Mundy spoke again in a flat, matter-of-fact manner. 'Helped by the fact that Anne Tweedale kept her will in her house and did not lodge it with her solicitior.'

'How can you prove that?' Geraldine Chisholm asked.

'I don't know . . . but I will trace William Tipton. I can do that quite easily,' Mundy replied. 'Whether he'll talk to me is another matter. That will remain to be seen . . . and that is if he is still with us. A lot can happen in twenty-eight years.'

Maurice Mundy returned to New Scotland Yard, presenting, to an observer, as a shabby-looking man in an ill-fitting rain-coat and an old, seen-better-days fedora. He took the lift up to the fifth floor and walked along the corridor to the small room which had been allocated to the officers of the Cold Case Review Team. He found Tom Ingram sitting in a chair with his feet on his desk, uncurling a paperclip. 'Overslept?' Ingram growled.

'Sorry . . .' Mundy peeled off his coat and hung it on the coat stand. He took his hat off and hung it on the peg above his coat.

'The young master has been enquiring as to your whereabouts.' Ingram tossed the paperclip into the metal waste bin which stood on the floor beside his chair. It clattered softly against the inside of the bin and came to rest silently on a layer of screwed-up paper.

'Pickering,' Mundy clarified, 'that particular young master?'

'The one and the same,' Ingram replied sourly. 'I stuck my neck out for you, said that I'd seen you, that you were in the building somewhere. Fortunately for you he's trapped in a case conference until . . . whenever.'

'Thanks, Tom.' Mundy sank into the chair behind his desk.

'Anyway, we're on our way.' Tom Ingram stood up.

'We are?' Mundy asked.

'Yes. Kenneth Cassey has asked us to visit. He's promised us a statement.' Ingram smiled broadly. 'A written statement, no less. So he says.' Ingram reached for his coat. 'Apparently.'

'Great . . . just give me a couple of minutes.' Mundy also stood up.

'What now!' Ingram put his coat back on the coat peg. 'Maurice, if you're pushing a personal agenda, so help me . . .'

'Two minutes,' Mundy promised. 'I'll be back before you know it.'

Mundy left the offices of the CCRT and took the lift down to Criminal Records.

'Once again, you're down in the depths,' Stanley Kinross greeted Maurice Mundy. 'This is getting to be a regular thing. You'll be wanting a trace?'

'Yes . . . please.' Maurice Mundy returned Stanley Kinross's smile. 'Just one more, Stan, then we'll have that drink. It's a geezer by the name of Tipton.'

'Tipton.' Stanley Kinross wrote the name on his notepad.

'Yes,' Mundy confirmed, 'William Henry Tipton. He's about fifty years old . . . about . . . probably one year either side of that.'

'OK.' Kinross looked at the name he had written down.

'You'll know him – he's got plenty of track,' Mundy advised.

'Well, if he's in there, I'll find him.' Kinross turned and walked from the Criminal Records reception desk. He returned a few moments later and handed Mundy a computer printout. 'He's known all right – one heavy-sounding geezer . . . Long list of previous . . . each and every conviction is for violence.'

'Black Country Bill,' Mundy read the printout.

'Home address is in Dudley,' Kinross remarked. 'Not my favourite part of the world. He's presently believed to be in East London.'

'Women are referred to as "wenches" up there.' Mundy grinned. 'So I am told.'

'Really!' Kinross gasped. 'Better not let the politically correct brigade hear about that. "Wenches", indeed, that would not amuse my wife. He's a big geezer,' Kinross added. 'Twenty stones of him. You'll need help if you're going to bring him in. So go carefully, Maurice.'

'I will. Bethnal Green . . .' Mundy glanced over the printout. 'Dudley to Bethnal Green. Hardly a man on his way up in the world.'

'Hardly,' Kinross echoed, 'and by way of many of Her Majesty's guesthouses.'

'Many,' Mundy read, 'but yes, I'll proceed with caution.'

'Can I ask why you're interested in him, Maurice?' Kinross asked. 'I'm just curious. He's a low-life thug and he's in his fifties, but that printout reads like it's the profile of a bloke with the emotional development of your average nine-year-old.'

'He silenced someone who was interested in a guy that I am interested in,' Mundy explained.

'Silenced?' Kinross spoke softly, 'As in murdered them?'

'No, as in frightened them into silence,' Mundy further explained.

'So then you must tread extremely carefully, Maurice.' Kinross's voice developed a serious tone.

'I will, but I am not a young woman straight out of university, which was the profile of the victim he silenced. I won't frighten that easily. In fact, if he tries to silence me it will only confirm my suspicions.'

'Still . . . softly, softly, Maurice. You promised me a beer, as you have just said.' Kinross's voice retained its serious tone. 'And I want to collect it.'

'Don't worry,' Mundy held eye contact with Kinross, 'I fully intend to keep my promise. I like a glass of beer and a chat as much as you do.'

The journey from London to HM Prison Blundeston was undertaken within a difficult silence which had developed between an angry Tom Ingram and an uncontrite Maurice Mundy. Ingram, at the wheel, drove slowly and steadily, and Mundy contended himself by watching the road ahead of them or gazing idly to his left at the flat fields of East Anglia. Upon arriving at the prison they were escorted to an agent's room and invited to take a seat within. The cheery prison officer said, 'I'll send for him. He'll be brought down from his landing. He seems to be in a talkative mood today. It's like he is very anxious to unburden himself of something.'

'Oh, that sounds encouraging.' Ingram sat at the table. 'That's the sort of thing we want to hear. It means that our journey will not be wasted.'

'Yes, very chatty.' The prison officer turned to go. 'I don't think that this will be at all a wasted trip for you two gentlemen. Anyway, I'll just go and send for him.'

Tom Ingram sat while Maurice Mundy continued to stand, and the awkward silence between them persisted for a matter of minutes until the calm of the prison was suddenly shattered by a deafening, nerve-shredding ringing of an alarm bell, over which cries of 'assistance!', 'assistance!' could be heard followed by the sound of running feet . . . many, many feet.

'I hope . . .' Tom Ingram broke the silence which existed between him and Maurice Mundy.

'I hope not also,' Mundy replied. 'I do hope not, but I am afraid . . . I have a feeling that it is . . . that it will be . . . that he has . . .'

'Inviting us up with the promise of a statement.' Ingram sighed. 'A talkative attitude so no one will suspect or fear . . . classic . . . it's just classic.'

'We couldn't have seen it coming.' Mundy leaned back against the wall. 'No one could have seen it coming.'

'It still may not be him.' Ingram laid a clenched fist gently on the tabletop.

'Don't get your hopes raised, Tom.' Mundy drummed his fingertips against the wall. 'The hairs on my old wooden leg tell me that it will be him.'

The two men once again fell into a silence, although this time the silence contained a bond between them which replaced the ill feeling. Thirty minutes elapsed and then the cheery prison officer who had escorted Mundy and Ingram to the agent's room once again entered. This time he looked to Mundy to be crestfallen and ashen-faced. He held a brown manila envelope in his left hand. He sat heavily in the chair across the table from Tom Ingram. He remained silent for a moment and then said, 'I suppose you two gentlemen can guess what has happened. You don't need me to spell it out for you . . .?'

'Cassey's topped himself,' Ingram said. 'We heard the commotion and you don't exactly look like the happiest man on the planet.'

'He slit his wrists,' the prison officer informed Ingram and Mundy. 'He seems to have snapped his toothbrush handle and pierced himself with the jagged edge. He seems to have been very determined.' The prison officer held the envelope. 'He left this for Mr Ingram.'

'That's me,' Ingram said, reaching for the envelope.

'We read it, we had to,' the prison officer advised, handing it to Ingram. 'It makes no sense to us.'

Tom Ingram opened the envelope and extracted a small sheet of paper. He read the note then passed it behind him to Maurice Mundy. Mundy took the note. It read:

This way I cheat the prison grounds. You'll find Ollie at 24 Lumley Walk, Chelmsford.

'It means,' Mundy explained as he handed the note back to Tom Ingram, 'that this way he'll be buried in sanctified ground; he won't be a convicted murderer interred in prison grounds.'

'I see.' The prison officer held his head down. 'Funny how

a man's mind can turn when he's locked in a little space for many hours a day. I'll have to take the note back with me.'

'Of course.' Tom Ingram handed the note and envelope to the prison officer.

'Who's "Ollie"?' The clearly much-shaken prison officer reread the note. 'It made no sense to us . . . "Ollie"? Is that another suspect or something?'

'It's our name for his partner . . . they were a two-man crew. We didn't know the identity of his partner,' Ingram explained, 'so we called him "Oliver".'

'"Oliver Hardy",' Mundy added, 'after his description. Can we have use of a phone, please? We'll have to notify the Chelmsford police of this and of the address of his . . . mate. It's their old pigeon now. Our job's done.'

'All done and dusted.' Tom Ingram slowly and casually stood up. 'Just the paperwork now – the jolly old paperwork to be done.'

Later that night, while walking home from a quiet and a reflective evening in the pub, Maurice Mundy found it to be true that when a person is dying the last sense that leaves them is that of hearing. Touch, speech, smell, taste all go . . . one by one, and hearing also goes, but is also always the last to leave, as consciousness fades and death envelops one. He was, as he recalled, walking slowly up Lidyard Road with the sound of the traffic on Archway Road hissing on wet tarmac when he then heard a sudden scuffling sound, followed by two rapid steps. He half turned as a blow to the rear of his head knocked him to the ground. He felt a foot impact with his stomach and managed to grab naked flesh near his attacker's ankle and scratch the flesh with his fingernail as the foot was withdrawn. He then felt a second blow to his head, but this one was much, much more powerful than the first blow, which had caused his knees to buckle. He felt then that he was lapsing into sleep as a darkness engulfed him and his sight faded. He felt himself drifting away and heard a voice say, 'Is that enough?' A second voice answered, 'Yes, no one can survive that. Now we walk . . . just walk . . . a man and a wench . . . just walk, it won't look iffy.' Then Maurice Mundy heard no more.

Maurice Mundy heard no more, that is, until he heard a soft clatter of metal on metal, an admonishing female voice say 'hush!' and a second voice, also female, say, 'sorry, sorry'. Minutes later, light penetrated the darkness and he saw a high ceiling again in a significantly dimmer light but heard no sound . . . and darkness then took him into her dreadful maw yet again. When the darkness once again left him he saw a woman standing beside him wearing a cap and a blue blouse. The woman glanced at him and he thought she looked worried. She turned and walked away and he heard her say, 'Sister! Sister!' A few moments later a second woman approached him, put her head close to his and said, 'Can you hear me?' Mundy nodded his head slowly in response. The second woman smiled and said, 'Good, you can understand me . . . that is a good sign . . . a very good sign. You're in hospital. You've had a bit of a bang on your head but you're safe now . . . all very safe . . . safe as safe can be.' She smiled again and then she withdrew, leaving Maurice Mundy alone.

Slowly, his senses returned. The smell of the hospital ward. The sounds, the touch of the coarse blankets. Later, a tall, youthful doctor called on him.

'You know, Mr Mundy . . .' the doctor had a warm voice, Mundy thought, and he also had a polished bedside manner. He felt reassured by the doctor's presence, '. . . if anyone ever calls you a numbskull or a thickhead in future, you can tell them how right they are. You see, you have an abnormally thick skull. There is a condition known as an eggshell skull where the skull is abnormally thin and even a gentle bump on the head can prove fatal, but you – you have just the opposite condition. You will have quite a groove across the top of your skull for the rest of your life, but you'll have a life . . . and if you can understand what is being said to you, and Sister Bateman told me that you understood her when she asked if you could hear her, then that means that not only will you live, but you have not suffered any brain damage.' The doctor, who Mundy noted by his lapel badge was called Dr Geeson, paused. 'Any normal skull would not have been able to withstand that blow. You were lucky your attacker didn't follow it up with further blows. Three or four such blows would have been fatal. But whatever he hit you with was very long, heavy and solid. It is often the way of it that people don't know that they have abnormally thin or abnormally thick skulls until they sustain a head injury. But anyway, you must rest now. Is there anyone we can contact for you?'

'Two people,' Mundy replied. 'Just two people. I can let you have the addresses of both.'

'All right,' Dr Geeson smiled, 'we'll do that for you. Someone will come along and take their addresses. You have a police officer waiting outside your room. This is an enclosed room within a ward. We usually use it for barrier nursing or VIPs and I reckon you count as a VIP. The police certainly seem to think so. The ambulance crew who picked you up off the pavement found your police officer's warrant card when they looked for something to identify you, and Scotland Yard insisted on putting a constable outside your door. We found blood under your fingernails. We sent it to the forensic science laboratory. If your attacker is known to the police his DNA will be on file . . . it will be enough to convict him.'

'Oh, he's known all right,' Mundy replied. His mouth felt dry and then he groaned loudly as his head suddenly felt as though it was being split open. 'He's well known.'

Dr Geeson smiled. 'You'll have a bit of a sore head for a few days. We'll give you some painkillers for that. You'll be detained for a day or two, just until we're sure there are no time delayed consequences. Then, with a bit of luck, you'll walk out of here.'

The following day, Roberta Loss sat in the upright chair beside Maurice Mundy's bed, sharing the bag of grapes she had bought for him and talking about inconsequential matters when there was a gentle tap on the door. The door was opened and Janet Thackery entered the room wearing a comfortable to the eye, pastel-blue raincoat and a ready smile.

'Oh . . .' Janet Thackery halted at the threshold of the room, 'I'm sorry. Is this a bad time?'

'No, no . . . not at all.' Mundy levered himself up in the bed. 'Janet, this is my daughter, Roberta. Roberta, please meet Janet. Janet is . . .'

'A good friend,' Janet Thackery explained. 'A very, very good friend.' Roberta Loss stood up and the two women shook hands.

Eagerly.

The two men sat facing each other across a table, staring at each other. They sat in an awkward silence. The room was spartan, upright chairs either side of a small table. The walls were painted a uniform cream. A slab of opaque glass was set high into the wall. A filament bulb behind a Perspex screen provided the illumination.

'I heard that.' William Tipton broke the silence. 'I heard that the criminal and their victims are going to be brought together so the victim can make an impact statement. I heard that on the radio. I just didn't expect it so soon.' Tipton spoke in a heavy Black Country accent, pronouncing 'so' like he was referring to a female pig. Mundy found the accent unpleasant to his ears, as Geraldine Chisholm had earlier described it as being. 'I thought it was supposed to happen after the guilty verdict.' Tipton continued, pronouncing 'verdict' as 'var-dict'.

'Oh . . .' Maurice Mundy inclined his head to the door of the room, '. . . they don't know I'm your victim. They wouldn't let me see you if they knew. I just showed my warrant card, said I wanted to see you and they brought you up from the cells. They expressed surprise that I was alone because coppers visit in pairs, but I said it wasn't an interview as such, it was just to confirm a couple of minor points since you're pleading guilty.'

'Yes, it's all I can do, my brief says.' Tipton spoke mildly. 'He says you've got me bang to rights.'

'Yes, we have, the police have . . . all that lovely DNA evidence.' Mundy shrugged his shoulders. 'Pleading guilty . . . well, that's your only option, William. It would be extremely foolish to plead not guilty.'

'That's what my brief says.' William Tipton looked down and to his left. 'I didn't feel the scratch at the time, I only noticed it the next morning, then I knew I was in real bother. I knew they'd scrape under your fingernails and I knew my DNA was on file. I couldn't run anywhere so I went to the boozer . . . then I went to the Caledonian Road and hired a brass. I knew I wouldn't be doing much of either for the next twenty years.'

'The brass you hired,' Mundy asked, 'it wasn't a mixed race girl, by any chance?'

'No, she was a young white wench,' Tipton replied. 'Very young . . . very white.'

Mundy sighed with relief.

'Why?' Tipton asked.

'Nothing.' Mundy held up his hand. 'It's not important. So you're pleading guilty?'

'Yes.' William Tipton was a large, well-built man with a mop of black hair. Mundy easily saw how he'd gravitate to the life of violent crime, making a living as a persuader or as an enforcer. 'Like I said . . . legal advice . . . but even so, the person I attempted to chill was a rozzer, a serving police officer, so I'm still looking at a twenty-year stretch, at least. My brief says that at the moment British justice is tending towards longer sentences.'

'It appears indeed to be the case,' Mundy agreed. 'It's a reaction to a period of lenient sentences which have brought complaints from all sides, all quarters . . . except criminals themselves, of course.'

Tipton heaved a laugh. 'Aye . . . they, we . . . wouldn't complain. We wouldn't complain at all. But if I get twenty years, well, I'll be in my mid-sixties when I get out, even if I get parole after fifteen years. That's my life over. I'll come out to a state pension and . . . nothing else. What a wasted life.'

'Yes,' Mundy nodded in agreement, 'you have to look at it like that. I'll be on the outside and you'll be on the inside.'

'I've been inside before . . . but twenty years.' Tipton closed his eyes. 'Twenty years of top security . . . of Category-A living, and Belmarsh. It's a tough prison.'

'Yes, so I have heard.' Mundy glanced up at the opaque slab of glass. 'I've heard that it is no holiday camp in here.'

'There are some bad boys in here.' Tipton opened his eyes. 'Some very hard old boys.'

'You should be able to take care of yourself, I would have

thought.' Mundy sat back in his chair. 'I mean, you're not exactly a lightweight, are you, William?'

'No, but they use the gang system,' Tipton explained. 'I can handle one . . . perhaps two. But five or six coming at you all with homemade weapons . . . you're constantly watching your back. All the time. You can never relax. Not for a second. Being in here with you is the first time I've felt safe all day.'

Mundy nodded. 'You're in a right old mess, William. You really need to start working for yourself.'

'That's what my brief says.' Tipton sighed. 'He says plead guilty and demonstrate contrition. From day one, he says, show a contrite attitude, nothing but contrition. Only that will get you an early parole. So I said, "Yes, OK, I'll show contrition", but I don't know what contrition means.'

'Accepting your guilt,' Mundy advised, 'showing regret, fully accepting responsibility for your actions . . . that sort of thing. Being repentant.'

'So, like not shifting the blame on to anyone else?' Tipton appealed to Mundy. 'Is that what it means?'

'Yes.' Mundy nodded. 'That's the idea. Fully accepting your responsibilities. No "all right I did it but I had a bad child-hood" . . . no abuse excuse nonsense, it won't help you. The parole boards have had quite enough of that attitude – it just won't wash any more.'

'All right, but I'll still be in prison for a long, long time.' Tipton once more closed his eyes, as though, thought Mundy, he was wishing himself to be somewhere else.

'Yes,' Mundy spoke softly, 'a very long time. You'll grow old in prison.'

'No one can survive top security for more than ten years,' Tipton whined, 'no one . . . so they say. You come out like a zombie.'

Maurice Mundy paused, then he said, 'Suppose . . . just suppose I drop my complaint against you.'

A silence fell in the room. Tipton's jaw dropped. He looked at Mundy. 'You'd do that?'

'Yes,' Mundy replied, 'I might . . . but I'd want something in return. Something really solid.'

'Solid?' Tipton looked curiously at Mundy. 'Solid. Like how solid? I won't be grassing anybody up. I'll tell you that now. I won't do that.'

'I'm not asking you to grass anybody up.' Mundy continued to speak softly. 'I'm not asking you to do that.'

'So what then?' Tipton demanded. 'What do you want from me?'

'How about the truth about Anne Tweedale's murder?' Mundy said matter-of-factly.

'Who's she?' Tipton asked. 'I don't know that name.'

'The elderly lady in Burnt Oak stabbed to death nearly thirty years ago. A big softy called Joshua Derbyshire was fitted up for her murder. That's who she is . . . or was.' Mundy paused. 'I know Duncan Spate was behind that but he wouldn't get his fingers dirty, and I know that you once put the frighteners on a newspaper reporter because she was asking too many awkward questions.' Mundy paused and then continued. 'And I know that he and his son are behind your attacking me . . . I did a CR check.'

'CR?' Tipton asked. 'What's a CR check?'

'A Criminal Records check,' Mundy explained.

'Ah . . .' Tipton nodded.

'So I did a CR check on you because I thought it highly likely that Christopher Spate would be automatically notified about it and that he'd tell his old man. I thought I'd get a warning.' Mundy exhaled. 'I did not think I'd be putting my old life on the line.'

Tipton looked intently at Mundy. 'This little chat is unofficial?'

'Completely. Totally. No tape recorders. No witnesses. Nothing will be signed,' Mundy assured Tipton. 'It is just you, me and the gatepost.'

'Well, yes . . .' Tipton avoided eye contact with Maurice Mundy. 'Yes, it was Spate who contacted me.'

'Which one?' Mundy asked. 'Father or son?'

'Duncan Spate. The old geezer. The father,' Tipton confirmed. 'He says you're being a right old nuisance. He wants you "taken out" . . . he wants you slotted . . . offed. You're causing him too much grief, too much aggro. He doesn't like grief. He doesn't like aggro.'

'So he's got something to hold over you?' Mundy suggested. 'Something heavy duty?'

'Heavy enough.' Tipton looked down at the tabletop. 'Try murder. It doesn't get much heavier.'

'Care to tell me?' Mundy invited calmly. 'No details, just the gist of it.'

'It was a long time ago. I was newly in the Smoke . . . just arrived from Dudley,' Tipton explained. 'I was a new boy in the big city.'

'That was before the murder of Miss Tweedale?' Mundy clasped both his hands together and rested them on the tabletop.

'Yes. Just before.'

'So it was that, the first murder, that enabled Duncan Spate to force you to murder Anne Tweedale?' Mundy clarified. 'Like, you do a little job for me which you won't be connected to and I'll make the evidence in respect of the first murder go away?'

'Yes.' Tipton continued to look at the tabletop. 'That was it exactly. He used those words: "make it go away". I was seventeen; I didn't want to go down for life. So me and this other geezer, we filled in the old woman.'

'There were two of you?' Mundy clarified.

'Yes.' Tipton looked down. 'Two of us.'

'Do you want to tell me the name of the other geezer?' Mundy asked.

'OK. He was called Carl Tate . . ."Spud" Tate.'

'Carl "Spud" Tate.' Mundy committed the name to memory. 'Tate as in potato, hence "Spud"?'

'Yes, that's it,' Tipton explained. 'He was from the West Midlands as well but he was in his thirties then. He was the main man and I was the boy.'

'Where can I find him?' Mundy asked. 'Does he have a record?'

'He's in the wind.' Tipton smiled. 'Well in the wind.'

'He's disappeared,' Mundy pressed. 'Is that what you mean, William?'

'No, I mean he's dead,' Tipton explained. 'He punched above his weight in a skirmish one night outside a boozer in Kentish Town and got his head well and truly kicked in. He

never regained consciousness. He was married and his old
lady had him cremated. So he went up the chimney . . . he's
in the wind. Like I said, well in the wind.'

'I see,' Mundy growled. 'So he can't help us any?'

'No. I think his old lady had him cremated because she
was frightened that he'd rise from the dead. He was an evil,
vicious little swine with a chip on his shoulder. In fact, he
had chips on both shoulders and really laid into the old woman.
He did more than me, much more. She was a tough old bird.
She kept getting up, just wouldn't lie down and die, and Spud,
he just kept pushing the blade into her again and again and
again. I know I'm equally guilty but Spud Tate really did it.'
Tipton kept his head lowered. 'He did the whole business.'

'So what happened then?' Mundy asked, speaking softly.

'Well, then we took some of the old woman's jewels and
one of the knives with her blood on it and planted them in
this geezer's drum, like Duncan Spate told us,' Tipton
explained. 'You see, Duncan Spate had something to hold over
Spud Tate as well as over me. He had us both in his pocket.
Oh . . . he – Tate, I mean – also smeared some of the old
woman's blood on a jacket belonging to this guy. Poor geezer.
He was well stitched up . . . well and truly stitched up. And
we had to search the house for the old woman's will and hand
it to Spate, which we did.'

'Did you know the geezer who was stitched up?' Mundy
relaxed, sitting back in his chair.

'No, no, we didn't,' Tipton replied, still bowing his head.
'Spate said it was better if we didn't know.' Tipton paused. 'I
felt a bit bad about it – I did then and I do now. I felt a lot
bad about it then and I still feel a lot bad about it . . . but it's
dog eat dog. If I hadn't done what I did Spate would have me
sent down for chilling my victim. If the other geezer didn't
go down, I would have. I was seventeen, scared, and I liked
a beer. I liked wenches. I wanted to own a fast car . . . it's
what I came down to the Smoke for. The good life like on
television.'

'It's not so glamorous, is it?' Mundy smiled wryly.

'London? London is a dirty, smelly mess.' Tipton raised his
head. 'But, you see, I couldn't go back to Dudley unless I had

made it . . . I was a bit proud like that – I wouldn't admit defeat. I still won't. So I stayed. And here I am.'

'Like so many before you,' Mundy sighed, 'and there'll be plenty still to come, and all will find that London is a dirty, smelly city where you are never more than three feet from a rat.'

'Really?' Tipton smiled briefly. 'Is that true?'

'So they say,' Mundy replied. 'It's a bit of an exaggeration. I've stood on Hampstead Heath in the middle of the day with not a rat in sight, but walking down the streets at night, well, then I know what people mean when they say that.' Mundy paused. 'So, anyway, let's keep this little chat focused. What has Spate got to hold over you?'

'My dabs on the murder weapon I used to off that guy, my first victim, when I was seventeen, and a signed confession that I did it. He can produce both and I'll go down for life, so he said. So he still says.' Tipton suddenly seemed to Mundy to look meek and fragile despite his bulk.

'It's an empty threat,' Mundy advised. 'Yes, he can produce that evidence, and if he does you'll collect your life sentence, but he can't produce it without ruining himself.'

'Really?' Tipton gasped. 'How?'

'Perverting the course of justice by wilfully withholding evidence,' Mundy replied flatly. 'He'll be prosecuted despite being a retired cop, and if his son is part of this, which he probably is, then he'll be finished as a police officer. It's the signed confession which will do it rather than your fingerprints on the murder weapon. The confession had to be dated.'

'It was,' Tipton replied.

'So he's suddenly going to flourish a confession which he's been sitting on for thirty years.' Mundy laughed. 'I don't think so.'

Tipton groaned. 'And me . . . I've been doing him favours all this time.'

'Now he can't hurt you, and he can't help you either, so you'll collect life for attempting to murder me.' Mundy spoke quietly.

'You're here to laugh at me.' Tipton's voice developed a hard edge. 'Is that why you're here?'

'No.' Mundy shook his head. 'I'm here to make you an offer – probably the best offer you'll ever be made . . . ever.'

'What's that?' Tipton scrutinized Mundy. 'What's the offer?'

'That I drop my complaint against you, like I said,' Mundy replied. 'That I withdraw it completely. How does that sound? Does that have any appeal for you?'

'It has plenty.' Tipton looked eagerly at Mundy. 'It has plenty of appeal.'

'But it's not a case of nothing for nothing,' Mundy explained. 'I want something in return.'

'Like what?' Tipton replied cautiously. 'I knew there'd be a catch.'

'A full confession but not to the murder of Anne Tweedale,' Mundy explained. 'A full confession to the planting of evidence which falsely incriminated Joshua Derbyshire. You'll be confessing to being a conspirator after the fact. You were not part of the murder, you were not there when it happened, but you helped the murderer, who you will name, after he had committed the deed.' Mundy paused. 'You'll collect five years. Max.'

'Five years max.' Tipton gasped. 'I can do that easily. You can do that for me?'

'You could be out in as little as eighteen months,' Mundy told him. 'It's that or collect twenty years for attempting to murder me.'

'That's some offer.' Tipton sat back in his chair. 'That's a really serious offer. But what guarantee do I have that you'll keep your part of the bargain?'

'You have my word,' Mundy replied solemnly. 'If you know me, William, you'd know that I am an Englishman of the old school. My word is my bond. If I break my word, I am nothing.'

'I believe you, sir,' Tipton replied. 'I believe you . . . and I can't hurt Spud Tate, but what about Duncan Spate? He can hurt me if I do what you ask.'

'No, he can't.' Mundy smiled. 'He's kidding that he's gaga. He's pretending that he's demented . . . he's pretending that he's got old man's disease so he can't suddenly stop pretending and try to implicate you in the murder you committed when you were seventeen. If he wants to avoid prosecution he'll have to continue to pretend that he's demented. So, as little as eighteen months or a guarantee of twenty years, minimum. It's your call. There'll still be beer and wenches aplenty in eighteen months' time . . . and you'll be young enough to enjoy both.'

'So what can I do?' Tipton appealed to Mundy.

'I used to be a boy scout.' Mundy reached into his jacket pocket. 'I've come prepared. I've got a blank statement form . . . I've got a couple, in fact. I'll write out your statement about planting evidence in Joshua Derbyshire's flat and you'll read it. If you agree with it you'll stick your moniker underneath it.'

'Then what?' Tipton asked.

'Well, then I photocopy it,' Mundy explained. 'I'll send one copy – the top copy, in fact, to Joshua's solicitor, Mr Greenall. He'll know what to do with it. I'll send it anonymously. He'll know who it came from but I'll send it anonymously anyway. I'll send another copy to a newspaper reporter who is angling to write a true crime book about the murder of Miss Tweedale. She will probably write to you asking to visit you when you're in prison. If she does you ought to cooperate with her. I'll send another copy to the Murder and Serious Crime Squad in New Scotland Yard, also anonymously. They will also know what to do with it. And I'll keep one copy for myself in a safe place . . . maybe two copies in separate safe places.'

'Got it all worked out, haven't you, boss?' Tipton said weakly.

'Yes.' Mundy smiled. 'It's all as clear as daylight, crystal clear.'

'Can I just say something, sir?' Tipton asked as Mundy took his ballpoint pen from the breast pocket of his jacket.

'Yes.' Mundy poised the pen over the statement form. 'Of course.'

'Well, if it means anything, now I've met you, I am just so pleased I didn't manage to kill you. I really thought I'd done the business.' Tipton spoke with a note of genuine regret.

'You would have done. Ordinarily you would have succeeded but I have an abnormally thick skull, apparently,' Mundy replied. 'It acted like a crash helmet. What did you use, anyway?'

'A camshaft from a car engine. It's long enough, heavy enough . . . and lumpy enough. I got rid of it . . . it's well out of it.'

'Well, I am also pleased you didn't manage to do the business. I've still got things I need to do.' Mundy looked to one side. 'I've got a daughter I want to turn round, for one thing . . .'

'She's doing crime?' Tipton asked.

'Shoplifting . . . she's a heroin-addicted brass who works the Caledonian Road.'

Tipton paled. 'So your question . . .?'

'But my daughter is of mixed race and you say you bought the services of a white, er . . . a white wench.'

'Yes. Definitely a white wench.' Tipton nodded. 'Definitely white.'

'Good. I mean, otherwise it would have been embarrassing for both of us. So, let's get this statement written.'

'Why are you doing this?' Tipton appealed to Mundy. 'I can't see what's in it for you, sir? If you don't mind me asking, sir?'

'It's personal,' Mundy replied. 'Just very, very personal.'

DCI Pickering took a pair of scissors from his desk drawer and cut Maurice Mundy's warrant card in half. Then he cut it into quarters.

'You are making sure all right,' Mundy growled. He sat motionless, with his legs crossed, in one of the chairs in front of Pickering's desk. 'No one can say you're not being thorough.'

'Look, Maurice,' Pickering replaced the scissors in his desk drawer, 'I don't like doing this, I'm not comfortable doing it, but . . . it's like the sergeant says. "Orders are orders". It's just the way of it . . . it always has been and always will be the way of it. Always. The king commands and we obey. The top floor wants it this way.'

'So the top floor gets it this way.' Maurice Mundy shook his head slowly. 'So it's "keep the boss happy" time.'

'That's about it, Maurice. That's about it. It's something that you should try doing instead of keeping yourself happy.

You know, earlier today I was thinking about you and, you know, you put me in mind of someone I hadn't thought of in years.' Pickering avoided eye contact with Mundy. 'That was my old maths teacher from school, Mr Parkin . . . a good man . . . and Mr Parkin once told us that we can sit a maths exam and get the wrong answer for every question and still pass, so long as we show that we understand the problem and that we have taken the correct steps to the solution. If the answer is two and we put three, we will still get a pass mark if we have got to our answer by following the correct route. All right, all right, it might not be a glitteringly high pass mark but it will still be a pass. He also said that the correct answer obtained by following the wrong route would conversely be a fail.'

'Yes, I can understand that,' Mundy said sullenly. 'Your point being . . .?'

'My point being that all right, you got the correct answers, you got the right results, but in this case the ends do not justify the means. You got to the right place but you followed the wrong route. You took the wrong steps and the top floor is not a happy bunch of jockeys right now.' Pickering paused. 'Yes . . . yes . . . all right, you did the job you were given, you solved the murder of the little boy who was found floating in the pond in the village green near his home . . . What was his name?'

'Oliver Walwyn,' Mundy replied. 'His name was Oliver Walwyn. One Oliver murdered by another Oliver.'

'Yes . . . Oliver Walwyn,' Pickering raised his voice, 'but you had no right, no right at all to shove your oar into the Essex force's investigation . . . I told you to keep out of their nosebag.'

'Excuse me,' Mundy also raised his voice, 'but me and Tom Ingram stopped a pair of serial killers in their tracks. The Essex Police were not even sure that those murders were linked. Their investigation had lost its focus . . . it had stagnated.' Mundy protested. 'And anyway, the geezer who topped himself . . . Kenneth Cassey . . . he would only talk to me and Tom. So what were we supposed to do? As soon as he gave up his mate's address we passed the information to the Chelmsford police.'

Pickering put the four pieces of Maurice Mundy's warrant card into a brown paper envelope. 'You should have refused to visit him, Maurice. It wasn't your pigeon, it was the pigeon of the Chelmsford boys. They know how to do their job and would have got there soon enough, especially since Cassey was clearly ready to talk. But I can tell you that the address you gave led to a good result. It belonged to another delivery-van driver called Sayers, Paul Sayers. Unlike Cassey, Sayers kept trophies of all their victims and he kept trophies from more women than the six victims that the Essex Police have thus far identified. You'll be reading about it, watching the story unfold on television. The press are already all over it, clinging to the story like a pair of wet denims. You'll likely be called as a Crown witness.'

'Well, I'm not likely to be going anywhere – not in the foreseeable future, anyway.' Maurice Mundy looked out of the window of Pickering's office at the dull, grey sky which hung like a blanket over central London. 'So what's going to happen to Tom Ingram?'

'He stays.' Pickering spoke firmly. 'Sorry, but he stays. You go, he stays. It might seem unfair but he didn't pursue his own agenda in respect of another case. You accessed Criminal Records, which you had no right to access, and you used your warrant card to gain access to felons who were serving prison sentences, all to pursue your own private agenda. It's just as well you withdrew your complaint against William Tipton because visiting the man who tried to murder you would have made his trial impossible. It completely compromised the Crown's case against him.'

'But William Tipton didn't know that and I got the signed confession, which is what I wanted,' Mundy growled. 'I got evidence that will overturn a wrongful conviction . . . not before time . . . and I exposed a bent copper in the process.'

'Not your job!' Pickering glared at Maurice Mundy. 'Don't you see? In neither case was it your job to do that. See what I mean? The right result by the wrong route. The moment you dug up dirt on Duncan Spate you should have notified A10. They investigate corruption in the Metropolitan Police . . . not you.' Pickering put the brown envelope which contained the pieces of Maurice Mundy's warrant card into his desk drawer and slammed it shut. 'You know, Maurice, you really should have taken that advice you were given in the lift as you left your disciplinary hearing that time, all those years ago. You were just never cut out to be a copper.'

'You were told about that?' Mundy raised his eyebrows.

'Yes.' Pickering took a deep breath. 'I was told. I had to be told before you joined the Cold Case Review Team why it was you never made it beyond the rank of detective constable. Not following procedure . . . A major felon walked free and potential prosecution witnesses were murdered, but that's for you to live with; that's for you to square with your conscience and rather you than me. You see, Maurice, back then you were too leftfield, you were just too leftfield, and you didn't learn from it.' Pickering paused. 'So, fifty-five years old . . . do you have any plans before you reach state retirement age? Your police pension won't be sufficient to live on, not when you're retiring from your lowly rank. You know, if you don't fancy driving a minicab some law firms hire ex-coppers as private eyes . . . It's just a thought, Maurice.'

'Funny you should say that.' Mundy stood up. 'In fact, I have a number to call. Please don't get up.' Mundy held his hand palm outwards. 'I'll see myself out. I know where the front door is.'

Maurice Mundy and Janet Thackery turned off the path and leaned against the gate. Mundy noticed that the wooden gate was new but the stone gateposts and the rusted hinges on which it rested belonged to a much earlier era. They stood side by side with their hands resting atop the gate, looking out across a field in which a group of horses stood, with one horse, a dapple grey mare, standing away to the left of the field. Beyond the field was a small wood of leafless trees, in the branches of which a murder of crows was cawing loudly. Above was a grey, thick, low cloud covering the sky. After observing the horses in an autumn landscape for a few moments, Janet Thackery pointed to the dapple grey mare and said, 'That's you.' Mundy thrust his hands into his duffel coat pockets and extracted a pair of leather gloves. 'Leftfield, you mean?'

'Yes,' Janet Thackery replied approvingly, 'very left.'

'I don't look particularly unhappy.' Mundy tugged the gloves on to his hands. 'In fact, if you ask me, I look quite content. It doesn't look like I want to be in the middle of the field.'

'I dare say that's the answer.' Janet Thackery let her eyes rest on the horse. 'Leave you where you are content. So what will happen now? What will happen to poor Joshua Derbyshire?'

'Poor, ill-served Joshua Derbyshire.' Maurice Mundy replaced his hands on top of the wooden gate. 'His case will be fast-tracked to the Court of Appeal, and with William Tipton's statement his conviction will be quashed, not just deemed unsafe but fully overturned. He will be declared not guilty of the murder of Anne Tweedale and released from custody.' Mundy paused. 'He will receive a massive compensation payment but compensation is just that . . . compensation . . . it dulls the cutting edge. It softens the blow but it does not right the wrong. How can you give a man back twenty-eight years of his life which was wrongfully taken from him? He went to prison when he was seventeen. He's never known a woman in the biblical sense . . . he's never been out with his mates for an evening in the pub . . . he's never travelled like young people do. In fact, he's never been out of London in his forty-five years. He has, though, occupied the moral high ground – he has that satisfaction, and he's proved that he could have coped with a mainstream education but he'll need a lot of help to readjust to life on the outside. Geraldine Chisholm . . .'

'Who is she?' Janet Thackery turned to Mundy.

'The reporter on the *Catford Chronicle and Advertiser*,' Mundy reminded her.

'Oh, yes.' Janet Thackery nodded. 'Yes, sorry.'

'She's taking a motherly interest in him and seems willing to steer him through the period of adjusting, but it will be difficult. He's going to have to learn to go into a diner when he's hungry and choose what he wants to eat from the menu rather than eating what is put in front of him. He'll have to learn to go into a supermarket and choose what to buy. He's never made decisions in his life, not day-to-day decisions anyway. Geraldine said that she will help him through that.'

'That's very good of her,' Janet Thackery commented.

'She's angling to get a true crime book out of it,' Mundy explained, 'so she's not being totally altruistic, as she might say . . . but she's there for him and that's the main thing.'

'And the Spates?' Janet Thackery wrapped her scarf more tightly round her neck. 'What of the father and son duo?'

'Dunno,' Mundy replied. 'Dunno . . . that wheel is still in spin. Spate the younger is facing a disciplinary hearing which will want to know why he arranged to be notified of any CR check on Joshua Derbyshire and William Tipton despite not having a professional interest in either of them. If he keeps his job his cards will be well and truly marked and he won't rise as far as he otherwise would . . . that's if he keeps his job.'

'What will happen to Anne Tweedale's fortune?' Janet Thackery shivered slightly.

'That will all depend on whether Spate the elder is prosecuted,' Mundy explained. 'If he is successfully prosecuted then the forensic accountants will try to trace her money but that won't be easy, not after thirty years. The Spates have had plenty of time to squirrel it away. But if the Crown Prosecution Service does not think that it is in the public interest to prosecute an eighty-year-old man who may or may not be suffering from senile dementia then the Spates will keep all Miss Tweedale's money and Spate the younger will most likely inherit it in the fullness of time.'

'That is so unfair.' Janet Thackery brought her fist down on the wooden gate. 'They had her murdered for her money and they get it—'

'Only if Duncan Spate is not prosecuted, but quite frankly I can't see that happening. So, yes . . . it is very unfair but life is unfair.' Maurice Mundy gazed across the field at the horses. 'If you look for fairness in life you'll make yourself unwell.'

'And you?' Janet Thackery turned to Maurice Mundy, 'What of you?'

'Me? Well, as you know I have been retained by Thomas

Greenall as a cash-in-hand plus expenses private eye to test the veracity of Crown witness statements. I'll be working against the police, which will be a bit of a change, but oddly I'm feeling quite enthusiastic about the prospect.' Mundy smiled. 'But, as Tom Greenall says, it's all to serve the ends of justice.'

'That's the leftfield coming out of you.' Janet Thackery returned the smile. 'Go with it. And Roberta . . . any development there?'

'Yes, she's accepted my invitation to risk my cooking. She's coming over for a meal and has agreed to stay the night in my little guest room.' Mundy looked up at the sky. 'So she'll be off the street for one night at least. That's a step in the right direction.'

'Good.' Janet Thackery paused. Then she said, 'Look, Maurice, why don't you come over to my house . . . both of you? I'd like to cook for you . . . I'd like to do that.'

Maurice Mundy laid his hand on Janet Thackery's and she laid her other hand on his. 'Thank you,' he said. 'Thank you so very much.'

Lightning Source UK Ltd.
Milton Keynes UK
UKHW03f2243270418
321779UK00001B/22/P